BABY LIES

A gripping detective mystery full of twists and turns

CHRIS COLLETT

JOFFE BOOKS

Revised edition 2018 by Joffe Books, London.

First published by Piatkus in 2007 as "Blood Money."

www.joffebooks.com

This book is a work of fiction. Names, characters, businesses, organizations, places and events are either the product of the author's imagination or are used fictitiously. Any resemblance to actual persons, living or dead, events or locales is entirely coincidental. The spelling is British English.

ISBN-13: 978-1-78931-001-6

To my sister, Judi.

Author's Note

This is the fourth mystery featuring Tom Mariner. It is set in the 2000s, when the internet was in its infancy, mobile phones had yet to evolve into smart phones, and people still read print newspapers.

Chapter One

Mariner was already awake when the digital alarm flipped over to three thirty a.m., a murmur of anticipation rippling through his stomach that was reminiscent of childhood, when getting up at this hour — the sky outside still inky black — meant it was either Christmas or the start of a long journey. He slid out of bed, careful not to tug the duvet and disturb Anna, only switching on the light when he was safely out of the bedroom. His clothes were where he'd left them last night, folded over the banister. Eyes grainy from lack of sleep, he stood under the shower and let his thoughts focus and sharpen in preparation for what lay ahead.

The wet spell they'd been having had temporarily abated, and the morning was still and dry, but there was an autumnal nip in the air as he crept from the house. Noticing that the *For Sale* sign positioned by the fence — now pleasingly covered with the word *Sold* — had fallen sideways, Mariner straightened it up before getting into his car. Five minutes later he drew up outside Tony Knox's house. His DS was looking out for him and appeared immediately. 'Good day for it, boss,' Knox said, climbing in beside Mariner and fastening his seat belt.

'Any day's a good day for this,' said Mariner, 'though the code name has to be someone's idea of a joke. Ocean Blue? Operation Open Sewer would be more accurate.'

'Won't you miss all this, boss?'

'I'm only on leave for a week. I think I'll manage.'

'No, I mean when your transfer comes through.'

'I'm sure they have their share of excitement in Herefordshire. If what you read in the press is accurate, rural towns are worse than anywhere for drugs and vice these days.'

'Won't be the same though, will it?'

'No, but I think that's the point. At least, it is where Anna's concerned.'

'You've got the whole of next week off too?'

'All seven days of it. The christening isn't until next Sunday.'

'The godfather, eh?' Knox hummed the opening bars of the soundtrack to the Coppola film.

'Only nominally,' said Mariner. 'I think Anna and I would have to be married to get the official title. But it'll do me. It feels like enough of a responsibility as it is.'

Up until now, and unsurprisingly at this hour, the traffic had been light. But passing the arts centre and turning into the outward-bound Pershore Road, they joined a steady queue of cars all turning right into Tally Ho, the police training centre. They must have looked like arrivals at some bizarrely timed party, but on the walk across the car park the mood was sombre, with just a few of the younger lads larking about as if they were going on a school trip. Around one hundred and fifty officers gathered from all over the West Midlands in the main conference hall. Chief Superintendent Marston kept it simple. Covert operation Ocean Blue had been months in the planning and anyone who wasn't clear on their role by now would face a disciplinary for sleeping on the job. 'Let's keep it swift and clean. Good luck.'

* * *

Curled in a foetal position on her grubby bed, Katarina lay with her hands locked together between her thighs where her body was sore. She should feel grateful. The night was over and she could relax, if that was what this state could be called. Waves of exhaustion lapped over her, if only she could stop shivering for long enough to drift away into blissful oblivion. But the room was damp and cold, and through the flimsy net curtains the light from the outside streetlamp lit up the condensation that crept down the window pane, collecting at the bottom of the rotting wooden frame. Despite the portable electric radiator, her shallow breaths steamed the air and the end of her nose tingled as she huddled in the blankets still in her clothes.

In search of some comfort she reached out, opened the drawer of the cheap bedside cabinet and took out her most precious possession, a much-handled photograph, one of the few possessions she'd retained from what now seemed like a whole other life. Even after all that she endured night after night, this was the most exquisite torture of all, as she considered what might have been, but for her own naiveté. With a will of their own, her thoughts ranged over her home and parents, her brother and sisters, as her chest contracted, forcing out a sob. She wondered if Alana in the room next to hers was suffering the same torment. It was impossible to tell if she too was awake. This was the time of night when the house fell silent. The last of the clients had been and gone and, but for the occasional passing of a distant car, the outside world seemed deceptively at peace.

Katarina must have dozed off because she was woken by a terrifying bang and shouting, followed by heavy footsteps stomping up the stairs. Scrambling to the end of her bed, she pressed herself against the cold wall in an attempt to make herself invisible, praying that this time she'd be left alone. But the door burst open and a man, a stranger, was framed in the doorway. Different from the others, clean and well dressed, he spoke in soothing tones, but in her panic she couldn't untangle the words to understand what he was saying. She saw his gaze take in the squalor and she closed her eyes to hide from the shame.

* * *

As the ram hit the door, bursting it open, it was the smell that hit them first: a combination of rising damp and the stale animal stench of sex and cheap perfume. Mariner, Knox and two uniformed officers stampeded up the stairs, flinging open doors as they went. In the first three rooms the occupants, two women and a man, were roused from their sleep, blinking uncertainly in the sudden glare of the bare light bulbs.

At the top of the house Mariner thought at first that the fourth room was empty. But as his eyes adjusted to the gloom he saw the bundle at the far end of the bed, eyes wide and terrified. 'It's all right,' he said. 'You're safe.' He held out his warrant card. 'I'm with the police. *Polizei.*' The girl shrank back further from him. Advancing slowly Mariner saw some kind of jacket slung over the chair, matted fur around the hood. He picked it up and held it up to her. 'You have to come with me.' When he was close enough he gently lifted the thin grimy blanket from her and took her bony arm.

Down on the street in the chilly dawn it felt like they were part of a freak show. Curtains twitched aside in the houses around them as the girls were bundled as quickly as possible into the waiting cars, one car containing the two arrested males sped away. Ocean Blue, for them, accomplished.

* * *

Emma O'Brien chuckled at a joke made by the radio presenter. 'What a silly man,' she said, gazing down at her baby daughter in her car seat beside her. Jessica rewarded her with a gummy grin, kicking her legs vigorously, and yet again Emma marvelled at the physical reaction that beautiful smile could evoke. The traffic ahead inched forward and she eased her foot off the clutch. Eight thirty. God, fancy having to do this journey every day. She'd known it would be slow getting into the city, so she'd allowed plenty of time, in fact she'd surprised herself at how relaxed she was feeling. It was down to motherhood, no doubt about it. Everyone had commented on the change. Six months ago she'd have been in the lecture theatre at the crack of dawn checking her presentation, making sure that all the AV technology was functioning and mentally rehearsing her opening remarks. 'Your mummy is a changed woman,' she told Jessica with another indulgent smile.

'Ghee,' grinned Jessica.

As Emma got nearer to the nursery, the first twinge of nervous apprehension kicked in. She tried to tell herself it was because she'd be standing up in front of a full lecture hall for the first time in six months, but part of her also acknowledged the true source of her unease. It was the prospect of leaving her seven-week-old daughter in the hands of relative strangers. Terrible things happened with tiny babies. Only recently she'd read in the paper about a nanny convicted of manslaughter for shaking a baby to death. 'Don't be ridiculous,' she said out loud. The crèche had been running for years, the staff fully vetted by the hospital. They were professionals. If there was any malpractice going on, the place would have been closed down long ago. Too late to back out now and, in any case, the one-off lecture paid so obscenely well that she'd have been out of her tiny mind to turn it down. The crèche arrangement would be just fine.

Half an hour later, her daughter happily entrusted to the kind and capable crèche manager, Emma O'Brien got back in her car and allowed herself a little cry, the separation from her daughter a tangible, physical pain even though – or perhaps because - Jessica had let her go without a murmur. Fumbling for her mobile Emma started to speed-dial Peter's mobile then abruptly severed the connection. He'd already be at work and in the first of his all-day meetings about the latest round of drug trials — he wouldn't thank her for the interruption. Far better to call him this afternoon when it was all over to report how well it had all gone. Blowing her nose hard, she shifted herself into professional mode.

* * *

At Granville Lane, while the FME was checking over the girls, up in the briefing room Mariner reminded his team of the drill. Eight girls in total had been brought back to Granville Lane from two establishments. Two men, their minders, had been arrested and all without casualties. It had gone smoothly and Mariner began with congratulations. 'But that was the easy part,' he said. 'Now comes the real challenge; building a case against these men and any others who have been picked up across the city, and finding out who's running the show. They're our real target — those further up the chain who are responsible for this whole obscene operation. Immigration have identified a number of suspects they've been monitoring for the last twelve months.' He held up half a dozen digital mugshots. 'But we need to make the connections. We want positive identification backed by credible witness statements. Some of the girls may have had direct contact, or overheard conversations. Immigration will continue to do their bit by going through any papers we've seized, but the taped and videoed interviews will be crucial.'

Looking around, Mariner was satisfied to see everyone, outwardly at least, fully focused. 'Of course, some girls are going to do better as witnesses than others, but what we're looking for are a couple of reliable ones who are also willing to testify.' He was aware as he said it that this was the biggest potential stumbling block. 'Most of these girls have been abused over long periods of time. They're young and scared and have learned the hard way not to trust anyone. We don't have much time to rebuild that trust. I don't have to remind you that we're interviewing victims, not criminals. We need to go gently and build confidence. These are potentially significant witnesses who must be carefully interviewed so that if and when any case comes to court we can be confident that there will be no accusations of leading the questioning.'

Mariner had split his officers into teams for interviewing — where possible, pairing male with female — in the hope that the girls would feel less intimidated. He and Knox would start with the minders, with a view to making some kind of deal that would lead them to the bigger fish.

As the briefing broke up, DCI Sharp came in, another woman following close behind. 'Tom, this is Lorelei Fielding, she's from the Daffodil Project,' Sharp said.

'Daffodil Project?'

'We're a charity that offers support to vulnerable women,' Fielding said. 'We act as advocates or counsellors and have several refuges across the city. We're here to offer our services. Our support workers can be present at the interviews and when you've finished what you have to do, we'll take the girls to one of our hostels overnight.'

'Thanks,' said Mariner. 'I'll let you know when we're ready.'

The FME was almost finished. 'You're beginning the interviews now?' he asked Mariner.

'We're just waiting for one of the translators to arrive.'

'You won't need it for all of them. One of the girls speaks pretty good English.'

'Really?'

'Her grandfather was over here during the war apparently. He taught her the basics. She's pretty fluent.'

'Which one is she?'

'Katarina. At nineteen she's one of the oldest, too, so you may find that she handles the whole process better.'

Mariner nodded his thanks. He and Knox would interview her as well.

'You'll go easy on them, won't you?' said Lorelei.

'Of course.'

But easy was only a one-way street. For Mariner and Knox the initial interviews with the minders were a frustrating experience. Except to give their names, the men refused to speak or to acknowledge recognition of any of the further suspects in the photographs. After only an hour Mariner gave up. 'If nothing else we've got them for living off immoral earnings. We can afford to let them stew. One of the girls might provide us with a way in. Let's make them the priority.' He wanted to start with the girl who spoke English.

Tony Knox, with DC Jenny Foster, was conducting an interview with a girl who looked no more than about twelve years old. Pale and scrawny, there were dark smudges under her eyes and her skinny arms were mottled with scars. She lowered her head as they entered the room, but not before Knox had noticed the gummy gap where her top incisors should have been, which gave her the appearance of a small child losing her milk teeth. She sat low in her chair placing as much distance as she could between herself and the officers, her arms folded protectively around her.

'Her name is Sonja,' the interpreter said, with a glance in the girl's direction.

'What happened to her teeth?' Foster asked the interpreter. 'Was she beaten?'

'They were removed,' the interpreter said after a short exchange. 'It would help her to do her work better.'

'Christ,' said Knox.

But Foster didn't get it.

'All the better for giving blow jobs,' Knox illuminated, his voice low.

His colleague turned a funny colour.

Sonja responded to their questions with the tiniest nod or shake of the head, and Knox was about to get up and leave the room, when suddenly she turned to the translator and spoke rapidly, her words gushing out in a torrent, tumbling over each other. For the first time she looked directly into Tony Knox's face with a desperation that wrenched at his insides.

'She wants to know how long this will take,' the translator said. 'She wants to go and find her child.'

'She has a child?' Knox failed to keep the incredulity from his voice.

The girl spoke again, the urgency in her voice increasing.

'A daughter. She's in an orphanage in Tirana. She wants to go and find her.'

'Jesus Christ,' breathed Knox, looking at the girl in front of them, who was little more than a child herself. 'Now I've heard it all.'

* * *

Walking into the interview suite along with PC Millie Khatoon, Mariner recognised Katarina as the girl he had brought down from the top floor of the house on Foundry Road. He'd never have believed she was nineteen, but in the safety of the police station, she seemed to have lost a little of her timidity. She clasped a beaker of tea between cupped hands. The room was cosy, with comfortable chairs and soft furnishings, but it had the same audio and video recording equipment you'd find in a standard interview room — and she looked anything but at home.

'You speak English?' Mariner confirmed.

Katarina nodded.

'I just want to ask you some questions. If there's anything you don't understand or anything you don't want to talk about, then you can tell me. Okay?'

She nodded again, and Mariner hoped for the sake of the recording equipment that she would eventually find her voice.

'How did you come to England, to Birmingham?'

Katarina took a sip from the cup and cleared her throat. 'I work as a waitress in a bar in Tirana where my family is,' she began, her gaze fixed on a point just to the left of Mariner's elbow. 'A man heard me talk in English to some American customers. He says that my English is very good, that he can get me a job as a translator and to teach our language in England. He says there's a big want for good translators and that I look nice and he can get me a good job in Brussels or in London, for good money. He says he work for the government.'

'Doing what?'

Her lip curled. 'I don't know. I tell him I have no money, but he said I can travel in his car and he will arrange the papers and the travel documents and I can pay him back when I have a job. He tells me about the kind of life I can have, with my own apartment and my own car. He says I must think about it and he will come back to the bar in a few days.'

'Did he tell you his name?'

'I only know Petya. I talk about it with my family and my father and he think it will be a great chance for me to have a good job. When Petya comes back to the restaurant I say I will go. I have to meet him at a place in the city early in the morning, five o'clock. I am surprised because he has good clothes but his car is old and dirty.' Her eyes glazed over as she remembered. 'But I think it's okay because there are two girls also waiting.'

'Did you know these other girls?'

'No. They are going to get a job with rich families, to look after the children. Petya took our passports for making them safe. He drive us to the border and a hotel where he says we will stay tonight. Two more men came and then Petya says that he must go back to Tirana on important government business and his friends will take us on the rest of the way to London.' She stopped for a moment and sipped her tea.

'You're doing really well,' Mariner encouraged her.

She took a deep breath. 'That night one of the men come in to my room and make me have sex with him.' Her lip trembled. 'I don't want it and I tried to fight him but he's very strong. Afterwards he locked the door. We stay in the hotel maybe three days, with the door locked. Sometimes a man comes, brings a little bit of food, some water, sometimes have sex or hit me.' The last words caught in her throat.

'Petya's friends?'

She nodded.

Mariner had heard of the process before, called 'seasoning,' in other words, beating the resistance out of the girls. He hated putting her through this, but they needed the evidence. 'Do you want to stop?' he asked. 'We can take a break?'

She shook her head but sipped again from her tea. Mariner couldn't help but notice the tremor in her hand.

'I know this is hard,' he said, 'but can you describe any of the men?'

'They have black hair,' she said, dully.

'All of them?'

'Yes. But one of them have very short.'

'Like my hair?'

She managed a brief look into his face. 'More short,' she said. 'And he tall man, thin man.' She measured out tall and thin with her hands. 'He don't have sex with me, but he bring food.'

'Were the other men tall, too?'

'Not so much.'

'They were short?'

'A little bit, and one is a bit fat and one more bit fat.' She gestured a generous gut. 'They don't shave and I think they don't wash very much. They smell like beer.' She grimaced with distaste, then a light sparked behind her eyes as she remembered something else. 'The fat man, he have a picture.' She stroked her skinny forearm.

'A tattoo?' Mariner confirmed. 'A picture on his arm?'

'Yes.'

'Do you remember what the picture was?' But she didn't.

'Sometimes I ask them about the job as translator but they laugh at me. They say I have a different job now. They have paid good money for me and I will work for them to pay it back.' She stopped abruptly and stood up. 'I have to pee now.'

'Of course.' They took a short break, during which Mariner went and stood outside in the fresh breeze, perhaps hoping that it might somehow cleanse him.

Ten minutes later they were back in the interview room. 'So you were at the hotel for three days,' Mariner prompted gently. 'What happened then?'

'They get me up very early and we leave the hotel. It's dark. We drive in the car again to Paris and go to another hotel. We stay - I don't know - two, maybe three weeks and many men come to have sex every night. They give us money, but the fat man take it for his money. Then another man come, tall man. We go on the train to London, and drive in a car to Birmingham. We come to the house where you find me.' Finally her eyes met his.

'The other girls were with you?' Mariner asked.

She shook her head. 'They stay in Paris. I don't know what happens to them.'

She seemed numb, quite devoid of emotion, but the air in the room was thick with suppressed outrage as Mariner and Khatoon listened.

'And since you came to Birmingham?'

She sighed. 'I do my job. I stay in the same house and the door is locked on my room except when I can go to the bathroom, or get food or when the men come.'

'How many clients . . . men?'

A shrug. 'Maybe fifteen, twenty each day.' She was beyond caring.

'And they pay you?'

'Stanislav take the money. I can't talk to the men and I must pretend I can't speak English.'

Mariner placed two photographs on the table. 'One of these is Stanislav?'

'Yes.'

'And the other man?'

'I don't know.'

'Do you know any of these faces?' Mariner placed the other photographs in front of her.

Her eyes fell on the third, a swarthy man with slicked back hair, and widened in surprise.

'You know him?'

'This is Petya.'

'He's the man who offered you work?'

'Yes.'

'Well done.' Crunch time. 'Katarina, we want to put Stanislav and Petya and men like them in prison, to stop them from hurting other young women. But to do that we need someone to tell the courts what they have done. Can you do that for us? Can you tell the court what you have told us today?'

'I don't know. I think they will be very angry.'

'If you tell your story, they'll be put in prison for a very long time and won't be able to harm you. We really need your help, Katarina. You're a good, strong witness.' They'd talk about defence cross-examinations later, much later, when she was physically stronger and would be more resilient.

'Okay. I try.'

'Thank you.' And if it hadn't been so wildly inappropriate, he would have hugged her.

* * *

By four o'clock all the girls had been extensively questioned, and they could do no more. It had been a harrowing day. Mariner should have been feeling elated, but instead depression kicked in, and he sensed that the others were feeling the same way. Tony Knox summed up the mood. 'The girl we talked to is fourteen,' he said, in disgust.

'That's only a year older than our Molly,' said Glover.

'And she's been working here for about a year, twenty blokes a day, protected and unprotected. She's a mess — physically and psychologically.' Knox looked emotionally drained.

'Makes me feel guilty to be going home to my family,' said Glover.

But Mariner was satisfied that they were building a good case. Of the eight, Katarina was going to make the most reliable witness. Even throughout the day she seemed to have grown in strength, her shoulders had loosened a little, the eye contact becoming more frequent. The other girls seemed to look up to her.

'What will happen to them?' he asked Lorelei, as he watched them piling into the minibus to go to the hostel.

'Tonight?'

'Long term.'

'After you've finished with them, most of them will be sent to an immigration centre, and then back home,' she said.

'Well, that's something.'

'Is it?'

Mariner should have asked her what she meant, but something told him he wouldn't want to hear the answer.

Instead he retreated to his office to write up his notes. He wanted to leave the case tidy for DCI Sharp in his absence, but he found it impossible to concentrate. Images conjured up by Katarina's account of her ordeal kept creeping into his head. She was just a kid, some of the other girls even younger. It was far too much for them to have gone through in their young lives and he couldn't begin to imagine the impact of their experiences. He felt tainted by it. Life as a country copper had to be preferable to this. When his phone rang he was glad of the distraction. It was DCI Sharp. 'Can you spare a few minutes, Tom?'

Mariner crossed the outer office and knocked on the gaffer's door. Going in, he recognised her visitor from the back of his head, a thinning crown of dark hair flecked with white flakes of dandruff. Councillor Derek Cahill was a regular crusader for the *Daily Mail*, an oily little man who saw the current climate of interagency co-operation as an opportunity to give the police as much grief as possible about what he called the 'moral decline' of the city.

'You know DI Mariner?' Sharp asked him as the two men came face to face.

Cahill managed a thin smile. 'We've met before.'

'The councillor came in to express his concern at the rise of prostitution in our area,' Sharp said, smoothly. 'I thought it might reassure him to know about the effectiveness of operation Ocean Blue today, and since you were on the ground when it happened, I thought you could help us out, Tom.'

'Of course, ma'am.' Mariner turned to Cahill. 'We're well aware of this as a growing problem, councillor. Which is why, at dawn today, we raided a number of premises in the city suspected to be brothels. We brought in a number of girls and not nearly enough papers for each of them. Most of them are from various places in Eastern Europe. Girls without identities. I don't have the official figures yet, of course. Those arrested are still being processed, but I can tell you that in the region of seventy women were brought in from across the city.' In truth Mariner had no idea how many it was, though he was pretty sure that seventy was a generous over-estimate. But he was doing what DCI Sharp had called him in to do – get this irritating little man out of her office.

'Yes, well, it's a start,' Cahill conceded. 'Though we all know that in a few weeks those girls will have simply been replaced by more.'

'Oh, we don't kid ourselves,' Mariner agreed. 'We might have broken this wave but we're a long way off stemming the tide.'

'I'm glad to hear that you're not being complacent.' Cahill was stymied. He'd chosen the wrong day to come in with his usual rant about how little was being done.

'You can depend on it,' said Mariner trying not to smirk. He looked up at DCI Sharp, engaged in a similar struggle. 'Is that all, ma'am?'

'Thank you for your input, Inspector.'

'Glad to be of help.'

Minutes later Mariner watched from his desk as Sharp strode across the main office seeing Cahill out of the building. The DCI cut an imposing figure and today, as always, was impeccably dressed. The little weasel was almost having to break into a trot to keep up with her. Mariner's phone rang again.

* * *

Mickey Mouse and Donald Duck winked down at Emma O'Brien from the windows as she walked across the car park to the entrance of the double-fronted Victorian villa, glowing with the prospect of her baby daughter's smile only moments away. She felt exhausted, the discipline of remaining mentally focused for a whole day was an unfamiliar one. She'd got through the lecture, that was the most she could say, and if she'd learned nothing else from today, it had certainly confirmed what she'd already known deep down; that in no way was she ready to consider going back to regular work.

Peter was going to be disappointed. With two households to support he was stretched about as far as he could be, so they could really use another income. Emma had an inkling that he was hoping today might have given her an appetite for what she was missing. In fact it had done quite the reverse. What was the point of having a baby if Emma wasn't going to spend time with her? And right now, that was what she wanted more than anything else in the world. Even she had been unprepared for what a wrench it had been, to have to leave Jessica today. The arrangement had been fine. The crèche had been convenient and the staff seemed competent and kind. It just wouldn't happen again, not for a very long time.

And now with the week at an end, she and Peter had nothing planned for the next two days except spending quality time together as a family. She pressed the buzzer and the nursery intercom crackled, as a tinny voice asked her for identification. 'Jessica Klinnemann's mummy,' she said.

A pause. 'Could you repeat that, please?'

'Jessica Klinnemann's mummy,' Emma yelled into the tiny speaker as the traffic roared by on the busy road behind her. It had been the same frustrating palaver first thing this morning too.

'Push the door,' instructed the voice, at last. Emma pushed open the heavy spring-hinged door and the warm smell of cooked vegetables hit her nostrils as she walked into a bright yellow vestibule, the thigh-high coat hooks crowded with tiny jackets and coats slung over Postman Pat and Bob the Builder bags. A notice board above displayed photographs of a dozen young women in identical tunics.

The office off to the left was empty and there was no one else around, so Emma crossed the hallway to the room where she'd dropped off her daughter five hours earlier. She levered down the high door handle and went in. She was confronted by chaos. Two infants lay in bouncing chairs and both were grizzling, while a tape of nursery rhymes provided a tuneful counterpoint. The girl who had been stooping over one of the babies turned, her freckled face flushed and damp with perspiration, fine red hair escaping from her ponytail and harassment written all over her face. She managed a brief smile. 'Hi.'

'Hi, I'm Jessica's mum,' she said to the girl. 'How's she been?'

The girl was looking at her as if she'd just requested half a pound of sausages. 'You're Jessica's mummy?' she said, uncertainly.

'Yes, that's right.' Scanning the row of crying babies, Emma noticed that Jessica wasn't among them. 'Is she being changed?'

As she spoke, a second young woman appeared from the bathroom carrying a dark-eyed baby on her hip. The two young women exchanged a look, momentarily disconcerted and a rumble of fear began deep inside Emma O'Brien.

'None of these children is Jessica,' she said, the sensation gathering momentum and rising up into her chest. 'Where is she?'

The girl frowned. 'I don't understand. The other babies have gone. These are the only children left.'

The rumble welled and broke to the surface and in an uncontrollable reflex reaction, Emma O'Brien let rip an anguished howl.

Chapter Two

Mariner picked up his ringing phone.

'Hi, again.'

Mariner smiled. 'Hello.' It was the third time Anna had called inside the last half hour. The attention to detail this week in Herefordshire was getting was worthy of a military campaign.

'Sorry. I thought we should take something smart to wear in the evening. Shall I pack your blue striped shirt?'

Did he even own a blue striped shirt? 'All right. Whatever you think.'

'And you're sure you won't be late? It would be nice to get there in time to have a relaxed—'

'I'm just about to leave,' he reassured her. She'd needed a lot of that recently — understandably, he conceded. At least planning this holiday had given her something else to focus on. He was looking forward to it, sort of. They certainly needed the break, what with the kind of hours Mariner had been working and the hassle of getting their houses on the market, and fielding the stream of people looking around. Disappointing though, that putting his own house up for sale hadn't resulted in the same positive outcome as Anna's.

As Mariner replaced the receiver DCI Sharp put her head round the door, briefcase in hand and coat slung over her arm. 'Thanks for earlier.' She was referring to Councillor Cahill. 'It should keep him off our backs for a couple of weeks.'

'My pleasure, ma'am. Good to give him one less excuse for complaining about us. He's a nasty piece of work.'

'So I understand. I've never had the full story on him. You must tell me sometime.' She glanced over Mariner's tidy desk. 'How did the interviews go?'

Mariner reported back on the day's events. 'Katarina in particular looks like a solid witness.'

'That's a great result. You're on a week's leave now, aren't you?'

'Yes, ma'am.'

'Well, you've earned it. Why don't you get yourself off?'

Out in the main office Mariner could see a few CID officers finishing up for the weekend, their pace unhurried. 'What, and run the gauntlet of smart-arsed remarks from that lot out there about the boss leaving early?'

'Hm. Remind me — what time did you start this morning?'

'We all started early today.'

'Okay then, yesterday? Probably while most of them were still wolfing down their eggs and bacon.'

'Not Tony Knox,' said Mariner. 'You have to be up early these days to beat him into the office.' Mariner could see his sergeant, his shaven pate bent forward in concentration, work currently a poor substitute for his non-existent social life. A passing phase, it had to be, but even so, Mariner made a mental note to ask him out for a drink when the next opportunity arose.

'He's the exception,' Sharp persisted. 'Go on, Tom. You have my permission.'

Mariner caved. 'Okay then, thank you, ma'am.' They'd come a long way since their first meeting when her opening gambit had been to caution him against bending the rules. 'You off too?'

'I wish.' She lifted her briefcase, simultaneously glancing at her watch. 'No. I've got the joys of a late budget briefing at Lloyd House, which started about ten minutes ago. Have a good week, Tom. Come back refreshed.'

'Thanks, I will.'

When the phone rang again Mariner was fully prepared for another last-minute amendment to his wardrobe, but this time it wasn't Anna. 'Tom? Louise Byrne from the Crown Prosecution Service. It's about Kenneth McCrae. We thought we should let you know.'

'Yes?' Mariner spoke calmly, as if a small whirlpool hadn't just started up in his stomach. Even from where he was languishing on remand, McCrae still had the capacity to crimp Mariner's gut and make the hairs on his neck bristle. The mere mention of his name triggered a vivid sensation of cold, dark, hunger and fear that nine months and occasional counselling hadn't yet fully dispelled. McCrae's trial was scheduled to start a week on Monday and was the other reason for taking a break: mental preparation.

'He's changing his plea to not guilty, on the grounds of diminished responsibility,' Louise Byrne went on.

Mariner snorted. Not guilty. Kenneth McCrae, the stepbrother who, until nine months ago, he'd known nothing about; the man who, fuelled by jealousy and greed, had gone on a rampage, shooting dead Mariner's estranged father, stepmother and their chauffeur in cold blood before going on to beat Mariner's grandmother to death, and finally abduct and imprison Mariner himself, leaving him to fester and die. He should have seen this coming. 'What are his chances?' he asked, evenly, ignoring the increased thudding of his heart.

'He'll be citing his tour in the Falklands, of course,' Louise said, dodging the question. 'Post-traumatic stress disorder.' So he was going for the jury's sympathy vote. Clever. 'But we're not beaten yet.' Her cheerfulness sounded forced. 'What McCrae did was planned and calculated, there's no doubt about that. All we have to prove is that the two are mutually exclusive. We still have a couple of weeks to prepare a counter argument and get some favourable psychiatric reports of our own.' But she'd been concerned enough to give Mariner the heads-up, which to him spoke volumes. 'It'll make your testimony all the more important,' she went on. 'McCrae was lodging with you at the time of the last killing and I need you to convince the jury that he was behaving perfectly rationally at that time.'

'I hardly saw him.'

'It will all help.' Code for: *we need anything we can get.* 'You and Mr Shipman are the only people to have had any contact at all during that time. And you are by definition a reliable witness.' Whereas Shipman, the agent who had let Mariner's flat to McCrae, was likely to be less secure in the courtroom arena.

'Thanks for letting me know,' said Mariner, ending the call. *Great note to sign off on.*

But when he looked up from replacing the receiver he saw a uniform hurrying towards him through the outer office, the urgency in PC Mann's stride catching everyone's attention. He wasn't the bearer of good news.

'We've had a call from a day nursery,' Mann gasped, arriving in Mariner's doorway, his face glossy with perspiration. 'One of the mothers came to collect her baby daughter, but she isn't there. The staff think she's been abducted.'

In police work there's one type of incident that, more than any other, requires an instant response and is guaranteed to galvanise the force. And this was it. Until they knew exactly what they'd got, no one would be leaving for the weekend. If Mariner had taken the gaffer's advice a bit more promptly it might have gone to someone else, but now his weekend was set to take on a completely different shape. Instructing Mann to gather together a team of uniforms, Mariner took Tony Knox and Charlie Glover and hurried down the stairs.

'You two up for this?' he asked the two sergeants. Only fair to give them an escape route now if they needed it.

'Fine with me,' said Glover. 'I've got the in-laws for the weekend.'

'I just need to make a phone call,' Tony Knox said, searching out his mobile.

'Cancelling a hot date?' Glover jibed.

Knox grimaced. 'No, calling in my dog-walker.'

'I didn't know you employed one,' said Mariner.

'The kid from across the road,' Knox illuminated. The boy had turned up on Knox's doorstep one Sunday afternoon a few weeks back, bucket and sponge in hand. 'Can I wash your car?'

Knox had looked out at his vehicle, put through the OCU car wash only the previous day. 'No, but you can walk my dog if you like.' After that it had become a regular arrangement.

It was by default that Tony Knox had ended up with Nelson, the canine orphan of McCrae's murder spree. Mariner had been all set to take him on, but then, with everything else that had been happening, it had seemed like not such a good idea. 'How about you though?' Mariner had said to Knox one evening over a pint. Knox's girlfriend, Selina, had moved out, taking with her the chocolate Labrador puppy that Knox had grown so fond of, so it had been an obvious question. And Nelson had settled in beautifully.

Compared with the puppy, Nelson was well behaved and low maintenance and, thanks to him, Knox had stumbled across a whole new world. His sights were set on a willowy brunette he'd met walking a maniacal springer one evening a couple of weeks ago, but though he'd been back to the same park regularly since, he hadn't been able to synchronise with her again so far. Not much chance for the next few days now this had happened, but he lived in hope.

Most of the family liaison team had also left for the weekend but Millie Khatoon remained. Mariner was glad. They'd worked together before. For several years now she'd brought to family liaison work the kind of openness and down-to-earth common sense that was instantly reassuring to families under duress. As they walked out to the car, Mariner talked through what Mann had told him, his own weekend obligations temporarily forgotten as his mind raced through the procedure. Right from the start with an incident such as this, there was a careful balance to be struck between acting quickly before the abductor had a chance to build any kind of relationship with the baby, and an equal need to be methodical and systematic so that no important details were overlooked.

Blues and twos eased them through the building rush-hour traffic that seemed to begin earlier and earlier on a Friday afternoon. As they drove, Mariner put in a call on his mobile to Anna, but the line was engaged. He didn't leave a message. 'I've never handled a baby-snatch before,' he said, to no one in particular. 'Haven't even been directly involved in an investigation.'

'I have,' Knox was grim. 'It didn't turn out well.'

After a couple of seconds it dawned on Mariner. 'Adam Teale,' he said, out loud. *Christ.* He'd forgotten that Knox was up on Merseyside back in 1993 when the toddler had disappeared, only to turn up three days later, strangled and beaten to death. 'This is different,' he said, sincerely hoping that the outcome would be, too. 'There it is.'

They'd almost driven past the nursery before Mariner spotted it, set as it was on the main through route connecting the suburbs of Selly Oak and Harborne. Mariner must have passed it hundreds of times before without noticing. There was no adjacent parking that was obvious, so continuing past, Glover manoeuvred them into a neighbouring cul-de-sac, Mann and his contingent following in convoy. The street was already lined with cars, but each driver managed to find a space to squeeze into, then they all trooped back the twenty or so yards along the main road. A little further up from the cul-de-sac and on the opposite side of the road they passed the entrance to the city's teaching hospital, the Queen Elizabeth. This was an area busy with traffic and pedestrians, Mariner noted, and instantly the odds began stacking against them.

Jack and the Beanstalk nursery was housed in a squat red-brick that stood apart from its neighbours in a tiny garden enclosed by high spiked iron railings. A red painted board in the garden advertised it as a *Private Day nursery for babies and toddlers aged 0—5 years.* A sticker affixed to the lower part of the board advertised free places for three- and four-year-olds, with a directive to enquire within. Someone was watching out for them, and as they passed through the gate and into the garden, the main front door swung open, on the other side of which stood a young woman in a royal blue tunic. Tall and slender, with shoulder-length blondish hair, she was young enough for her hormones to still be playing havoc with her complexion.

Mariner had his warrant card ready, though with PCs Mann and Khatoon in uniform it hardly seemed necessary. 'I'm DI Mariner and I'm here with DC Knox, DC Glover, PC Mann and PC Khatoon.'

'Samantha.'

The introductions, like Samantha's limp-fingered handshake, seemed a strange formality under the circumstances. As they all crammed into the narrow lobby she shut the front door, blotting out the traffic noise. 'I'm the deputy manager.' Her voice was thin and nervous. 'Mrs

Barratt who owns and manages the nursery has just popped out.'

'Where to?' Mariner asked.

'She had an emergency, personal I think, and after that she might have gone to the cash and carry. She'll go ballistic. I've tried to get her on her mobile, but she must be driving. It's switched off, so I've left a message. I wanted to wait until she came back but Jessica's mummy insisted that we call you straight away.'

'Quite right,' said Mariner. 'We can't afford to lose any time.' He gestured towards the two uniforms. 'These officers will need to search the building and grounds. It may seem unnecessary but we need to ensure that Jessica is definitely missing.' On Mariner's signal, Glover, Mann and their team headed off. 'Meanwhile I have to ask you some questions. Is there somewhere we can go to talk?'

'The main office is in here.'

Stepping past them Samantha pushed open the nearest door on their left, which opened into what was little more than a large cupboard crammed with two desks at right angles, a tower of filing cabinets and shelves bowed beneath the weight of dozens of ring binders. Every inch of wall space was covered with paper. A monochrome split-screen CCTV played four mini silent movies at them from one of the desks.

Squashed into the tiny area of free space, knees almost touching, were two more women. The younger one wore a uniform identical to Samantha's and seemed to be ministering to the other, who from the raw, swollen face, Mariner deduced to be Jessica's mother. 'Thank God!' she jumped up recognising immediately who they were. Her face contorted with emotion. 'Somebody's taken my daughter. You have to find her.'

'We will Mrs O'Brien—' began Mariner, recalling the details passed on by Mann.

'I'm Detective Inspector Tom Mariner and I'll be leading the search for your daughter. First of all I need to speak to the staff to establish exactly what has happened. While I'm doing that, Millie — PC Khatoon — who is a family liaison officer, is going to sit with you for a few minutes, and will be able to explain to you what's going on.' Mariner glanced up at Samantha. 'Is there somewhere more private where PC Khatoon can take Mrs O'Brien?' Mariner asked.

'They could go upstairs to the staff room.'

'Mrs O'Brien—' Millie stepped in to take control.

'*Miss*,' the distraught woman cut in, automatically.

'I'm sorry?'

'It's *Miss* O'Brien.'

'Sorry, Miss O'Brien. Why don't you come with me?'

'It's at the top of the stairs and on the—' Samantha said.

'We'll find it.' Khatoon was already halfway up the stairs, shepherding a bewildered Emma O'Brien ahead of her.

Mariner watched them go before entering the office. 'Okay, Samantha. Let's just go through the sequence of events.' Samantha automatically placed herself behind the desk, leaving Mariner and Knox to the chairs on the opposite side recently vacated by Emma O'Brien and her consoler. She'd picked up an elastic band and was stretching it over her fingers as Mariner spoke.

'When did you first realise that Jessica was missing?' he asked.

'About four o'clock, when her mummy came to fetch her. She just wasn't there.' That was fifty minutes ago.

'How many ways are there in and out of the nursery?'

'Just the entrance where you came in. There are patio doors at the back of the nursery that lead into the garden, but they can only be opened from the inside. And there's a fire door off the kitchen, but if someone wanted to get in through there they'd have to get over a high fence at the side.'

'And the main entrance has a security pad. Who knows the code for that?'

'Only permanent members of staff.'

'You don't give it out to parents?'

'They have to ring the bell.'

'So everyone gets buzzed in by you, in this office?'

Samantha shook her head. 'Sometimes Mrs Barratt or I get called away, so there are door releases in a couple of the rooms too.'

'Do they have cameras too?'

'No, but there's an intercom.'

'So people can be let in by simply identifying themselves verbally.'

'Yes.'

'But everyone who comes in would have to ring the bell and make themselves known to a member of staff,' Mariner clarified.

'Yes. Unless . . .' she tailed off, uncertainly.

'Unless what?'

'Sometimes people hold the door open for each other. We ask parents not to do that, but it's just good manners, isn't it?'

'So, if they chose the right moment, someone could get into the nursery without ringing the bell and without having to explain themselves to a member of staff.'

She thought about that for a moment. 'I suppose it's possible, yes. It shouldn't happen like that but . . .'

'And once they're in the building they are free to go anywhere?'

'Yes.'

'So potentially, if they'd chosen the right moment, someone could have just walked into the nursery off the street without any of the staff being any the wiser.'

'It shouldn't—'

'*Could* they?' demanded Mariner.

'It's *possible*, yes,' she repeated, becoming increasingly rattled.

'And they could just take a child without anyone noticing?' Mariner exchanged a brief glance with Knox. He couldn't quite believe that.

'No,' said Samantha. 'The children are never left unattended.'

'But I don't understand,' Mariner was floundering. 'It means that someone must have seen the abductor take Jessica.' He allowed himself a moment of optimism. Maybe this wasn't as bad as it had first appeared, and they would at least get a decent description.

'She did, but she assumed it was Jessica's mummy.'

Mariner was flummoxed again. 'Didn't she know Jessica's mother?'

'Jessica was a crèche baby,' Samantha said as if that explained everything. When she realised it didn't, she went on: 'In the main nursery staff do get to know the parents, because the children come here regularly over a period of time. We haven't had any new children for several months. But we also have an arrangement with the hospital to provide a daily crèche for medical professionals who attend conferences at the medical school, and for visiting consultants. Most of those children just come here for a day or maybe two and that's it, although we have a handful of regular users. The children are booked in advance, so that we can plan the right staffing levels.'

'And Jessica was a crèche baby, so she'd never been here before,' said Mariner finally beginning to grasp the situation.

'It was a complete one-off,' said Samantha.

'So the staff didn't know her mother. Isn't that a bit of a risk?'

'Everyone who comes into the crèche is meant to sign the visitor's book when they come in and go out.'

'And in practice?'

'It doesn't always happen,' she admitted. 'If parents are in a hurry—'

Mariner still couldn't make sense of it. 'But surely the staff would have seen Jessica's mother when she dropped the baby off this morning. Wouldn't they expect the same person to pick her up?'

'Miss O'Brien brought Jessica early. The crèche staff work a nine till five, so any children being left earlier than that are received by Mrs Barratt. It happens sometimes.'

'So up until she came to collect Jessica, the staff in the room had never met Miss O'Brien.'

'That's right.'

'And the only person who had met Jessica's mother — Mrs Barratt — wasn't here. Meaning that anyone could have come in and announced themselves as Jessica's mother and wouldn't have been challenged.'

Samantha was beginning to lose her cool. 'It wouldn't usually have been possible, because Mrs Barratt would have been here. And parents are supposed to sign the book and staff are meant to ask for identification—'

'Except we've already established that your security systems aren't exactly what we'd call watertight, are they?' said Mariner.

'No.' Samantha's flimsy veneer of confidence had all but dissolved. She looked about to cry and it crossed Mariner's mind that she was far too young to be burdened with this much responsibility.

There was a light knock on the door. Charlie Glover peered in and, catching Mariner's eye, gave the faintest shake of the head. Baby Jessica was definitely gone. But then, Mariner knew that now anyway. A member of staff had stood by and watched it happen. The priority now was to get a good description and start to fan out the search.

Leaving Samantha for a moment, Mariner went out to the hall to brief Glover, and Brian Mann. 'Get someone from uniform to retrieve as much CCTV footage as they can from a half-mile radius, then gather as many bodies as we can, and as soon as we have a description we'll start talking to people within a five-mile radius. See if the other

OCUs can spare any troops. And call the technicians to get someone down here so that we can start to monitor phone lines going in and out.'

As Mariner returned to the office, a buzz sounded and the top of a shaven head filled a segment of the split-screen CCTV.

'That's Josh's dad,' said Samantha. 'All the nursery parents will be here to fetch their children in the next hour or so. We've still got quite a few left.'

Shit. This was going to be a logistical nightmare. Ideally Mariner would want to keep everyone at the scene to be interviewed as potential witnesses, but if they did that, the place would be packed with agitated parents and kids.

'Okay, as long as you're certain these are parents you know, you can let them go, but PC Mann will screen them and take details before they leave. We'll need to talk to them later. Is there somewhere he can do that?' The hall would be far too cramped.

'The room across the hall there is empty at this time of day.' Samantha opened the door opposite onto what looked like a tiny classroom.

'That'll be fine,' said Mariner. He turned back to Glover. 'When you've instructed uniform, stay here by the front door with Mann, to supervise people going in and out.'

'How much do we tell them about what's going on, boss?' Mann wondered.

Mariner thought about that. Ordinarily in an investigation you'd want to keep everything under wraps to avoid creating panic, but in this case they needed as many pairs of ears and eyes working for them as possible. 'Everything,' he said. 'They've probably seen the cars and they'll certainly notice the uniforms. And we need them working with us. Someone might have noticed someone or something when they dropped their child off this morning.'

The buzzer sounded again, more insistently and an impatient face turned towards the camera.

'You know him well?' Mariner checked with Samantha.

'Josh has been here since he was a baby.'

'Okay, you can let him in.'

Samantha pushed the button on the telephone intercom and the shaved head bobbed and disappeared from the screen as, behind them, the main door opened and Josh's father stepped in. 'Everything all right?' he asked Samantha, seeing that clearly everything wasn't.

'Fine,' Samantha smiled weakly.

PC Mann stepped forward. 'Would you like to come in here a moment, sir?'

'What about anyone else who's been in and out this afternoon?' Mariner directed his question at Samantha.

'I'll have to talk to the girls in all the rooms to find out who they've let in.'

'DC Glover will do that,' said Mariner. Taking his cue, Glover came across from where he was standing. 'Interview separately and in isolation if you can,' Mariner told him. 'Come back to me if we get anything worthwhile.' He turned back to Samantha. 'We'll then need a list of addresses and contact details to go with the names so that we can get in touch with anyone we know has been here this afternoon.'

Mariner turned his attention back to the screen. 'The CCTV covers the whole nursery?'

'It moves from room to room automatically, but it hasn't been working very well.'

'Are the images stored?'

'Only for about ten minutes, it's just a monitoring system.'

Shame.

'Who was it who saw the person who took Jessica?' Mariner asked.

'The girls in the crèche. It's been a busy day, so there's one permanent member of staff, Christie, and two agency staff, Leanne and Kam.'

'How long has Christie been with you?'

'About eight months.'

'That's permanent?'

'In child care, yes. A lot of the girls start young and then leave young to have their own babies, or move to other settings.'

'Have Kam and Leanne worked for you before?' Mariner was wondering about an inside job.

'They've worked in the nursery but not in the crèche, so they're not so familiar with the procedures in there. But it's a reliable agency. They've supplied us for years.'

'And they're the only people to have been in that room this afternoon?'

'Apart from the parents who have already been to collect their children,' Samantha said. 'The hours vary but the girls will be able to tell you more.' She was fidgety now, wanting them to move on before her efficiency was further called into question.

'Right,' Mariner stood up. 'We'll speak to them next.'

'They've still got children down there. Is it all right if you talk to them in the room?'

It wasn't ideal. Ideally Mariner would have wanted to interview the girls separately and in the proper conditions, to get admissible witness statements, but they would have to make the best of it with preliminary interviews.

'I don't see why not,' he said. It was a decision Mariner would regret within minutes. Outside the confines of the office, they crossed the hall, following it round alongside the staircase to a room at the back of the building. Samantha hesitated outside the door.

'Can you be gentle with them? Leanne especially, well, she's not the sharpest knife in the drawer, if you know what I mean.'

'And she's responsible for looking after young children?'

Samantha shrugged. 'There probably wasn't much else in the way of careers options.' This afternoon was turning out to be a revelation. Allowing Mariner to absorb that fact, Samantha pushed open a door panelled with safety glass onto a twelve-by-fifteen playroom, children's artwork on the walls and the partially carpeted floor littered with fluorescent plastic toys. An alcove off to the left opened into a bathroom with fixtures and fittings in miniature. Going in, Mariner and Knox had to dodge a path through painted paper leaves that dangled from the ceiling. A baby lay on the carpet happily batting at an arc of dangling rattles, but what first assaulted Mariner's senses was the high-decibel wailing of the second small child, which seemed to reverberate back at them off the walls. The two young women in the room seemed oblivious, engaged as they were in half-heartedly tidying up, picking up toys from the floor and tossing them into plastic crates.

'This is Leanne and Kam,' Samantha said, by way of a crude introduction, raising her voice above the sound of the screaming baby. The women looked up at mention of their names. 'Girls, this is the police. They need to talk to you.'

Samantha had referred to them as 'girls' and that was exactly right. They looked barely old enough to take care of themselves let alone other people's children. And both of them looked decidedly wary of their visitors.

'What about the third girl?' Mariner asked.

'Sorry?'

'You mentioned Christie?'

'Oh, she's upstairs in the toddler room with one of the older children,' said Samantha. 'She wasn't here when—'

'Okay.'

'Do you mind?' Kam, an Asian girl with wide heavy-framed glasses, gestured towards the bawling infant, who up until now had been summarily ignored.

'No, please do,' said Mariner; anything to stop the awful racket. A pang of anxiety tweaked at him as he thought of what could be to come. He'd only been in here half a minute and already it was getting on his nerves. But maybe it was different when it was your own child. He hoped so. He watched as Kam eased the child out of its bobbing canvas seat, and grabbing a tissue, expertly wiped the snot and tears from its face in one stroke. The yelling diminished to a whimper, but the baby's face remained contorted with displeasure. Tony Knox stepped forward and offered a finger, which the child grabbed, dragging Knox's whole hand up towards its mouth.

'How old is she?' Knox asked. So it was a girl. Mariner was impressed that Tony Knox could identify the gender so quickly, given that she was wearing neither giveaway pink nor blue. The huge dark eyes gazing gravely at them from the pale face could have belonged to either.

'She's about three months, I think,' Kam told him, using her free hand to nudge her glasses higher up her nose. 'Though she's quite small for her age.'

'It's a long day for her,' Knox gave voice to Mariner's thoughts.

Kam rolled her eyes. 'Tell me about it. She hasn't been too thrilled, either. I think she's teething because her tummy's been upset all day. I've lost count of the number of times we've had to change her. She'll be glad to see her mummy again.' Talking about the baby seemed to relax Kam a little, though Mariner sensed she was glad to have the distraction of the child.

While they'd been focusing on the baby, Samantha had grouped some child-sized plastic chairs into a semi-circle, which Leanne, a large and lumbering girl, with freckles and red hair, came and perched on, leaving Mariner and Knox no other option than to fold their legs and do the same. Samantha took the more comfortable option of a table just behind them. To Mariner's right Leanne worried at a hang nail, and was unwilling to meet his eye. Kam remained standing, gently swaying, the child propped on her hip.

'How many children have there been in here today?' Mariner began.

'Six altogether: three babies, two toddlers and a pre-schooler.' Though he'd addressed Leanne it was Kam who spoke up from where she stood jiggling the child on her hip. 'Four this afternoon after Christie took Samuel up to the pre-school room, to play with his own age group. And after, Jessica . . .' she tailed off.

'And Christie was out of the room from what time?'

Leanne abandoned her nail and looked up. 'About half past one.'

'Leaving the two of you alone in the room, with the children.'

'It leaves us well within ratio.' Though it meant nothing to Mariner, Samantha's tone was defensive and the unease in her eyes seemed to infiltrate the other girls too. These were nothing more than frightened kids, not so very different from the young women they'd been interviewing earlier in the day for Ocean Blue. 'And then what?' he asked.

Again it was Kam who answered his question. Mariner tried to read the look in her eyes. 'It was an ordinary afternoon,' she said. 'The babies had a sleep after lunch and woke up gradually. We put out toys for them to play with. Mr Singh collected Rajid at about two o'clock.'

'And Mr Singh—?'

'Definitely took his child.' Samantha intervened. 'I was in the office when they left the building, and he's one of the few parents who has used the crèche before. I know him. And, well, it was obvious, wasn't it?'

'And then?'

The girls exchanged a nervous glance. Finally Leanne chipped in. 'It's been mad. A couple of the children have had loose nappies. We've been in and out of the bathroom all afternoon.'

'Loose . . . ?'

'I think she means the contents, boss,' said Knox, the experienced family man, looking up from his pocketbook. Since he'd ceased entertaining the baby girl, he'd been scribbling as the girls talked.

'Oh.' That was an image Mariner didn't care to linger on. 'And all this was going on when the woman came in for Jessica?'

'Yes.'

'Who was in here at the time?' asked Mariner.

'Just me,' said Leanne and suddenly all eyes were on her. She shrugged casually. 'I thought she was Jessica's mummy.'

Chapter Three

Leanne glared defensively at Kam. 'You were in the bathroom changing Connor and I was trying to comfort Ellie. Like you said, she's been crying all day. This woman came in and sort of smiled and went straight over to Jessica, so I thought—'

'So this woman definitely took Jessica?' Mariner felt a numbness spreading along the underside of his left thigh and shifted in an effort to get comfortable.

'Well, she must have done, mustn't she? Because when Jessica's real mummy came in later, Jessica wasn't here.' She turned to look at Samantha. 'I didn't know she wasn't — I mean, how was I supposed to know?' The belligerence faded and her face began to crumple in the way that Ellie's had moments before.

'Nobody's blaming you, Leanne,' Samantha said, though it seemed to Mariner that her words lacked a certain sincerity.

'It's great that you saw the person who took Jessica, Leanne,' he said, conscious of the need to keep her on side. 'It means we stand a much better chance of finding her.'

'I should have stopped her though, shouldn't I?' she said miserably. 'If I had we wouldn't be in this mess, and poor Mrs O'Brien—'

Mariner was pretty determined that this young kid wasn't going to bear the responsibility for what appeared to be pretty lax security all round in the nursery. 'It has happened but now we need to put it right. You can do that by telling me everything you can about this woman. What were you doing when the door opened and she came in?' He knew that re-setting the scene would help her recall.

'I was sitting on the carpet there, on a bean bag and I was cuddling Ellie, trying to make her stop crying.'

Mariner got up and walked over to the bean bags. 'Here? And where was Jessica at this time?'

'In her car seat on that side of the carpet, there.'

'So, she was about three feet away from where you were sitting.' Mariner picked up a little chair and plonked it where she had said. 'And the woman came in. What did she do?'

'She stood in the doorway and said hello.'

'And you looked up and saw her. Just take a minute to think carefully. This is really important. Now, what did she look like?' They'd get as much as they could now, and if necessary bring in a psychologist later to take her back over the events again.

Leanne shrugged, and Mariner's hopes sank a little. 'She was ordinary, no different from the other mums who come here. I only glanced at her for a second.'

They sank further. 'Had you ever seen her before?'

'I don't think so.'

'What about her hair colour?'

'It was sort of brown, I think. But it might have been blonde.'

Mariner was beginning to see Samantha's point about Leanne's intellectual capacity. 'Was she tall or short?' he asked.

Leanne looked around her as if trying to judge alongside them all, but failed to come to a decision.

'Thin or overweight?' Mariner persisted.

Another shrug.

Mariner bit back his frustration. From where he stood by the bean bag he glanced over at the door. He squatted down to the level at which Leanne would have been, and from that perspective, suddenly he could see why Leanne's memory was hazy at that point. The autumn leaves would have obscured most of her view. 'Okay,' he said. 'Let's try something different. How did this woman behave?'

'What do you mean?'

'Did she hesitate at all?'

'She might have done, I don't know. I was trying to quieten Ellie.'

'Okay, she was standing in the doorway. What did she do next?'

'She went over to Jessica.'

'And how did Jessica react?'

'She didn't. She was asleep in her baby seat. She'd nodded off.'

'Her baby seat?'

'Yeah, you know — the ones with the handle that you can strap into the car.'

'All right. Then what happened?'

'I think I said, "Oh, hello, you're Jessica's mummy."'

'So you told her the baby's name before she said it.'

She blushed again. 'I suppose I must have done.'

'Did she say anything else?'

'Something like: "oh, there she is, my little sweetheart. Mummy's come to take you home" — the usual stuff that they say. Then she asked how Jessica had been and I said, "Fine."

'She asked me when she'd been fed and changed, so I said that we'd had to change her when she was sick, and that her feeding chart was on the wall by her coat and bag.' Leanne nodded towards the little row of pegs with name labels above, that ran along one wall of the room. 'She went and got them, then picked up Jessica's car seat, said thanks and went.'

'And she gave you no reason to think that there was anything wrong at this time?'

'No, there was nothing . . . she just went straight over to the baby. I mean, what mother doesn't know her own child? And I was pretty busy trying to stop Ellie from crying. To be honest I was glad we'd have one less to think about.'

'What time was this?'

'About half past two.'

Christ, it had happened hours ago. The woman could be anywhere by now. They'd have to go national with the publicity right away. The press office would need to get busy with this one with maximum exposure. It would make a change from trying to keep things under wraps.

'And when did you first realise something was amiss?'

Kam spoke up. 'Not until Jessica's real mummy came to collect her and we found that she wasn't here. At first we couldn't understand what had happened. It didn't make sense.'

Leanne's face had creased into a frown as if it still was a mystery.

'What was Jessica wearing?' Mariner asked.

'A yellow babygro with a cardigan over the top,' said Leanne, but even this detail was not straightforward.

'No, it was green,' Kam chipped in.

'It was yellow.' Leanne stuck to her story. 'She was sick at lunchtime so I'd had to change her.'

Kam didn't look convinced. They'd have to go with an either or.

'And a babygro is one of those little suits like Ellie is wearing?' Mariner interrupted.

'Yes.' From where she stood Kam went in to the bathroom and returned with a mint coloured stretchy suit.

'It was exactly like this. We keep a supply for the babies who run out of clothes.'

'Except it was yellow,' muttered Leanne under her breath.

'Can we keep that?' Mariner asked Samantha. 'We can show a photograph when we do the appeal. It would have this same label in the back?' A manufacturer's label was sewn into the neck.

'Yes, Mrs Barratt bulk buys them as we don't always get them back.'

'It doesn't look much for this weather. It's cool outside.'

'Jessica had a coat but her mum — the woman — just covered her with it and tucked it in. She said she didn't want to wake the baby.'

'She took her in the car seat?'

'Yes, most of them do,' Samantha said. 'We don't have many babies whose parents live close enough to walk. They bring them in the seat in the morning and it stays here with them.'

'What colour was the seat?'

'It was dark blue, with a sort of checked pattern. The woman said that it was heavy and that she'd got to walk a long way.'

'Do you think she would have parked round the corner, in the cul-de-sac, like we have?' Mariner thought hopefully of the CCTV.

'Either that, or she might have left her car up in the hospital car park,' Samantha said. 'They're not really meant to, but some parents do that if there's no space here.'

So they'd need to get hold of any CCTV footage on the hospital site, as well as anything from the local streets. 'Anything else?'

'She thanked us for looking after Jessica so well. It was a bit over the top really. She seemed sort of relieved. I thought maybe it was the first time she'd left her with anyone.'

Knox looked up from his notepad. 'Is it the case with all the crèche children that the staff might not have met the parents?' he asked Samantha.

'Not all of them,' she said. 'Christie would know parents who leave their children for more than one day, and sometimes parents do the drop-off later in the morning, when all the staff are here.'

Knox caught Mariner's eye. 'So if this woman had approached a different baby — Ellie, for example — you would have known that it wasn't her baby?'

'No, we don't know her parents either.'

'But at the time the woman came into the room, Jessica was the only unattended baby . . .' said Mariner. So there was no way of telling whether this was a random snatch or if Jessica had been targeted.

'Thanks, Leanne, you've been a great help.' Mariner lied. He motioned Tony Knox to one side of the room.

'I'll have a quick word with Miss O'Brien then I need to see what progress Charlie Glover is making with the rest of the staff,' he told Knox. 'Find out from him if anyone else encountered this woman entering or leaving the nursery at around two thirty. Let's hope to God that they did and we can get a half-decent description, otherwise we're fucked. We can't hit the streets until we've got it sharpened up or we'll be bringing in just about every woman in south Birmingham. Let the team covering the CCTV footage know that, at the moment, we're looking for any woman in the area carrying a baby in a car seat around two thirty this afternoon, possibly, though not necessarily, walking up to the hospital site, maybe behaving strangely.'

Out in the hall it was chaos. PC Mann was trying to take details from the remaining parents, but there was a backlog and a queue had formed — around which the unoccupied children were running and squealing.

'Leopold, do stop!' shrieked one of the mothers in desperation. She wore a hospital name badge and was presumably on her way home from work.

'Please tell me that isn't really that child's name,' Mariner murmured.

'You'd be amazed,' Samantha said.

Leaving the mayhem temporarily behind, Mariner climbed the stairs to the first floor and found his way to the staff room. Pushing open the door, Emma O'Brien's anxiety ridden eyes turned on him immediately, with a desperation Mariner had seen etched on many faces over the years, and which today he could do little to alleviate. He'd have liked to reassure her with what they knew, but in this case it wasn't much. Someone had made her a hot drink and she was clutching the mug like a prop, but it remained full almost to the brim, an oily skin forming on the surface.

Mariner sat down on one of the low seats facing her. 'What we know is that at around half past two this afternoon a woman came into the nursery and took Jessica as if she was her child.'

Emma O'Brien let out an involuntary moan.

'It may not sound like it, but it's good news,' Mariner said, quickly. 'Because once we've firmed up the description we will know, to some extent, who we're looking for. We also have at least one eyewitness who should be able to recognise her.' He wouldn't tell her yet that what they had so far was less than useless or that, without some clue about the woman's motive, they were pissing into the wind. 'The woman also cared enough about Jessica to ask about when she'd been fed and changed — so she is concerned about your daughter's wellbeing. What I want to do next is release information to the press so that we can enlist the help of the public,' he went on, gently. 'Do you have a recent photograph of Jessica?'

Like any proud new parent, Emma O'Brien carried several in her bag. Her hands shook and her eyes dripped as she fumbled for them. Mariner isolated the one that presented the clearest shot of blonde, blue-eyed Jessica, then went back out into the corridor and gave it to Knox.

'She's a cracker, isn't she?' said Knox, taking the snapshot from him. It was true; she was a beautiful child. Even Mariner had noticed that much. Had it been what had attracted the woman to her?

'Stupid question, I know,' said Mariner. 'But do you think there's any way this can have been a simple mistake?'

But Knox shook his head, echoing Leanne's words. 'Any mother knows her child from day one.'

Mariner sighed. 'Okay. Fax it through to the OCU along with the description of the woman and get it released to the press along with the time and location. We particularly want to hear from anyone who might have been on or around the hospital site at around two thirty this afternoon — especially anyone who happened to be driving past here. That includes bus drivers. It's a busy road and we're hours too late, but you never know. We need to know if anyone else saw this woman entering or leaving the nursery. I want a couple of officers to stop any vehicles leaving the hospital site and uniform can start a house-to-house along this street and in the immediate vicinity. There's building work going on at the hospital, too. Make sure somebody talks to the workmen. They're the sort of people who might just have noticed this woman.'

'What about a press conference?'

'We haven't got enough for that yet,' said Mariner. 'But call the press office and have them on standby, with a view to getting something out for the late evening news. We'll set up the incident room at Granville Lane. There's nothing big enough here.' Mariner glanced at his watch. 'The gaffer should be out of her meeting at Lloyd House by now, too. See if you can raise her.' *And ruin whatever plans she might have had for the weekend, too.*

'She'll be thrilled,' said Knox, though they'd no way of knowing what DCI Sharp's reaction might be. So far they knew her career history: a top-level Hendon graduate who'd worked her way rapidly through the ranks and covered ground too. She'd had four years in Manchester, five in West Mercia, seven with the Met. She knew both city and rural forces. But her personal life was a closed book. Mariner had a vague impression of someone at home, but that was it. It was something they'd never talked about. Suddenly Mariner remembered his own weekend commitment. He'd meant to call Anna back, but hadn't got round to it. 'Shit! I should let Anna know what's going on too,' he said, thinking aloud. 'I'm meant to be on annual leave from tonight. When I spoke to her an hour ago I pretty much told her I was on my way. But I can't get into it all now.'

It was left for Knox to say: 'You want me to call her?'

'It'll be simpler coming from someone else.' It was pragmatic, Mariner told himself. It had a better ring to it than cowardice. 'Tell her I'll speak to her as soon as I can.'

'Sure.' Knox went outside to make the call.

'Where the hell—?' Anna launched in, when the line connected.

'Anna it's me,' Knox interrupted. 'Tony. I'm sorry. Something's come up that the boss has got to deal with, something urgent.'

'Like what?' Her voice was shot through with suspicion.

It was the last thing she'd want to hear. 'It's a missing baby,' he said. 'If you switch on the news in a bit, you'll see.'

'How long will he be?'

'I don't know. As long as it takes.'

'I'll get the luggage out of the car then.'

'Yes.'

'What about next week?'

'I really don't know, luv. I'm sorry.'

'Yeah, you and me both.'

Afterwards Knox made a mental note never to do the boss's dirty work again.

* * *

Mariner had returned to Emma O'Brien. 'Have you been able to let your husband know?' he asked.

'My *partner*,' she corrected him again. It seemed to be a sensitive issue. 'He's on his way here.'

'From?'

'Cambridge. It's where we live and where Peter works.'

'You're a long way from home,' Mariner observed.

'I was guest speaker at a conference today at the hospital. I'm something of a specialist in my field.'

'What field is that?'

'Sorry? Oh, sleep disorders,' she said, absently. 'I was honouring an arrangement I made last year to do a guest lecture on the course here. Jess was a bit of a surprise when she came along. I've given up my job but I didn't feel that I could let down the hospital.' She gave an apologetic smile. 'The money was good, too.'

'So you drove over here today?'

'No, we came over last night and stayed with friends in Knowle. A hotel would have been an unnecessary expense.'

'And today was the first time you've been to the nursery?' asked Mariner.

'No, there was a meeting for all the speakers about a month ago. I came to have a look round and met Mrs Barratt. Originally I was going to ask my parents to look after Jess, but it would have meant an extra journey over to Suffolk and back, and the hospital sent information about the crèche service, offered free. It seemed much more convenient.' A sob escaped her. 'Oh, God. It's the first time I've ever left her with anyone except Peter or my mother. Why did I ever think—?' Her composure crumbled and Mariner allowed her a few seconds to regroup. Millie passed a fresh box of tissues.

'So you dropped Jessica off at what time this morning?' Mariner asked after a respectable pause.

'About twenty past eight. The lecture wasn't until ten, but our friends suggested I come in early to beat the traffic. It gave me plenty of time to do last-minute preparation, too.'

'And you handed Jessica over to Mrs Barratt.'

'That's right.' She frowned. 'Where is Mrs Barratt? I haven't seen her this afternoon.'

'We're trying to locate her,' Mariner said. 'And you didn't notice anything unusual, anyone hanging about, watching or following you?'

'No, though I wasn't really looking of course.'

'Is there any chance that someone else could have collected Jessica for you, one of your friends perhaps?'

'No. No one else knew exactly where the nursery was. And why would they do that without speaking to me?'

'We just have to cover every possibility,' Mariner explained. 'One of the things I need to ask you to do is come up with a list of all the people who knew, or might have known, you were coming here today, including the friends you stayed with last night.'

She looked alarmed. 'Are you suggesting this could be someone we know? That's ludicrous.'

There was a knock on the door. It was Tony Knox. 'Can I have a word, boss?'

'I know, it's unlikely,' Mariner said to Emma O'Brien, getting to his feet. 'But we have to explore all the options. Would you excuse me? If anything develops I'll keep you informed.'

'Thank you.'

'I think we've got a description,' said Tony Knox, outside on the landing. 'Charlie Glover's found a girl who saw the woman when she first arrived.'

'Thank Christ for that.'

Charlie Glover had found interviewing the staff a frustrating and tedious business. 'The most any of them can remember is buzzing from the rooms to let several people in during the afternoon, but none of them can remember specific times or what was said,' he grumbled as they descended the stairs. 'Except Christie.'

'The girl who went from the crèche to the room upstairs,' Knox reminded him.

Glover took them down the landing to what was normally some kind of storage space, where Glover had cleared enough room for a couple of chairs to conduct his makeshift interviews. 'This is Christie,' he said. 'She met a woman in the hallway at about the right time.' Glover looked at the girl. 'Tell Inspector Mariner what you told me.'

Christie's colour rose as she spoke, but not enough to hide the dark red shadow, like a birthmark, that ran down the side of her face partially, but not fully, concealed by makeup. 'I was up in pre-school but had popped down to the office for some craft paper,' she said. 'I was on my way back up the stairs,' she said, 'when the woman was buzzed in.'

'Do you know who let her in?'

'No. It must have been one of the upstairs rooms. She was sort of hovering in the hallway and looked a bit uncertain of herself and I didn't recognise her, so I asked if I could help. She said she'd come for her baby, then she asked if Mrs Barratt was here, but I said no, I didn't think so. I asked her if everything was all right and she sort of hesitated, so I asked if her baby was in the crèche, because those are the mums who never remember where to go, and she said yes, so I reminded her where it was, and she went along there.'

'Were those the exact words: "I've come for my baby?"'

'Yes, I'm sure. I didn't quite catch it at first. She had an accent.'

'What kind of accent?'

'From up north, like Deidre.'

'Deidre?'

'Off *Coronation Street*.' She was distraught. 'I thought I was helping.'

'Of course you did. You had no way of knowing what was happening.'

'But now I think about it, she seemed sort of anxious and a bit out of breath. I thought maybe she was in a hurry because she'd left her car on the double yellows outside. People do that all the time.'

'Okay, so you rationalised her behaviour. There's nothing wrong with that. She must have known Mrs Barratt,' Mariner said. 'She asked for her by name.'

'Except that Mrs Barratt's picture is on the notice board in the hall, right where she was standing,' Christie reminded him. 'She'd have seen it.' What a contrast, Mariner thought. If Christie had been in the room with Jessica, she might never have been taken.

'Perhaps she was just checking that there was no manager on the premises,' offered Knox.

'And you got a good look at the woman?' Mariner said.

'Yes.'

Thank God for that. 'Okay, off you go.' He held his breath.

'She was white, about the same height as me — sort of average — and slim with a good figure.'

It was a promising start. 'What about her hair?' Mariner asked.

'It was tied back, and it was brown, I think, quite a nice reddish brown colour.'

Charlie Glover was checking his notebook for consistency with what she'd already told him.

'And how old would you say she was?'

Christie grimaced. 'I'm not very good on ages.'

'Was she your age — younger, older?'

'Older than me, sort of middle-aged, I suppose. I don't think she was wearing any makeup and sometimes that makes women look younger, doesn't it?'

'You're doing brilliantly, Christie,' Mariner could hardly contain his relief. 'Do you remember what she was wearing?'

'Trousers, I think.'

'Trousers or jeans?'

'No, definitely dark trousers and a nice top and jacket. She was quite smart, as if she'd been to work, like, in an office or something.'

'What colour was the top?'

'I couldn't see much of it.' She wrinkled her nose. 'But it was, like, a cream colour with some kind of pattern on, embroidery or sequins. It looked expensive, like cashmere or something. I remember thinking I quite liked it. And she had some kind of jewellery.' Her hand went up to her throat. 'She had a gold chain or something round her neck.'

'And the jacket?'

'It was dark, navy or black.'

'Anything else, shoes, a bag?'

'I don't think I looked at her shoes. She was holding something in her hand, could have been car keys, I suppose.' She stopped to think for a moment. 'That's all I can remember, there's nothing else.'

'That's a great description, Christie, well done. Will you go to the police station and help us to put together a computer image of this woman?'

'Take Christie straight to Granville Lane to meet with the e-fit team,' he said to Knox. 'The quicker we have an accurate image of this woman the better.'

'Tony.' As Knox was leaving, Mariner called him back. 'You spoke to Anna? How did she take it?'

'She was okay about it,' said Knox. 'Calm as you like.'

But Mariner didn't like the sound of that. He knew what she was thinking: *I hope this isn't going to happen when . . .*

She'd been so excited when she found out that she rang him at work, unable to contain herself. 'You know all that crap they used to give us in sex education lessons about how babies are made?'

'Yes.'

'Turns out they were right. I'm pregnant.' He'd never known her so happy. It had happened so much sooner than either of them had imagined it would. Her euphoria had lasted a month to the day, until that morning when he'd awoken in the early hours to find the duvet turned back from ominous stains and Anna perched on the side of the bath sobbing uncontrollably.

'It's far more common than you might think,' the doctor had reassured them, 'and really nothing to worry about. Absolutely no reason why you can't go on to have a healthy baby.' But his words weren't much comfort. Anna had wanted that baby. The experience had frightened her, too. Since then Anna had insisted that they do as the doctor suggested and wait a few weeks, and somehow the weeks had evolved into months and she remained reluctant. But then, it was she who had gone through all the physical and emotional turmoil and he could understand why she'd be afraid of it happening again. They hadn't really had much opportunity to talk about it and Mariner was loath to raise the subject because he knew how much it upset her. Sometimes when he looked at her she seemed so tired, and a light had gone out behind her eyes that he so wanted to re-ignite.

'I'm sure she'd prefer to speak to you though, boss,' Knox said, bringing him back to the present.

Knox was right. He could snatch a couple of minutes now. But when Mariner stepped outside into the gathering dusk to try and ring Anna, he was side-tracked by the appearance of a tank-like four-by-four that bounced up onto the pavement drawing to a halt outside the nursery, completely disregarding the parking restrictions. The side window bore a sticker for Jack and the Beanstalk Day Nursery. A big busted woman, fiftyish in suit and heels, with glossy scarlet fingernails that perfectly matched her lipstick, climbed out and went round to the tailgate of the vehicle, from which she began to drag a huge cardboard box. As Mariner approached her, she eyed him with suspicion, a lone male prowling outside a children's nursery.

'Mrs Barratt?' Mariner ventured a guess.

'That's right, I'm Trudy Barratt. Can I help you?' She paid him scant attention, more concerned with the task at hand.

Mariner took out his warrant card. 'I'm here to help you,' he said, reaching into the car and holding it out where she could see it. 'One of your children has gone missing.'

The box was teetering on the rim of the boot when he spoke and she almost let it drop. 'That's impossible.' She was aghast, until pragmatism took over. 'Someone's made a mistake. The girls have got you here for nothing.'

'I'm afraid not,' said Mariner. 'Jessica O'Brien has been taken from your nursery.'

She froze, and pocketing his phone Mariner pulled the bulky cardboard carton from where it precariously rested on the lip of the boot. It wasn't as heavy as it looked.

'Thanks,' she said, absently and slammed shut the tailgate — now intent on getting into the building as quickly as possible. She punched in the code and stepped aside to let Mariner through with his load, which he deposited in the now blissfully empty hallway. The full circumstances explained, Mrs Barratt's response became somewhat repetitive. 'I don't understand how this can have happened,' she kept saying. 'I need to talk to the girls.'

‘We already have,’ said Mariner. ‘As far as we can ascertain a woman walked into the crèche unchallenged at two thirty this afternoon and took Jessica O’Brien, as if she were her own child.’

‘And they let her go?’

‘No one had any reason not to. Your staff didn’t know that the woman wasn’t Jessica’s mother. You were the only person who would have known that.’

‘And I wasn’t here.’ Mariner hadn’t intended his comment as a judgement but she’d clearly taken it that way. ‘Oh, my God.’

Samantha appeared, hurrying down the stairs. ‘Have you heard what’s happened? A woman came into—’

‘Yes, I know. I’d like to have a few minutes . . .’

The last was directed at Mariner and as he nodded affirmation the two women disappeared into the office and Trudy Barratt closed the door politely but firmly behind them. Raised voices followed, before finally Samantha emerged, shaken but still keeping it together.

‘I’ll go and check if all the other children have gone,’ she said, unnecessarily to Mariner as she crossed the hall and climbed the stairs. He watched as Mrs Barratt went to pick up her phone and spotted the recording device, her hand hovering in mid-air. He pushed open the door. ‘We have to track all the calls made from now on,’ he said.

Mrs Barratt looked panicked. ‘Can I use my mobile?’

‘If you tell me who you’re calling.’

‘My husband.’

Chapter Four

Mariner allowed Trudy Barratt some privacy, and as he watched her through the window, pacing her office and jabbering into the phone, her expression grim, Charlie Glover appeared at his side.

'She's jittery,' Glover observed.

'Wouldn't you be? She's responsible for other people's children and she's just lost one of them. The publicity could ruin her. She's scared. Her reputation, her business and her livelihood are on the line.'

As they watched, Trudy Barratt became increasingly animated, the phone conversation becoming heated. 'She told me she wanted to speak to her husband. Do you get the impression he's not taking it well?' Mariner wondered aloud. He turned to Glover. 'What did you need?'

'Some of the staff are asking how long we'll be, sir,' Charlie Glover said. 'They've got families at home, and some have got their own kids to collect.'

Mariner nodded. 'As long as we've got statements and contact details from all of them, then you can let them go. Warn them that we may need to get in touch with them over the course of the weekend though.' Glover went to pass on the good news. Mariner allowed Trudy Barratt a further couple of minutes then knocked lightly on the door and, without waiting for an invitation, walked in.

'I'll call you back,' Trudy Barratt said, decisively, and ended the call.

Mariner waited expectantly. 'My husband,' she said, eventually.

'He's a partner in the business?'

'Oh, no. I just wanted him to know that I'd be late.'

The call was clearly about more than that, but Mariner let it go.

There was another knock on the door and one of the girls brought in a baby car seat. The baby he'd met earlier, Ellie, was, by now, sucking strenuously on a pink dummy, dark eyes surveying all around her. It was after six.

'Ellie is staying late,' Mariner said. 'Shouldn't her parents have collected her by now?'

Trudy Barratt remained loyal to her clientele. 'We try to be flexible to accommodate parents' needs,' she said, tactfully.

'It must make your life . . . unpredictable.'

'On the contrary, it's what we're here for.' Trudy Barratt took the seat behind her desk.

Mariner sat down on one of the plastic chairs opposite. 'Samantha told us about the arrangement that you have with the hospital regarding the crèche. How exactly does that work?'

'We undertake to keep open a certain number of places on particular days, up to a maximum of eight, for the children of visiting consultants and so on. The crèche is advertised through the hospital and parents ring us to book their child in for as many days as they would like.'

'And what do you get for offering this service?' asked Mariner.

'The hospital pays us for the nursery places taken.'

'A retainer then,' Mariner concluded. 'Do you have to submit some kind of records to the hospital?'

'Oh, yes. The Trust needs to know that the service is being properly used and I like to be as transparent as possible.'

'What form do these records take?'

'They're fairly basic, just details of the child — name, address, date of birth.' She pulled open a drawer. 'I have one here.' She handed Mariner a pre-printed form with a pink carbon backing. 'I send the top sheet up to the hospital, and keep a copy on file here.'

'At what point do you send the originals up to the hospital?'

'On a weekly basis as the bookings come in.'

'And when did Emma O'Brien book Jessica's place?'

'Oh, several weeks ago, let me check.' She reached up onto the shelf beside her and took down a blue lever-arch file, which contained a number of the pink carbons. 'Let me see . . .' She rifled through them until she found the one she wanted. 'Yes, Mrs O'Brien made the booking over the phone in the middle of August.'

'Can I see?'

'Yes, of course.' She passed across the bulky file. From it Mariner learned that the baby's name was actually Jessica Klinnemann, her name taken from her father, Peter Klinnemann, it gave her date of birth, her home address, and the date and times when Jessica was booked into the crèche. A circled 'No' at the top also told the reader that Jessica had never been placed there before. It was information that would have been useful to someone planning an abduction. The form had been completed on 8 August. A glance up at the wall planner behind Trudy Barratt's desk told him that it had been a Tuesday.

'So you would have sent Jessica's form along with others up to the hospital some time ago?'

'Yes. At the end of that week they would have gone to the main administration centre.'

'How do you advertise the crèche?' Mariner asked.

Trudy Barratt dug around among the piles of papers on her desk and came up with a glossy leaflet bearing the nursery logo, with photographs of the facilities on offer. 'This leaflet is on display on notice boards up at the hospital in the relevant departments,' she told Mariner. 'The hospital also sends them out routinely with their information for visiting lecturers and conference delegates. It has our phone number on the back so that parents can contact us directly. The conference that Mrs O'Brien was speaking at was advertised as having a crèche.'

Miss, Mariner wanted to remind her. Instead he said, 'But anyone else visiting the hospital could also see them?'

'Yes.'

'So people outside the nursery would be aware of particular days when the crèche is being used?'

'Yes.'

'And anyone working in the hospital administration department could have known that Jessica Klinnemann would be here today.'

'Yes, I suppose they could.' That was bad news too.

The buzzer sounded and DCI Sharp's face filled the CCTV screen. Trudy Barratt hesitated, her brow knitted to a frown.

'It's my gaffer,' Mariner enlightened her. 'She's quite safe.'

Trudy Barratt followed him out into the hallway to meet the DCI and Mariner made introductions. After a short and expectant pause, Trudy Barratt took the hint. 'I'll leave you to it, shall I?' And she went back into her office and closed the door.

'So what the hell is going on?' Sharp asked, when she and Mariner were alone.

'All we know so far, is that at about two thirty a woman came into the nursery, collected a baby, Jessica Klinnemann, and walked out with her.'

'And no one stopped her?'

'They had no reason to,' said Mariner. 'The girls working in the room had never met Jessica's mother, so assumed that it was her. Mrs Barratt seems to have been the only person who had met the mother, Emma O'Brien, and she was out of the building at the time.'

'This woman just walked in off the street?'

'Security exists here, but it's not that great. That is, it would be fine if it worked, but it's a bit hit and miss. It's not clear if this woman rang the bell and was buzzed in by one of the staff in the rooms, or if someone leaving the building let her in. There was no one in the office to challenge her, and the deputy manager was elsewhere in one of the other rooms. Added to that, the girls in the room where Jessica was are temporary, and one of them, frankly, isn't all that bright.'

'So we don't know if this woman had the nerve to announce her arrival or if she sneaked in when no one was looking.'

'Aside from the girl in the room we have another member of staff who encountered the abductor in the hall and has given us an excellent description. According to her, the woman was definitely edgy and wanted to know if Mrs Barratt was around.'

'So she knew Mrs Barratt by name?'

Mariner allowed his eyes to drift up to the wall behind where they were standing. 'Not necessarily. It's on the board outside as well as up there. When Christie — the girl who actually spoke to her — explained that Mrs Barratt wasn't here, the woman told her she had come for her baby, so Christie showed her through to the crèche. She reasonably assumed that the uncertainty was because the woman was unfamiliar with the nursery.'

'So how does this crèche work?'

Mariner briefly outlined what he knew.

'I've never come across that kind of setup before,' said Sharp. 'But I suppose being so close to the hospital it makes sense.'

'It's the woman's behaviour inside the room that starts to get interesting,' Mariner said. 'And I think it might demonstrate a level of understanding about how the crèche works. If this had just been a chancer walking in off the street you would expect her to have waited until the children were left unattended, and snatch one without being seen. But this woman went into the room when there was a member of staff present and just took the child right in front of her eyes. That was a huge risk, and depended on the girl working in the room not knowing what the mother of the child looked like. If she'd been caught she would have no doubt claimed confusion, that she was in the wrong room, but everything played her way. She wasn't afraid of being seen. Unless it was a professional disguise, she seems to have made no effort to hide her appearance.'

'That's remarkable in itself,' said Sharp. 'But all of this so far points to it being more than simply an opportunistic enterprise.'

'Exactly,' said Mariner. 'This woman was a gambler. She must have known that there would be security procedures operating in the nursery, and that she could potentially have been challenged at any time. I don't think this is your average baby-snatch.'

'The woman was on her own?'

'She came into the nursery alone, but until we know what she did once she was outside again, we've no way of knowing if she was working solo. There may have been an accomplice waiting in a vehicle to take them away. Leanne, the girl she met in the crèche itself, got the impression that she'd had to park some distance away, so she must have had transport.'

'Buses pass right by the front door,' Sharp pointed out.

'But the timing would have had to be right,' said Mariner. 'Once outside with the baby she wouldn't have wanted to hang about, would she? As it was, no one realised Jessica was missing until her real mum came to collect her at four o'clock, but Mrs Barratt could have come back at any time and realised that something was wrong.'

'It's still a possibility.'

Mariner nodded agreement. 'I've got someone talking to the drivers working the route this afternoon.'

'Do you think it's any coincidence that we're very close to the maternity hospital?' asked Sharp.

It had crossed Mariner's mind. 'In the past when babies have been snatched it's generally been from maternity wards. But security has tightened considerably in the last few years, particularly after Naomi Carr was taken from Good Hope. All newborns are tagged.'

'Well, it can't be ignored. Someone should follow up with the hospital to check on any women who might have recently lost a baby. It's an unusual way of doing it, but if she couldn't get hold of a newborn, maybe Jessica was the next best thing.'

'There's also a fertility clinic up at the hospital, so we could be looking at a woman who's unable to conceive.' Mariner explained about the marketing for the crèche. 'It'll be interesting to see exactly where the flyers are pinned up. They might have given someone the initial idea. I'll find out if there have been any general enquiries about the crèche recently, someone who wanted the information but didn't then go ahead and book in a child.'

'So you're thinking it's premeditated?'

'I think it has to be, at least to some degree. It would be a hell of a risk to just walk in off the street and try to take a child. All sorts of things could go wrong. And I think she has to have known about the crèche.'

'Unless she was just incredibly lucky.'

It was the word 'incredibly' that Mariner found hard to disregard.

'We are *sure* it's a woman?' Sharp said, suddenly.

‘Absolutely. The description’s been corroborated by both Leanne and Christie: a woman, white, middle-aged with short or tied-back dark hair. We also have a sound description of what she was wearing. Christie got a better look and seems to have more about her, so I’ve sent her back to Granville Lane with DS Knox to put together an e-fit, which we’ll get out to the media as soon as it’s ready.’

‘Good.’ Sharp seemed to drift off for a moment. ‘This is any mother’s worst nightmare.’ It was spoken from the heart. ‘How’s she doing, the mother?’

‘About what you’d expect,’ said Mariner. ‘Millie Khatoon is with her.’

‘Right, I should come and meet her.’

As she spoke, the buzzer sounded again, making them both jump. Mrs Barratt appeared from her office, Ellie’s car seat over her arm. Mariner and Sharp stood back and watched as she opened the door to a young woman who, to Mariner, looked far too young to be a consultant in anything. There was no greeting exchanged and there seemed to be a mutual lack of interest between her and the baby. The child was handed over with no more sensibility than if she’d been a package. Mariner remarked on this as they watched her carry the baby seat down the path and put it into the back of the car parked right outside.

‘The au pair,’ said Mrs Barratt, anticipating Mariner’s next question. ‘Ellie’s mother called a little while ago to say that she’d been held up so would be sending her. I don’t think she speaks much English. Young, inexperienced and probably paid peanuts, poor girl.’

Poor girl? Mariner thought back to the girls who had travelled with Katarina, expecting to be employed looking after other people’s children. They’d have happily traded places with Ellie’s au pair. Compared with those girls her life was charmed, though she didn’t appear to appreciate her good fortune and her eyes seemed to carry that same haunted look. But maybe she was just homesick.

'Is she working here legally?' Mariner couldn't help but ask.

'I've no idea,' said Mrs Barratt, tightly. 'That really is none of my business.' Even DCI Sharp gave him a stormy look.

'At any rate not very deserving of a car,' Mariner observed, noting the battered Escort that pulled away. The wall clock said a little after twenty past six.

'Ellie can't see a lot of her mum,' DCI Sharp remarked.

'This government wants women back in the workplace,' replied Mrs Barratt. 'It keeps me in business, but the consequence, to be truthful, is that lots of children don't see much of their parents.' She didn't indicate whether or not she agreed with the principle, but presumably she was complicit, as she was making her living from it.

'How long have you been open?' Sharp asked, conversationally.

'Nearly ten years.'

'A lot must have changed in that time.'

'There's more paperwork, if that's what you mean,' said Trudy Barratt, with feeling. 'Endless guidelines and regulations.'

'I was thinking more about the huge expansion in childcare provision. It must have created more competition. Any rivalry with other local nurseries?'

Mrs Barratt smiled. 'In my view there's nothing wrong with a little healthy competition. It helps to keep us on our toes. And there are plenty of children to go around.'

'Your contract with the hospital must help,' said Mariner.

'It's a useful cushion, yes.'

Nicely understated, thought Mariner. 'There must be other nurseries who would like that contract,' he said.

'I daresay there are, but they haven't discussed it with me.'

'Which other nurseries are closest to you, geographically?'

Trudy Barratt gave them a couple of names, which Mariner mentally noted.

'And they're doing well?'

'You'd have to ask them that.'

'One of the things we must consider is whether this could be personal,' DCI Sharp went on. 'Can you think of any reason why someone might want to bring your nursery into disrepute?'

'No.'

'Anyone who might simply want to make life difficult for you? What about any staff who have recently left?'

Trudy Barratt smiled. 'You're clearly unfamiliar with the early years childcare sector Chief Inspector. Staff moving on is a feature of life.'

'Anyone who went under a cloud?' asked Mariner.

'Not that I can remember. Generally staff leave for promotion, or to go and work in schools where the hours are more favourable, or to start their own families.'

'All the same, we'll need a list of all those who have left in the last six months.'

'It will be a substantial list.'

Mariner followed Trudy Barratt back into the office, where she was about to take another file off the shelf when on the CCTV monitor they saw a man appear at the nursery gates. He looked disorientated and harassed, and by the time he'd reached the door Mariner had already correctly identified him. The buzzer sounded and in a rare traffic-free moment he spoke into the intercom. 'Peter Klinnemann' he said, breathlessly into the microphone. 'I'm Jessica's father.'

Chapter Five

Tony Knox had taken Christie back to Granville Lane, where the station had erupted into the activity levels more typical of a weekday morning. 'We'll go up to DI Mariner's office,' he told receptionist Delrose, signing Christie in. 'It will be quieter.' And away from prying eyes. 'Can you let the e-fit tech know when he gets here?'

An incident room was being created adjacent to CID on the first floor and Knox had to steer Christie past officers laden with files and equipment, holding open doors and letting others take precedence.

In Mariner's office Knox closed the door on the pandemonium. 'Have a seat,' he told Christie. 'Can I get you a drink?'

Christie declined. She was staring at the computer printout pinned to the board above Mariner's desk, depicting the face of a young woman. 'Who's she?'

'Madeleine,' said Knox, hoping they could leave it at that and spare her the grisly details. When Mariner had first stuck the picture there, eight months ago, anyone coming into his office had reacted in the same way, their attention drawn to the haunting image. Charlie Glover had even accused Mariner of being macabre, but it was interesting how quickly they'd all become inured to it — Knox included. He didn't even know why the boss had kept it. There were plenty of other unsolved murders festering in the filing cabinets. Why should this one be different? Could it be because she was a young female, or because she'd so recently given birth, meaning that somewhere out there was a child without its mother? Or perhaps the frustration was that she wasn't strictly unsolved.

Christie was watching him expectantly, waiting for more. Knox hesitated. 'She's a young woman who was murdered last year,' he told her.

'Oh.'

'She was found dumped down a drain, tied up with duct tape and wrapped in bin liners. There wasn't much of her face left, so what we've got there is a computer mock-up.'

He'd said too much. Christie had paled, the mark on her face standing out more lividly. She swallowed hard. 'Did you catch the person who did it?'

'Not exactly.'

It was Charlie Glover mostly who'd been instrumental in tracking down the Albanian national whose prints they'd found all over the tape; the same man they were certain had first strangled Madeleine with his bare hands. But now he was dead, too, gunned down in his home city of Tirana before extradition procedures could be implemented and the case against him brought and proven.

No, the real mystery about this young girl was that she remained without an identity. Despite widely circulating the image both here and in Albania, no one had come forward to claim her as a daughter or a sister. Charlie Glover had named her Madeleine after Caravaggio's *Mary Magdalene*, his wife's favourite painting. And they hadn't yet come up with a real name to replace it. It was the kind of loose end everyone hated.

Christie was transfixed by the image. 'I thought I might know her. I thought she came into the nursery.'

'She did?' Knox's heart beat a little faster.

Suddenly Christie seemed less certain. 'Well, someone like her, anyway.'

'Oh.' *Someone like her.* They'd lost count of the number of people who'd said that. They waited less than five minutes for Susan Cohen, the e-fit technician to arrive.

'I'll leave you to it,' Knox said, getting up to leave. He saw Christie's face. 'We have to be sure I don't influence what you say,' he told her. 'Sue will look after you. I'll go and get us a cuppa. How do you take it?'

'Milk no sugar,' she said, meekly.

After forty-five minutes Cohen called Knox in again and presented him with a computer generated image of the woman who had abducted Jessica. 'Fantastic,' he said studying the portrait.

'She's done really well,' Cohen seemed genuinely impressed. 'Very observant.'

Christie blushed again, unsure of what to do with the compliments. 'I thought about joining the police, once,' she told Knox, after Cohen had packed up her things and gone.

'What's stopping you? You might be good,' said Knox.

'Jimmy would never let me.'

'Jimmy?'

'My boyfriend. He doesn't have a very high opinion of the police. Besides, he wants us to start a family, and he thinks it would be too dangerous.'

'Do you want a family too?'

She smiled, one of the rare moments since they'd got here when she appeared relaxed. 'I'd like a little girl one day. I'd call her Chantelle.'

'You always let your boyfriend tell you what to do?' Knox asked, deliberately steering the conversation.

'Oh he's not like that, not really.'

'Is that how you got that bruise on your face?' Silence. 'It's all right, Christie,' Knox said, quietly. 'It happens. It happened to me.' Unbuttoning his shirt cuff, Knox rolled up his sleeve to show her the scars on his forearm that were only just beginning to fade. She looked up at him, wide eyed. 'My girlfriend was in an . . . accident,' he said. 'She blamed me. And in a way I could understand it. If it hadn't been for me she wouldn't have been there, the place where it happened. So she used to hit me and scratch me, and throw things sometimes too.'

'Jim can't help it,' Christie said, softly. 'His business isn't doing very well. It gets him down and sometimes he has trouble controlling his temper.' She sipped her tea, then lifted her eyes to fleetingly meet his. 'What did you do?'

'I put up with it for a while,' Knox said casually. 'I told myself my girlfriend couldn't help it. She'd been in an accident and was just having trouble controlling her temper.' He shot her a meaningful look. 'Then I realised that it wasn't enough of an excuse, so I got out.' Knox got to his feet. 'Come on, let's get you home.'

Dropping the e-fit in at the press office to be immediately circulated, Knox drove Christie himself. 'We'll need to talk to you again,' he said. As she got out of the car Knox handed her a card. 'Here's my number in case you think of anything else that might help us with finding Jessica. And if things get rough, give me a call, eh?' he said. 'Remember, you don't have to put up with it.' As Knox glanced up at the modern terraced starter-home a figure appeared at a ground-floor window. 'Do you want me to come in and have a word?'

'No! Really, I'll be fine.' Christie looked down at the card then back at Knox. 'Thanks.'

Knox watched her let herself into the house before driving off.

* * *

Mariner took Peter Klinnemann straight up to the staff room, where he and his wife held one another tightly, their hands locked together. When they were ready to talk he had to ask Klinnemann to spell his name.

'It's Austrian,' Klinnemann said. His English was flawless with barely a trace of an accent, but Mariner noticed that he pronounced his words carefully and some of the phrasing was unusual, betraying him as someone for whom English was not his mother tongue.

'You live here permanently?' Mariner asked. He couldn't help but also remark that Peter Klinnemann was significantly older than Emma O'Brien, mid-fifties perhaps, compared with her late thirties.

'I have dual citizenship,' Klinnemann said. 'It was granted when I married my wife. She's English.'

'His first wife,' Emma O'Brien added pointedly.

'What line of work are you in, Mr Klinnemann?'

'I work in the field of research.'

'And you're based in Cambridge?'

'That's correct. I don't understand, how has this happened?'

'That's what we're trying to work out too,' said Mariner. 'All we know is that at about half past two this afternoon a woman came into the nursery, told staff that she was here to collect her child, picked up Jessica and walked out again. Unfortunately, the people who were in the room at the time hadn't met your wi— your partner, so they had no reason to question her actions. At the moment we have no way of knowing what the motive was—'

'So she could be some crank,' Emma O'Brien broke in. 'Someone with mental health problems, like the woman who stole that baby from the hospital!'

'We don't know that,' Mariner tried to reassure her. 'There could be any number of reasons why this has happened. This woman appeared outwardly fairly calm and collected. It's one of the reasons the staff didn't challenge her. Nothing about her demeanour set alarm bells ringing.'

'That doesn't mean anything. She could have just been a good actress.'

'There's that possibility,' Mariner conceded. 'But we've every reason to think that Jessica is being well looked after.'

With some effort Peter Klinnemann disengaged himself from his partner. 'I should phone the children and let them know what's going on. If they should happen to see this on the news—'

'Surely they can manage for a few hours without you?' Emma O'Brien retorted.

'Of course, but they will be worried.'

'I doubt it. They'll be rubbing their hands in glee.' The bitterness in her voice took Mariner aback. He and Millie exchanged a look.

Peter Klinnemann flashed an uncertain smile. 'That's nonsense, darling, and you know it.'

'I don't want them here.' Emma was adamant.

'I'm just going to let them know what's happening, that's all.'

When Klinnemann left the room, Mariner followed him down the stairs and into the hall, waiting at a discreet distance while he made the call. After a substantial pause, Mariner heard him speak at length, uninterrupted. He was leaving a message.

'I didn't know that Jessica has brothers and sisters,' Mariner said when he'd finished.

'A half-brother and half-sister; they're the children from my first marriage,' Klinnemann said, almost apologetically. 'They're grown up now but Paul often stays with us. He'll be devastated if he sees the news. I don't want him dashing over here.' It was unconvincingly said.

'They must be very fond of their little sister,' Mariner said.

Klinnemann didn't appear to hear the remark, but Mariner bided his time. 'Actually, they're not terribly thrilled,' Klinnemann admitted eventually. 'Emma and I began our affair two years ago, while I was married to their mother. Jessica was a surprise to us all. I was still living at home when Emma discovered that she was pregnant, so things are rather raw. My first wife took it very badly and of course the new baby effectively ended our marriage, perhaps sooner than I had planned. Even though their mother and I knew that it was over, the children do seem to have cast Emma as the wicked witch.'

'Were you able to reassure your son?'

Klinnemann glanced down at his handset. 'He's not answering his phone. I had to leave a message.'

The two men climbed back up the stairs together. 'Which company do you work for?' Mariner asked.

'I head up a team at Hamilton.'

The name seemed familiar to Mariner but he couldn't quite place it. 'Researching into what?'

'Healthcare products most of all.'

Klinnemann seemed reluctant to elaborate and Mariner was none the wiser, though he'd have someone on the investigation team follow it up. He gave a neutral nod, holding open the door of the staff room for Klinnemann to enter.

Emma O'Brien had been crying again, and was vigorously blowing her nose. She grabbed Klinnemann's arm as he sat down beside her.

That'll be good for the cameras, thought Mariner, at the same time hating his detachment. 'I need to ask a couple more questions,' he said. 'We have to consider that this may not have been a random snatch.'

'What do you mean?' Emma O'Brien asked.

'We just have to look at all the options. It's routine procedure. Who did you talk to about coming here today?'

'I might have mentioned it to a couple of people.'

'Did you mention the crèche?'

'I don't remember. I suppose I was worried about leaving Jessica, so I might have mentioned it to a couple of girlfriends. The leaflet has been pinned to the board in the kitchen for a few weeks too.'

'Did your children know?' Mariner asked Klinnemann.

'It's very possible, but are you implying that they are involved?' Klinnemann was incredulous. 'They wouldn't do something like this.' Emma O'Brien's face said she wasn't so sure. It was something they'd have to come back to, perhaps when she was alone.

'We'd like you to be present at a press conference to be broadcast on the mid-evening news.' Mariner said. 'All we will do at this stage is appeal to Jessica's abductor to let us know that she's safe.'

'Oh, God.' Emma O'Brien looked about to faint. Klinnemann tightened his arm around her.

'It won't be necessary for you to speak on this occasion,' Mariner said. 'And I'm sorry to ask you to go in front of the cameras at a time like this, but we have to let the abductor know how much distress she is causing.'

Klinnemann squeezed his partner's hand. 'Yes, of course. We'll do anything.'

Mariner stood up and DCI Sharp did the same. 'We'll keep you posted,' Mariner said, and followed Sharp out of the room. They reconvened in a darkened playroom next door that overlooked the main road.

'What do you think?' Sharp asked.

'They're holding up pretty well considering,' said Mariner.

'What an ordeal to have to go through.'

Glancing out Mariner saw the brand-new Jeep Cherokee parked half on the pavement, with its nursery sticker in the back window. 'Mrs Barratt seems to be doing very well out of the business. How profitable do you reckon it would be, a setup like this?' he queried.

'She's got a captive market,' said Sharp. 'This has to be the most convenient nursery for hospital staff to leave their children at. I noticed the list of charges on the wall though, and the rates seem pretty competitive.'

Mariner wondered how she knew that. 'Doesn't seem right somehow,' he said. 'Leaving kids here at such a young age. Shouldn't they be with their mums?'

Sharp allowed herself a wry smile. 'Only a man would say that. In theory, of course, being home with your baby is a great idea. But have you any idea of the impact a break in career has on a woman? If you don't have qualifications then you're consigned to the lowest paid jobs that can accommodate childcare, and if you are qualified and experienced you drop countless rungs on the career ladder. Some women never catch up. If there was no alternative we'd have considered this for ours.'

'I didn't know you had kids.' Mariner couldn't keep the surprise from his voice.

This time she laughed out loud. 'Three of them: nine, seven and two.'

Mariner tried to reconcile this with what he'd been told of her career history. There had been no mention of maternity leave and certainly not three lots of it. And if she'd taken all that time out, her rise to DCI had been even more meteoric than he'd thought. Maybe the kids were adopted. 'So who looks after them?' he asked.

'We made the decision early on that my partner would be the stay-at-home parent.' She placed her own interpretation on Mariner's silence. 'You don't agree with that?'

Mariner shrugged. 'I'm old fashioned, I suppose. I still tend to think the main carers would be the mothers.'

'She is their mother.'

'Ah.'

'I'm disappointed in you, DI Mariner. It's the good detective's mantra. *Never make assumptions about anyone,* including your colleagues.' There was mischief in her voice. She'd got a buzz out of stringing him along.

Across the road in the hospital entrance they could see the fluorescent jackets of the officers stopping the drivers, and further along a couple of uniforms consulting on the house-to-house. Now that all the children and most of the staff had gone, it was time to close the nursery.

'So, what next?' Sharp asked.

'I think we've done what we can here,' Mariner said. 'We should move across to Granville Lane.'

'I was thinking the same thing.'

Mariner went back into the staff room to break the news to PC Khatoon and Jessica's parents, who gathered together their things. Brian Mann would remain on the premises until Trudy Barratt left and would seal off the building, but the rest of them would decamp. Charlie Glover went out in advance to bring round a car.

The press office was doing its job and outside a gaggle of reporters had already begun to assemble, but for once, Mariner didn't mind. It was one of those rare occasions when press interest was to be actively encouraged.

'Chief Inspector!' someone called out. 'Baby Jessica has been missing for several hours now. Do you think she's still alive?' yelled a voice from the back of the pack.

Mariner cringed. That they could do without. Too much to expect that Emma O'Brien hadn't heard.

Once they were bundled into a car and safely on their way, accompanied by Millie, Sharp responded, approaching the nearest reporter. 'There will be a press conference at around seven o'clock at Granville Lane police station when we'll be able to give you more details.'

'Chief Inspector! Do you think what's happened here this afternoon is a consequence of the government's growing policy of forcing mothers to return to work, leaving their babies in the care of the state?'

Sharp ignored the question that came from a middle-aged woman in dungarees and Doc Martens, who stood apart from the group, and unlike the others seemed to carry no recording equipment or notebook.

'Should have known that she'd crawl out of the woodwork at some point,' Sharp muttered as they walked back along the road to the cul-de-sac where Mariner's car was parked, now in isolation.

'Who is she?' Mariner asked, unlocking the car.

'Marcella Turner. She's a longstanding campaigner for a return to the "traditional family unit." Runs an organisation called "Families Come First." She thinks that women should stay at home to care for their children, and be paid by the state for doing so. In many ways I agree with her views but she takes them to the extreme. Breastfeeding children until they go to university and all that.' Sharp saw Mariner's face. 'Okay, I exaggerate, but some of her group have been known to infiltrate day nurseries posing as potential parents, then make official complaints to Ofsted in an attempt to close down the settings. I don't doubt that she'll cash in on what's happened here and get the press all fired up.'

Minutes later in the car, Sharp said, 'Are you happy about taking the lead on this one, Tom?'

'Any reason why I shouldn't be, ma'am?'

'I just thought with the upcoming trial . . . you must have a lot on your mind.'

'I'm fine, thank you.'

'Good. So let's find out what all this is about.' And she'd moved on, just like that. She was starting to trust him, Mariner realised with some satisfaction.

* * *

Back at Granville Lane, Mariner left Millie to settle Emma and Peter Klinnemann in a side room, making them as comfortable as possible, then headed up to the incident room on the first floor adjacent to the press room. There was no shortage of volunteers for overtime and he opened the door onto a dozen or so uniformed worker-bees, either fielding phone calls or working at computer stations, logging information as it came in. It was crucial at this stage that every detail be recorded. Something seemingly insignificant could prove to be of the utmost importance later on in the enquiry.

A whiteboard took up the length of one wall. In the middle of the organised chaos was Tony Knox, sticking up an enlarged version of the e-fit. 'How's it going?' Mariner asked. 'This is the picture Christie gave us?'

'This is it,' said Knox. 'She did a really good job in the end. I think she quite enjoyed it.' The two men stood back for a few seconds and studied the image of the woman with tied-back brown hair framing an unremarkable face.

'She looks so bloody ordinary, doesn't she?' Mariner complained. It wasn't going to help them.

'But somebody knows her,' said Knox. 'It's gone out to the press and we've set up a voice bank of up-to-date information that the media can tap into. We're getting a big response from the initial appeal, close to a couple of dozen calls so far, but nothing yet in the way of concrete sightings.'

'What we could really do with is a link to a vehicle or transport of some kind.'

'Well, if she did get into a car, no one's come forward yet to say they saw her.'

Glover, Khatoon and DCI Sharp appeared and gathered round one of the tables at the quieter end of the room, while Mariner summarised what had been learned so far. It wasn't much. 'I think the most helpful way of approaching this is to consider the motive,' he said. 'If we can understand *why* Jessica has been taken it will lead us to who may have taken her. There are a number of possible scenarios: this could only be a one-off, so I think we can rule out the possibility that Jessica has been taken for some kind of commercial gain. Similarly if the baby has been taken as part of a religious ritual, I can't believe that the abductors would go to all this trouble just for one child. I think we can also discount the idea that the baby has been taken in error. I don't believe that a mother would mistake her own child and this woman behaved as if she knew Jessica.'

'And if she simply took the wrong baby, where is her baby — the one she left behind?' said Millie.

'Precisely. I do think, however, that we have to explore a possible link with the hospital. It's too close to ignore. The crèche facility is publicly advertised there, and details of the children booked into the crèche are sent to the admin office. What we don't yet know is whether the reason for the snatch is personal to the abductor, or if there's some kind of external motive.'

Millie spoke up first. 'If you think about the baby snatches that have happened in the past, in most of those cases the abduction was the result of some kind of psychological disturbance, a woman who has recently lost a child and was desperate to fill the hole that's been left. The nursery is right next to the hospital's maternity wing and the fertility clinic, so we could be talking about a woman who has lost a baby, or who has been told that she can't have children.'

'Yes, but in the last couple of years since Naomi Carr, security in maternity units has been stepped up big time,' Knox pointed out. 'They electronically tag all newborns, they have coded locks on the doors and the staff are trained to be alert to strangers.'

'So perhaps this woman saw the nursery as the next best thing,' Millie came back. 'The women who do this kind of thing aren't thinking rationally, are they? Normally theirs is an act of desperation. She might even have started off in the maternity wing, and when she saw that she wouldn't get away with it, the nursery was the next best place.'

'But this doesn't sound like a desperate woman,' Knox countered. 'The nursery staff describe her as being reasonably calm. At the time they didn't particularly notice anything odd about her behaviour. Would she have been that composed?'

'It might depend on how deeply delusional she is.' Sharp chipped in. 'In the past, abductors have managed to pose convincingly as health visitors or social workers. If this woman has concocted the fantasy that she is Jessica's mother, and she truly believes her own fabrication, then she may appear outwardly calm.'

'That would tie in with her encounters with the staff in the nursery,' Knox said. 'In the first instance, when Christie asked if she could help she said, "I've come to collect *my* baby." Christie was quite clear on that. It was the only time the abductor was put on the spot and her automatic response was to claim Jessica as hers.'

'So we're looking at a woman who has already thought herself into the role of the baby's mother and, when she takes her, truly believes that Jessica is rightfully hers. If she knows about the crèche arrangement this woman could have simply convinced herself that she'd deposited her baby at the nursery that morning, and that all she had to do was go and collect it. Blonde, blue-eyed babies fit most people's ideal, so this woman goes into the nursery, into the crèche, sees Jessica and picks her.'

'But that line could equally have been rehearsed,' said Charlie Glover. 'The success of the abduction depended on the nursery staff believing the woman to be Jessica's mother, so she would have practised it.'

Knox remained unconvinced. 'I still don't think a day nursery is an obvious place to abduct a child from if you're just wanting any child. Surely a woman who's lost a baby or who can't have kids is going to want a newborn; one that they can pretend is their own, not a child who already belongs to someone else. Nurseries are more associated with young children than newborn babies.'

'Naomi Carr was taken to sustain and protect a relationship,' added Millie. 'The abductor thought that having a baby would make her partner stay with her. She faked the whole pregnancy thing.'

'That's what I mean,' said Knox. 'The success of what she did depended entirely on her friends and family believing that she had given birth to Naomi. You couldn't do that with a child that's even a few weeks old.'

'But the nursery does take very young infants,' Glover pointed out. 'We saw that today.'

'The abductor wouldn't necessarily have known that. And Jessica Klinnemann is seven weeks old. She's hardly a newborn, is she?'

'The other aspect to this is the staff,' said DCI Sharp. 'In most nurseries the staff would be too familiar with the parents to allow this to happen.'

'You think this woman knew about the crèche?'

'It's the feature that makes this nursery unique and vulnerable. The strategy wouldn't have worked in another nursery.'

Having sat back and listened thus far it was time for Mariner to step in. 'I'm inclined to agree with DCI Sharp,' he said. 'That this isn't a conventional baby-snatch. It was neither random nor impulsive. There was too much that could have gone wrong.' The murmurs of agreement signalled that they were all coming round to that way of thinking. 'It's no simple thing to walk in off the street and take a baby,' Mariner went on. 'So this operation was carefully planned and executed, meaning that the abductor must have had pretty in-depth knowledge of how the crèche operates and the shift patterns of the staff. It's interesting too that the snatch took place while Mrs Barratt — the one person who could have identified Jessica's real mother - was out of the building. The abductor even double checked that Mrs Barratt wasn't there.'

'But that was a risk,' said Knox. 'How would she know that Mrs Barratt had gone?'

'That car is distinctive enough,' said Mariner. 'And if she knows how the crèche operates then she'll know that the staff in the crèche wouldn't recognise the person who'd brought the child in, and that the crèche is staffed by agency workers who may also be less familiar with security procedures. And, if we're in agreement that this was a planned operation, then we have to conclude that either this child or this nursery were targeted for a reason.'

'We should start looking at former nursery employees and anyone linked to the crèche up at the hospital.'

'How long has the crèche been open?' asked Millie.

'About seven years,' said Mariner. 'Look at former members of staff, especially those who haven't yet had children, or possibly even married. The nursery has a high staff turnover and I've asked Mrs Barratt for details of those who have left in the last six months. Tony, I want you to go through that and find out if there's anyone who has reason to hold a grudge against Mrs Barratt.'

'It could even be an inside job,' Glover suggested. 'Two of the girls are temporary agency staff.'

'I'm not sure that any of those girls are up to it. Samantha, the deputy, seems the most experienced of them and she was clearly panicked. The others just look too young to front it out. But we're doing the usual background checks, using DBS records as a starting point.'

'Somebody could have got to them.' Mariner turned to Knox. 'You've spent some time with Christie. She's given us the best description of the woman.'

Knox was doubtful. 'She seemed genuinely eager to help. But did you notice that bruising?'

'The mark on her face?'

'She's in an abusive relationship. I mean, she didn't come out and say it, but she didn't deny it either, so I did a check on her boyfriend, Jimmy Bond.'

'And?'

'He's on our books. Three years ago he was convicted of tax fraud. He runs some kind of garage and vehicle distribution business.'

'Okay, well it's hardly an obvious link but there's a financial element there so it's something else to keep an eye on. It's another motive.'

'That someone's in this for financial gain?'

'It's a possibility, in which case we can expect a phone call at any time.'

'But why this nursery, this child? Is it likely to be that lucrative?'

'I agree,' said Sharp. 'The nursery is an independent business. If someone wanted to make serious money out of this surely it would be better to hit one of the larger chains of nurseries.'

'So there may be a personal element,' said Mariner. 'Tell us more about Marcella Turner; is there any way she could have orchestrated the snatch, as a way of demonstrating that children aren't safe in day-care provision?'

DCI Sharp turned down her mouth. 'It's way beyond the scale of her normal protests, but that's not to say she wouldn't. It would be an interesting stunt and perhaps one born of frustration. And it's making people sit up and take notice. We certainly need to keep a watch on anyone who's involved, even on the periphery, which brings us to the parents. How do you think they're handling it?' Sharp addressed her question to Millie.

'They're beside themselves with worry, which is about what you'd expect.'

'Their home life is not as happy as it might be,' Mariner said. Suddenly everyone was interested.

'It's the second time around for Klinnemann,' Millie said. 'But that doesn't necessarily mean—'

Mariner shook his head, slowly. 'No it's more than that. There's tension with his ex and the children from his first marriage. Emotions were running so high when they were mentioned I could practically feel it. Klinnemann told me — his wife didn't even know he was having the affair with Emma O'Brien until Jessica was on the way.'

'Oops.'

'His two adult kids didn't think much of the development either. The son — Paul — has gone AWOL,' Mariner said. 'I'd like to track him down.'

'So maybe it's not the nursery that's under attack, but the Klinnemanns.'

'Anyone else get a sense that money is tight too?' Mariner asked. 'A couple of times during our initial conversation Emma O'Brien mentioned economising — with the crèche place and by staying overnight with friends.'

'Setting up a second family doesn't come cheap,' said Knox. 'And she's not back to working regularly yet.'

'It seems to me that we could do with a bit more background on the Klinnemanns,' Sharp said.

'I'll give Cambridgeshire police a call, ma'am,' Mariner said.

'And we'll get the press conference done.'

'On the plus side, none of the options we've discussed would lead us to believe that the abductor means to harm Jessica in any deliberate way. She might be working alone or with an accomplice, but we just have to hope that she has the skill, instinct and inclination to take proper care of her.'

All the time they'd been speaking, Mariner had been scribbling on the white board, creating an image that resembled a spider with far more legs sprouting from it than was biologically possible. A number of lines of inquiry to follow up, while at the same time the clock was ticking, challenging them to get to baby Jessica before any harm could come to her. A map of the immediate area had been pinned alongside the diagram, but so far it was blank. So far they had not a clue where Jessica had been taken.

Chapter Six

When the others went off to pursue some of those avenues, Mariner remained with DCI Sharp and PC Khatoon to plan the press conference.

'How do you intend to play it?' Sharp asked him.

'Well, whatever has happened, the approach we'll adopt is the sympathetic one. We need the abductor on our side,' Mariner began. 'At the moment we have no way of telling why this baby has been abducted, but what we don't want is to panic this woman or anyone she may be working with into abandoning Jessica. She wouldn't survive more than a few days alone. We'll try to make contact, but starting from the angle that all we want is to know that Jessica is safe, and we try to convey the anguish Jessica's parents are going through. She needs to see them as real people who will be understanding and non-judgemental.'

'Will the Klinnemanns say anything?' Millie asked.

'Not yet,' said Mariner. 'We'll have them there, but we'll need to keep something back for a further appeal if nothing comes of this.' He couldn't shake the thought that, in so many of these appeals, the guilty party turned out to be one of those sitting alongside the police. 'I'd better go and smarten myself up.'

* * *

Millie went to prepare Emma O'Brien and Peter Klinnemann for what would be happening next. While she was doing that, Mariner went to splash water over his face in an effort to wake himself up a bit. Back in his office he put on a clean shirt, kept for just such an occasion as this, and was straightening his tie in the reflection from the window when Millie walked in. 'Very nice, sir,' she grinned, and Mariner had a sudden flashback to the occasion a couple of years earlier when he and Millie had worked together on the disappearance of a young Asian girl. It, too, had been an emotionally charged time and on one memorable occasion they had ended up in bed at her flat.

Mostly the incident went unspoken between them, a brief, impulsive episode, but she'd never quite let him forget it. Mariner caught sight of her ring. For the last six months Millie had been engaged to a man her parents had 'found' for her, something she'd always sworn she would resist. 'But he's actually okay,' she'd confided, shortly after she and her intended had met. Turned out he was more than okay.

The chain of thought reminded Mariner that he should try again to speak to Anna, but there really wasn't time before the conference.

Minutes later, under the glare of the press-room spotlights, Mariner flanked DCI Sharp as she read out a prepared statement, looking directly into the camera and appealing to Jessica's abductor. She was good, thought Mariner. And Emma O'Brien alongside them needed no coaching to look suitably distraught. She wept intermittently throughout. Peter Klinnemann remained composed, his arm around his partner, and Mariner could see the milky gleam of his knuckles as he tightly clutched her hand. The e-fit compiled with Christie's help was flashed onto the screen while Mariner gave a more detailed description of Jessica's abductor, omitting a couple of key details so that they could rule out the hoax calls that would inevitably follow. Giving the phone number of the incident room, he appealed to the public to come forward if they noticed any sudden new additions to the families of friends or neighbours, or if they noticed anyone acting suspiciously. The whole performance was to be broadcast on local and national evening news. As Millie ushered Emma and Klinnemann out of the press room, he and Sharp began taking questions.

'DCI Sharp, this has happened very close to the maternity hospital. Do you see a parallel with the Naomi Carr case?'

'It's just one of many possibilities we're exploring.'

But as Emma and Klinnemann were exiting through the side door, another of the journalists called after them: 'Mr Klinnemann, am I correct in thinking that you are the same Peter Klinnemann who works for Hamilton Sciences? And if so do you think this could be the work of animal rights activists?'

The question took them all by surprise, horror spreading like a domino effect across their faces. Someone had either made a huge unfounded assumption or had thoroughly done his homework. Judging from the look on Klinnemann's face it was the latter. Before Klinnemann could say anything, Mariner cut in with the standard reply: 'At this early stage we're not ruling out anything.' His eyes locked with DCI Sharp's. Christ, if that journalist was right then it took this case to a whole new level.

After he'd finished his stint in the press room Mariner went to see Klinnemann and Emma. Millie was approaching from the opposite direction.

'You've got them in somewhere?' Mariner asked.

'The Cedar Wood Hotel.'

‘Good.’ It was a couple of minutes’ drive away, and discreet. The couple would need a break from the press attention. As Mariner and Millie drew nearer to the room they could hear raised voices.

‘If this is down to them, I’ll never forgive you!’ they heard Emma O’Brien shriek. As Mariner tapped on the door, the voices ceased abruptly and Mariner went in to see Klinnemann and Emma O’Brien both on their feet, just inches apart, Emma O’Brien leaning in aggressively towards her partner. Seeing the police officers her whole body seemed to deflate as the adrenaline subsided, and she looked shattered.

‘I’m sorry to have put you through that,’ Mariner said, referring to the press conference and ignoring the tension in the air. ‘But it’s the most effective tool we’ve got for communicating with the abductor.’

‘We understand,’ Klinnemann swallowed hard, speaking for both of them.

‘We’ve booked a room for you at a local hotel, where you’ll be more comfortable. It’s out of the way so you should get some peace from the media. PC Khatoon will take you there. I realise it may not seem possible, but it will be a good idea if you can try to get some rest. If you wish we can arrange for the FME to give you something—’

‘We don’t need anything,’ Peter Klinnemann said quietly, catching on immediately. ‘We just need you to find our baby daughter.’

‘Of course,’ said Mariner. ‘It goes without saying that we’ll keep you informed of any developments.’ God, he got sick of that phrase.

Taking her arm, Millie guided Emma O’Brien out of the room. Mariner moved to follow Peter Klinnemann, but he hung back until the two women had turned the corner, before rounding on Mariner. ‘How in the name of God did that reporter know about my work place?’ he demanded to know.

'I've no idea,' said Mariner, truthfully. 'Perhaps your name—'

'They have no reason to make that connection. One of your officers must have told them.' Klinnemann was incensed.

'I can assure you,' Mariner said, coldly. 'That none of my officers had even made the link themselves. And even if they had, they certainly not would have disclosed that kind of information without first clearing it with me. I'm very sorry that it came up, but I've no way of knowing how the press found out.'

'Then it must have been one of the nursery staff.'

'I can't speak for them, of course. But it' something that would have emerged sooner or later. I'm disappointed that you didn't see fit to be more forthcoming about the nature of your work right from the beginning. It's another obvious line of enquiry and we might have lost valuable time by not pursuing it. You must know how these people operate. They have whole networks of intelligence. It really would have helped if you'd been more open with us.'

'I didn't want to make Emma any more afraid than she is already. These people put the lives of animals above human lives and will go to extraordinary lengths to make their point. Can you imagine what it will do to her if she believes that one of those barbarians might have our daughter?'

'I'm sorry the press found out, Mr Klinnemann, but our priority remains to recover Jessica safely.'

It seemed to bring him up short, the anger dissipating as quickly as it had flared. 'It was a mistake. I apologise.'

'It's a difficult time,' Mariner said, but they both let the understatement pass. 'What exactly *is* the substance of your work?'

'I'm researching into the effectiveness of a drug that treats Alzheimer's disease.'

'And it involves the use of live animals?'

'Yes.'

While he had Klinnemann on his own it seemed, to Mariner, a good opportunity to raise some other sensitive issues. He steeled himself. 'Mr Klinnemann, this revelation makes it more likely that, at some stage, we may be contacted by the abductor. Is there something about Jessica, some distinguishing feature that wouldn't be commonly known, a mole or birthmark perhaps?'

Klinnemann rubbed a hand over tired eyes. 'Yes,' he said. 'She has a *muttermal*, a . . .' he sketched a round shape on the back of his hand.

'A birthmark?' Mariner guessed.

'Yes, about one inch, but here,' Klinnemann touched his neck, 'underneath the hair.'

'Also,' Mariner went on, 'we may need something like a lock of Jessica's hair.'

'Yes, I think—' the significance of the request dawned on Klinnemann. 'Oh God.'

'It's routine,' Mariner reassured him quickly. 'Nothing more. It's just easier to do it now.' *Instead of leaving it until later when we need it.*

'Yes, yes of course. I'll see to it.'

* * *

'What is Hamilton Sciences?' Millie asked, coming back into the incident room after leaving Jessica's parents at their hotel.

'It's a research centre that's been a target for animal rights activists,' Mariner filled her in. 'It gets in the news all the time, thanks to them.'

'That's why it sounded so familiar.'

'Yes, he told me the name of the company he worked for hours ago, but I didn't make the connection. I wish to God I had.'

'Didn't they follow home some guy who worked there, and beat him senseless in front of his wife and kids?' Knox asked.

'Among other things,' said Mariner. 'Christ, if they're involved we're into a whole different ball game. Why the hell didn't Klinnemann tell us that?'

Millie looked shaken. 'Perhaps he didn't want to consider it a possibility.'

'More fool him. He leads a research team. He's a prime target.'

'If it is them, they'll have done their homework. Someone will have found out that Emma O'Brien was coming here today and would have done a recce of the nursery in advance.'

'It's possible. There are active cells of animal rights all over the country who gather intelligence and communicate via the internet. It would be a big operation, but they are highly organised and something could have been set up. The nursery has the crèche contract with the hospital and details of the children using the facility are passed on. Someone there could have easily seen an opportunity. It might be worth checking if Jimmy Bond has any leanings in that direction, too.'

It added a whole layer of further work to be done. 'Someone could do with identifying any likely candidates here, and I'll add that onto the list of things to ask them in Cambridge.'

Mariner returned to his office to make the call to Cambridgeshire police himself. DI Ruth Tunstall had been nominated to liaise with him and Mariner was pleased to pick up the professional tone at the other end of the line. Ruth knew the family from previous involvement and had already made it her business to have the paperwork available. Even so, he was surprised at the level of detail.

'Peter Klinnemann left his wife Mary in March, when Emma O'Brien was seven months pregnant,' she told him. 'Mary took it very badly and was hell bent on revenge on Peter and on Emma. It was all good bunny-boiling stuff, but nothing terribly original. Peter initially moved into Emma's flat in Cambridge. Mary followed him there and, on several occasions subsequently we were called out to disturbances; mostly Mary standing in the street below shouting abuse at them both, sometimes throwing fruit and eggs at the windows. On one occasion she dumped all Peter's clothes outside Emma's flat in black bin bags. It seemed perfectly reasonable until he opened up the bags and found his best suits and shirts liberally seasoned with tomato ketchup, mustard and HP sauce.'

'Ouch,' said Mariner.

'Quite. Mary also admitted to making nuisance calls to Emma O'Brien at home and at work and there were instances of vandalism to their cars — lipstick on the windscreen, a knife in the tyres. It wasn't so much the seriousness of the attacks as the persistence and in the end Peter Klinnemann was forced to take out an injunction against her.'

'And has it worked?'

'Yes. I mean this all happened months ago, and Mary's been pretty quiet since. I've been keeping an eye on her too. We've talked a lot and she seems to listen to me.'

Mariner wasn't surprised. Ruth Tunstall seemed the kind of person who would inspire confidence. 'When did you last see her?'

'I've just come from her house — their house as I suppose it technically still is. You can rest assured that if she is in any way involved it's not in the front line, and I would doubt that she has anything to do with it. I don't think she's particularly sorry that it's happened but neither is she up to organising anything like it. She's on anti-depressants and pretty spaced out.'

'What about the children?'

'Lisbet is lovely. She lives away from home now, up in Peterborough, but she's been spending a lot of time with her mum. She's been very supportive.'

'And Paul?'

Ruth Tunstall began to measure her words carefully. 'Paul is different,' she said. 'The whole business has hit him a lot harder. He was pretty angry with his dad.'

Mariner sensed she was holding back. 'And?'

'Look, don't read too much into this, but Paul has had his problems in the past. About three years ago he was cautioned for possession of cannabis and he moved from that to the stronger stuff. I think he's clean at the moment but his dad's activities haven't exactly helped the healing process.'

'He has a drug habit? Even if he's not behind this, someone could be using him to get at his father. He wasn't at home this evening?'

'No, but as I said, that isn't unusual. He's away at university — UCL — he may well have gone back a bit early.'

'His father tried to contact him earlier today, but his phone was switched off.'

'Do you want me to see if I can track him down?'

'I want to know where he is,' said Mariner.

'Of course, I'll talk to Mary and see if she has any ideas about where he might be.'

'And any close friends.'

'Sure,' said Tunstall. 'But if you want my honest opinion, I can't imagine that either of the kids would be caught up in this. Okay, they were angry with their father, but they wouldn't want to hurt him.'

'What do you know about Klinnemann's finances?' Mariner asked.

'Nothing specific. Naturally Mary is threatening to screw him for everything he's got, and so far she's hung on to the house and the Freelander. As far as I can make out, Emma O'Brien sold her flat and the happy couple have moved into a place in Witham, a village just outside the city.'

'What sort of place is it?'

'Compared with the family home it's a pretty modest little cottage, but no property in or around Cambridge is ever cheap.'

'How much longer has Paul Klinnemann got at uni?'

'He's in his final year. You know where Peter Klinnemann works?'

'We do now, but only because one of the local hacks found out ahead of us. Klinnemann didn't see fit to mention it. We'll need to know if there's been any activity with cells in your area.'

'I've got a couple of people working on it already. They'll be making a few house calls. There's nothing yet, but I'll keep you posted.'

'Thanks.'

'And good luck. This is not the sort of case any of us wants.'

Thanking Tunstall again, Mariner rang off. Following the press conference, the phones in the incident room were red hot. Specially trained officers had been brought in to answer them, weeding out the calls they thought might be significant. Tony Knox was overseeing the evidence gathering process.

'How's the house-to-house doing?' Mariner asked him.

'No one saw anything at that time of day. Most people were out at work or picking up kids from school. One lead though. One of the bus drivers on that route has come forward. He drove past at about two forty. He didn't pick anyone up, but he did stop to allow a woman across the road who was carrying a baby in a car seat. It's about the right time and what little he could remember about her appearance fits with what we've already got.'

'So from that we can gather that she parked, or had transport waiting up at the hospital.'

'Looks like it, boss. We've also isolated what we think is the relevant CCTV footage. And there's another possible sighting by one of the site workmen of a woman struggling to carry the seat up the hill towards the main hospital car park. He noticed her because she was making heavy weather of it, switching from one arm to the other. He remembered thinking that the poor baby was getting a rough ride.' Knox took Mariner over to a map of the area that was pinned to the wall beside the white board. 'It's most likely that she was going up to the south car park, here.' He traced the route with an index finger. 'It's the nearest one to the nursery.' Coloured spot stickers littered the map, marking the position of the cameras, but there wasn't one here. 'It's a new car park and they haven't finished installing the system yet, but the building site where the brickie was working, over here, has footage, so we've concentrated on the vehicles they picked up coming down the exit ramp at around that time. Do you want to see it?'

'Let's give it a look.'

'Okay. This is the action between two thirty and three thirty. I can't imagine she'd have wanted to hang around here any longer than necessary.' Knox played the video, fast forwarding though the quiet patches. 'This is what we've got starting at half past two.'

Mariner stared at the video. For several seconds nothing happened then a medium-sized, dark car proceeded down the ramp, turned into the road and drove off to the right towards the main road. From then the exiting traffic was intermittent, a couple of cars every minute or so. All these vehicles would need to be traced. The quality of the film was disappointing — grainy and indistinct — and the camera angle meant that, apart from a fraction of a second before each car rounded the corner, the registration numbers were not in view. It was difficult at first glance even to ascertain the makes of the cars. Mariner said nothing. He had every confidence in the tech team to work their magic, and could only hope they'd be able to come up with something.

Meanwhile they could appeal to anyone who may have been in the car park at that time and noticed a woman with a baby getting into a vehicle, but again they were relying on members of the public to come forward, all of which took up precious time. Something that they couldn't really afford.

'That's good work,' Mariner said. 'But we really need to identify what vehicle she got into, or we're stuffed. Linking her to a car is the best chance we have of finding out where she went. Anything else?'

'We've talked to the friends Emma O'Brien stayed with last night,' said Knox. 'They're old college friends apparently, both of them now doctors. According to them they may have mentioned to a couple of people in the last few days that Emma was coming to stay, but they claim not to have spoken to anyone about the arrangements for Jessica. They didn't even seem to know anything about the nursery, only that it's a crèche connected to the hospital, so I'm inclined to believe them.'

'Okay, that makes sense. I can't think what they'd have to gain from this. I think we can safely leave them for now.' But there were more uncomfortable questions he'd have to ask Peter Klinnemann.

DCI Sharp burst into the office, carrying a portable radio, which she plugged in and switched on. 'You may want to hear this, Tom.'

The programme she'd tuned in to was a late-night radio phone-in. It took Mariner mere seconds to recognise Marcella Turner's voice. 'This was a tragedy waiting to happen,' she was saying. 'Babies and young children get dumped in places like this for hours on end, the young girls responsible for their welfare barely out of school themselves, without the faintest clue how to care for them.'

'But surely nurseries provide a valuable service for working parents,' the presenter countered.

'Exactly. It provides a service for the *parents*. No one ever considers the effect it might be having on the child. What this government is doing is reinforcing a culture of "children as accessories," encouraging couples to have children without the inconvenience of having to raise them. Hand them over to someone else to bring up and make them someone else's responsibility. No wonder the family unit is disintegrating.'

'So what would you suggest, Ms Turner?'

'That women are given a genuine choice; the mother's role is fully recognised and that women are paid a decent wage for staying at home and looking after their children. And that these glorified baby farms are closed down.'

'Is that all?' commented someone drily.

'Someone get me some more background on her,' said Mariner, to no one in particular.

* * *

Mariner had been putting off the inevitable phone call to Anna, mainly because he didn't want to face her disappointment, but suddenly he found himself at a loose end and could find no further excuse within himself. If he left it much later she'd be in bed. She picked up on the first ring.

'I'm really sorry about the holiday,' Mariner began.

'I know,' Anna said. 'It can't be helped.' Now that she'd had time to think about it, she seemed philosophical, her voice unemotional. 'I can't imagine what those poor parents are going through, but if I was in their shoes I'd want you out there looking for baby Jessica, too.'

'I don't deserve you,' Mariner said.

'You're right about that. Something you'd do well to remember sometimes.' But it was said with a hint of playfulness. 'Has there been a breakthrough? Is that why you're calling?'

'I wish. No. I just wanted to check in. I can't do anything about this. You do understand that?'

‘Of course. It’s just . . . I was just so looking forward to you finally meeting everyone down there.’

‘I will, eventually. This situation could end at any time.’

‘What are baby Jessica’s chances?’ she asked.

‘I really don’t know. It’s certainly putting me off the idea of nursery day care,’ Mariner said. ‘What’s the point of having children if you’re not going to look after them?’

‘I agree. So how long will you be taking?’

‘What do you mean?’

‘How many years’ paternity leave will you get?’ Unable to see her face Mariner couldn’t tell if she was joking or not. ‘I mean, if we’re not going to put the baby in a nursery, one of us will need to stay at home with him or her,’ she continued. ‘Are you assuming it will be me, just when my career is picking up and getting interesting again? Have you any idea what another break would mean?’

Mariner bit back the retort he wanted to make, along the lines of, *you’re the one who wants children*. Instead he said: ‘As a matter of fact I do. The guv’nor filled me in.’

‘She’s got kids? You didn’t tell me that.’

‘Only found out myself today,’ as he spoke he saw that the hands of the clock had moved past midnight. ‘Well, yesterday. She’d kept that one to herself.’

‘How many?’

‘Three. Her partner is their mother.’

Anna took a few seconds to absorb that nugget. ‘Wow.’

‘Yes, wow.’

‘Well, good for her.’ She was thoughtful for a moment.

‘I’d better go,’ said Mariner.

‘Okay, well, loads of luck. I hope you get a break soon, and a good one. And not just for my own selfish reasons.’

‘Thanks. Sleep tight.’ Mariner felt a sudden longing for his bed.

'I will.'

* * *

Information continued to filter in throughout the night, but frustratingly nothing as yet that stood out as significant. Mariner left the incident room early the next morning, just as breakfast was being delivered. After a night's activity with the whole team the room was becoming unbearably hot and stuffy, and he was glad to get out into the cool morning air. His first stop was the Cedar Wood Hotel, where he met Millie with a view to giving Klinnemann and Emma an update. She took him up to their hotel room, where he could see immediately from the condition of the bed that it hadn't been slept in. One look at the couple confirmed it. Emma O'Brien's face was puffy and swollen and he guessed that she'd been shedding tears on and off all night. Peter Klinnemann's face looked pale and shadowed.

A breakfast tray sat on the desk largely untouched, though the cafetière was almost empty. Mariner was invited to take the one easy chair, while they sat on the bed. 'Mr Klinnemann, your son isn't anywhere to be found,' he began. 'Have you any idea where he might be?'

'No, but it's not unusual for him to go off for a weekend,' Klinnemann seemed a touch defensive. 'He's a student.'

'I have to ask you, does he have any sympathy for the animal rights cause?'

Klinnemann's eyes hardened. 'I'm his father. He is loyal to me.'

'How well do you know his friends?'

'We've met one or two, but he's in his final year at university in London — so naturally we don't know them all.'

'Are you aware of any who might disapprove of your work?' asked Mariner.

'Paul has never mentioned it.'

'But it's not out of the question?'

'I suppose not.' That might prove tricky.

* * *

From the hotel Mariner doubled back to the Queen Elizabeth Hospital admin department. The office was normally closed on Saturdays, but Mariner had called the previous evening to arrange for the office manager to meet him there. Marjorie Allen was also responsible for administering the crèche. She was babysitting Josh, her three-year-old grandson, this morning and had brought him with her.

'I'm sorry to call you out at the weekend, but I'm sure you understand why it's important,' Mariner said.

'Of course. I saw it on the news last night. That poor lady. I can't imagine how she must be feeling.'

'Could you talk me through the record keeping system for the crèche?'

'As I'm sure you already know, we publicise the crèche and then parents contact Mrs Barratt to make a booking. Mrs Barratt takes all the details and sends a copy of each booking form up to us.'

'Does Mrs Barratt bring it here?'

'No, one of the hospital couriers used to collect it for us, but they let us down a couple of times. Sheila Fry, one of the staff in the unit next door has a child in the nursery, so she brings them up for us. At least then we know they're getting here.'

'In an envelope?'

'Yes, a sealed envelope, because of confidentiality.'

'What happens to your copy of the records?'

'They're filed in here.' She went over to one of two steel filing cabinets.

'Could you check and see if you still have the copy of Jessica Klinnemann's booking?'

She opened up the filing cabinet and sorted through the alphabetically arranged folders. 'Yes, here it is.' She passed him the carbon copy of the form he'd seen in Trudy Barratt's office. It didn't mean a thing. Not three feet away from where they were standing was a photocopier.

'And the filing cabinet is kept locked?'

'Outside office hours, of course,' Marjorie told him. 'During the day some of the other files need to be regularly accessed.'

'So who else would access them?'

'No one, just me,' she said.

Mariner looked across at the two other workstations next to where they were standing. 'You share this office with two other people?'

'Yes, but neither of them would have any cause to go into this filing cabinet.'

So trusting. 'I'll need their details anyway,' said Mariner. 'Do you always remember to lock the filing cabinet when you're out of the office?'

'At the end of the day, yes, of course.'

'What about lunchtimes?'

Marjorie Allen flushed. 'Well, er . . .'

Meaning no. So if they'd got the timing right, anyone could have had access to Jessica Klinnemann's records. 'This area is covered by closed circuit cameras?' asked Mariner.

'Yes.'

It was something, if only more CCTV footage to trawl through. When Mariner reported this information in to Granville Lane, he learned that Sheila Fry was already on record for the investigation, and as he took her details from Tony Knox, Mariner realised that he must have already met her. According to the notes she'd been collecting her son late on Friday afternoon when they were at the nursery. When she opened her front door to him twenty minutes later he immediately recognised her as one of the parents who'd been standing in the hall waiting to go. Mariner wondered if hers was the child so unfortunately named Leopold.

'I understand you deliver the details of crèche babies up to the hospital,' Mariner said.

'Yes, I think there was a mix up with the couriers once or twice, so Trudy asked if I wouldn't mind helping out. As I go up there every day it seems to make sense.'

'Has anything unusual occurred in the last few weeks? Someone stopping you, for example, or showing an interest in the forms?'

'No, nothing at all.'

* * *

Mariner walked back into the incident room, where, apart from the growing pile of empty takeaway cartons, nothing seemed to have changed since he'd left. 'Anything new?' he asked Knox.

'Sorry, nothing boss,' his sergeant said, with the same air of despondency. 'We're stuck in the mud. It's like this woman disappeared off the face of the planet. What about Sheila Fry?'

'I don't think she's a contender. She's got a child in the nursery herself. She wouldn't want strangers wandering around. It's possible that someone could have gained access to Jessica's record at the hospital, but we could be looking at thousands of people, and unless we can come up with a motive—'

'Sir?' It was one of the officers stationed at the phones who called across and there was something in her tone of voice that made everyone stop what they were doing and look up. She was holding the receiver a little way from her ear, covering the mouthpiece. 'The caller wants to speak to you. He's asked for you by name.'

Chapter Seven

As Mariner moved across the room to a phone with a recording facility, she took her hand off the mouthpiece. 'I'm just putting you through.'

Mariner pressed the button that would record the call and prompt the team working in the next room to begin tracing it. 'This is DI Mariner,' he said, his heart thumping in his chest.

'I've got baby Jessica,' said a deep, disembodied voice.

'I'm sorry, could you repeat that?' said Mariner.

'Don't piss me about,' said the voice, muffled and with a tinny distortion to it. 'I've got baby Jessica. She's safe and well, at the moment. For her return I want two hundred and fifty thousand euros in used notes, or I won't be responsible for what happens to her. No electronic marking or sequential numbers. I'll be in touch to let you know about the time and the location.'

'How will we recognise you?' asked Mariner, playing for time. 'We need a name, a code word . . . we're taking dozens of calls so we have to be able to single you out right away.' Mariner knew that this would appeal to the caller's sense of self-importance and it could also provide a clue as to who they were talking to. 'We also need some proof that you are holding Jessica.'

There was a pause, then: 'You can call me Zion.' The line went dead.

Mariner played the tape back for everyone to hear.

'It's to the point,' said Sharp. 'Did we trace it?'

'It's a mobile number. It'll take us a little while to get the registered owner.'

'Get it done.'

'And I'd better go and talk to Jessica's parents,' said Mariner.

* * *

'We'll pay!' Emma O'Brien was predictably in no doubt whatsoever as to the right course of action.

Klinnemann looked devastated. 'I haven't got that kind of money, Emma.' He looked despairingly at Mariner. 'I really haven't.'

'But we could raise it somehow.' Emma O'Brien's voice was high with desperation. 'My parents—'

'It's not as simple as that,' Klinnemann said.

'I don't see how it could be any simpler,' Emma O'Brien cried. 'This maniac has got our daughter and wants money from us. If we can find it from somewhere, we'll get her back. If Jessica has been taken because of your job, then Hamilton should pay. God knows they put you through enough stress anyway.'

'They won't pay,' Klinnemann said.

'Why not? They make millions. Two hundred and fifty thousand euros would be nothing to them.'

Peter Klinnemann looked beaten. 'That's not the point,' he said wearily.

'Then what *is* the point??'

Mariner intervened. 'They won't pay, Miss O'Brien, because they can't be held hostage. If they're seen to give in to this demand then it will be the start of many. But we're jumping the gun here. The first thing we have to do is establish if this is a genuine call. It could just be a hoax, someone trying to cash in on the situation. We're attempting to trace the number, and we'll have a negotiator on standby for when the abductor next makes contact. I just needed to let you know what's going on. Is there anyone, beyond who we're already considering, who might have a motive for extortion?'

'No. None of it makes any sense at all,' said Peter Klinnemann.

* * *

Back at Granville Lane, Mariner turned back to the diagram on the whiteboard. 'Okay, if this is purely about money, then who are the likely candidates?'

'Can we rule out Klinnemann, trying to extort money from his employer?' queried Millie.

'Unless he's good at bluffing, I think we can. And he knows that Hamilton would never give in to this kind of blackmail. He more or less said it.'

'What about Trudy Barratt?' Knox offered.

'The nursery manager? I don't think so. A stunt like this would be counterproductive for her. The adverse publicity could wreck her business. There's no indication that it's in any trouble and I don't get a sense that she's looking for a way out. Judging from that car she drives, she's doing very well out of it, so why put all that in jeopardy? You've been doing the background checks. Any of the staff stand out?'

'I've been through all of them pretty thoroughly, but like I said before, I don't think any of them are up to it,' said Knox.

Charlie Glover had joined them. 'They're pretty badly paid,' he pointed out.

'But would they have the organisational skills for something of this nature? What about Christie's boyfriend, Bond?' said Mariner. 'Wasn't there something about him?'

‘It’s possible,’ Knox said. ‘He’s flouted the law before.’

‘If Christie is in on this and covering up for him she could have given us a completely false description,’ said Millie.

‘Shit.’

‘She hasn’t,’ Knox said, confidently. ‘I know she hasn’t.’ All the same, he grabbed his coat from the back of the chair. ‘I’ll go and talk to her.’

* * *

It was the middle of the afternoon when Knox arrived for the second time outside the house Christie shared with Jimmy Bond, and the driveway was empty. He rang the doorbell and hammered on the door and eventually Christie appeared. She was surprised to see him, but not unduly worried. ‘Where’s Jimmy?’ Knox demanded.

‘He’s not here. He’s at work, why? What’s this about?’

‘Do you ever talk to him about the nursery?’

‘Sometimes. Everybody does, don’t they, talk about work? Look, do you want to come in?’ Knox followed her into a small rectangular lounge decorated in varying shades of beige. A cream leather sofa took up one third of the space and shelves of DVDs and computer games lined one of the walls, but what dominated the room was a huge plasma screen TV with a DVD and PlayStation. Christie perched tentatively on the edge of the sofa but Knox declined the offer to sit, choosing instead to pace the room. He took a couple of computer games from the shelf, inspecting the covers before putting them back. ‘Did you tell Jimmy about the crèche?’ he wanted to know.

‘I might have.’

‘Would he know how it all works?’

She shrugged. ‘Not necessarily. Half the time I don’t think he even listens to me. You can’t think that Jim—? I know he’s not perfect, but he’d never do anything like this.’

'You told me that his business is in trouble.'

'Yes, but—'

'We've had a ransom demand.' Knox saw from her face that now, suddenly, she wasn't so sure of her boyfriend. 'What's his mobile number?'

'Wait, it's stored on my phone.' Fetching her phone from a white leather handbag, Christie brought up the number in her phone book and handed it to him. 'And yours?' Knox asked. But when he looked, neither was the number they had for Zion. The opening digits were entirely different. 'Does Jimmy have another phone?'

'He has one for the business but I don't know the number.'

'Give him a call, would you?' Knox asked. 'On his personal phone.'

Christie did as he asked, but the phone was switched off. 'It usually is when he's at work. He's probably with customers.'

Before leaving Knox said, 'Do you mind if I have a look round upstairs?'

'No.' She seemed unsure, but Knox felt certain it wasn't because she had anything to hide. She was worrying about what Bond would say if he found out. It didn't take him long to scrutinise the small, boxy bedrooms and bathroom — where he found nothing that looked out of place — and when he glanced out of the window and into the garden he saw only a small patch of green lawn surrounded by bare wooden fencing. Nowhere to hide anything — or anyone — out there.

'Christie, if you're protecting Jimmy, you're in big trouble and there's nothing I can do to help you. You understand that, don't you?' Knox said, fixing her gaze.

She didn't falter. 'Of course I do.'

* * *

The address she gave Knox for Jimmy Bond's garage, led him to a street corner off the Pershore Road in Balsall

Heath, close to the city centre. But when he got there it was all closed up. Knox peered through the plate glass windows, but alongside the row of dubious-looking 'pre-owned' cars, there was no sign of human life anywhere. So where the hell was Bond?

He'd told Christie he was going to work as usual, and surely Saturday was a good day for the used car trade. He couldn't afford to close unless he had some other, more pressing business to attend to. Knox crossed over to the other side of the road and stood back to have another look at the garage building. The showroom itself was a wide single-storey structure, but built on at the rear he could see a higher two-floor structure, with an iron fire escape snaking up towards a single window. Had those curtains been closed when he got here?

Walking round the side of the garage Knox came to a high wooden gate. It was unlocked. Knox walked in and crept up the fire escape and when he got to the top, banged his fist on the panelling of the door as hard as he could. God, that hurt. 'Police! Open up, I know you're in there.' He could have sworn he heard a sound. The door looked flimsy and unsubstantial. He probably could shoulder it if he needed to. 'If you don't open up we'll break it down,' he shouted, giving himself some imaginary backup. 'Five seconds . . . four . . .'

This time there was definite scuffling and the door opened a crack, behind it a white male, twenties, overweight and wearing nothing but boxer shorts. Knox could see why Bond had shortened his name — 007 he wasn't. He peered over Knox's shoulder to ascertain how many he was up against. He was in for a disappointment.

'Jimmy Bond?' said Knox, holding out his warrant card.

He didn't deny it. 'What the hell do you—?'

Catching Bond off guard, Knox shoved open the door and forced his way in, slamming it shut again behind his back. He'd walked straight into a room that offered little more refinement than the houses they'd raided on Ocean Blue, and contained a double bed that, judging from the state of the sheets, had seen a lot of very recent action. In an alcove off to the left a woman stood, wearing a look of indignation and probably very little else under the thin duvet that she hugged around her. Small and slim, as far as Knox could tell, she had coffee coloured skin and her cropped black hair was in tight curls. 'What is this?'

Ignoring her Knox strode over to where she stood and peered in. It was a tiny bathroom of the most basic kind. Not much doubt about what was going on here, and it had nothing to do with Jessica Klinnemann. Set to vibrate, Knox felt his phone ringing. He ought to respond to it and there was nothing else to be done here. 'Christie know about all this, does she?' he sneered as he walked back past Bond. 'You piece of shite.'

Back out on the street Knox checked his phone. The call was from Mariner. He returned it straight away.

'Meet us up at the Lickeys.' Mariner's voice was grim, and there was a background roar. He was in a car. 'Coven Lane behind the chapel. Some baby clothes have been found, including a pale green babygro.'

'Oh, Christ.'

'Yeah. We'll see you up there.'

'Right, boss.'

* * *

Mariner drove up the steep incline of Rose Hill, with the dread of anticipation tight in his chest. He'd ordered the area to be cordoned off and called for back up from the dog handling team. He drove past the little church and into the lane that ran between a row of detached houses to their right and woodland on the left, and pulled into a rough lay-by behind a pale blue minibus. The call had come from the leader of a Scout group who were out on an orienteering exercise in the woods. Now a crowd of boys in bottle green jumpers milled around the back of the bus, some of them swigging from sports bottles, all of them high with excitement as they watched the drama unfold.

Uniformed officers in fluorescent green jackets were already stretching crime scene tape to the side of the group, around the trunks of the beech trees whose leaves were a bright orangey-gold in the late afternoon sun. Mariner sought out the woman in charge of the boys, who introduced herself as Akela. She, in turn, took Mariner over to Ryan, the eight-year-old who had found the clothing.

'We were having a leaf fight,' the boy explained, 'and I grabbed this little baby suit by accident, with a handful of leaves. It was all dirty. Then I remembered what they said on the telly last night about that baby that got taken so I went to tell Akela.'

As he was talking Mariner was aware of another car pulling into the lay-by. Tony Knox.

'Can you take us to where you found them?'

'I left my neckerchief there to mark the spot,' the boy said proudly. 'Akela told us to leave the clothes where they were.' Good old Akela.

Impressively in a thickly wooded area where each tree looked precisely the same as all the others, the boy was able to lead them, unerringly, to the exact place, about a hundred metres into the woods, where he'd come across the clothing. A couple of minutes in Mariner was able to spot the bright red and yellow scarf up ahead.

'Well done Ryan,' Mariner said. 'You did the right thing. Now, can you go back to your friends exactly the same way as we just came?' Taking out a business card he handed it to Akela. 'Give me a call when all this is over and we'll arrange a visit for them all to Granville Lane.'

'Thanks.'

When Ryan and Akela had retreated back to the road, Mariner turned his attention to the crumpled garment, still half-buried and difficult to identify at all from where it now lay. Pulling on latex gloves, and with Knox squatting beside him, he gingerly picked it up. The little suit was filthy with soil and leaf mulch and around the neck and down the body was a more distinct dark brown stain that to him was all too familiar. 'It fits the description,' he said. It did, even down to the same manufacturer's label that had been on the one they'd seen at the nursery yesterday afternoon. Bagging it up, he noticed the condensation that immediately began to form on the inside of the polythene packet. He and Knox walked around the spot but there was nothing else to see.

'This isn't consistent with the ransom demand,' Knox observed.

'It could be,' Mariner said. 'We'll have to wait and see. Maybe it's Zion's way of letting us know how serious he is. Or it might be nothing at all,' Mariner said. 'It could simply be that the abductor has discarded the clothes because they're identifiable.' It didn't explain the ominous stains, but Mariner wasn't ready to pursue that line of reasoning.

'He came a long way from the road to dump just a baby suit,' said Knox, as they started back towards the road, following the dying light of the sun through the trees. 'If that's all there was, why not just throw it into the trees from the road? It would still have been pretty well hidden.'

'Perhaps that's what he did and an animal, a fox or something, picked it up and brought it further in.' Mariner said, avoiding the other, more obvious alternative. As he walked his foot kicked up something greyish white among the dead leaves. He picked it up. It was a chunk of plastic-looking material backed with some kind of wadding.

'Is this what I think it is?' he asked Knox.

'It's a chunk of nappy.'

If his theory was correct they'd a highly organised fox on their hands.

Back at the roadside a couple of vans were disgorging police dogs and their handlers. The clothing was dispatched to the lab for analysis and uniformed officers, some enlisted from the incident room, were pulling on forensic suits to commence a fingertip search of the immediate area. All of which would take at least a couple of hours to complete.

It began to drizzle. 'We can't do anything more here,' Mariner said. 'We may as well go back to base and do something useful.' *Whatever that might be.*

'Will you tell the parents?'

Mariner watched the group of young lads piling back into their minibus. 'I'll have to. It's only a matter of time before the press will get wind of what's going on up here. I'm amazed they haven't already.'

In the car Tony Knox had the opportunity to fill Mariner in on his visits to Christie and Jimmy Bond. 'So we can rule him out?' Mariner concluded.

'He hasn't taken baby Jessica. He's been too busy for that, but there's something about him—'

'Aside from the fact that he cheats on his girlfriend and beats her up?' said Mariner. 'He's just a pathetic loser.'

On the way back they stopped off at the hotel to break the news, Mariner taking Peter Klinnemann on one side to tell him. 'It doesn't necessarily mean the worst,' Mariner stressed. 'All we've found is clothing, nothing else.'

'I've made some calls,' Klinnemann said, chalk white. 'I can raise the money.' So Emma O'Brien had talked him round.

'Let's just wait and see what happens next,' Mariner said. He looked at his watch. 'Zion could call back at any time.' But almost the whole day had passed and Zion had remained silent.

* * *

Back in the incident room everyone seemed to have stopped working. Manpower was depleted, thanks to the search, but even so . . .

'What's going on?' Mariner asked.

'You didn't get the message, sir? Shortly after you left the scene the search officers found the body of a baby close to where the clothing was discovered. It's on its way to Croghan's office.'

* * *

Mariner and Knox drove to the mortuary in silence, Mariner unable to believe what was happening. How could the case be over so soon when they'd made so little progress on it all? What had they done that was so wrong, and what could they possibly have done differently? Did Zion know they were onto him, or did he think they weren't taking him seriously?

They arrived at Newton Street just as the tiny body bag was being transferred from the mortuary ambulance, and had to endure frustrating minutes while Stuart Croghan prepared himself for the examining room having pushed back all his other work to look at the findings. After what seemed an interminable wait, Mariner and Knox were allowed in.

'The good news for you guys is that it's not Jessica,' said Croghan.

Mariner felt a surge of relief. 'How can you tell so soon?'

'The body is in a much too advanced stage of decomposition. It's been there many months, I'd say, possibly up to a year. And the baby is small too, I'd say only a couple of weeks old.'

'Is it likely that the clothes belonged to this baby?'

'They'd swamp him a bit, but yes he could have worn them, and he's still wearing what looks like the remains of a vest, with a bloodstain pattern very similar to the one on the babygro. It looks as if an animal of some kind has had a good chew on it too.'

'So it's pure coincidence that the babygro is the same make as the one that Jessica is wearing?'

'It would seem so. I'm guessing these garments must be pretty widely available.'

'Any idea how this baby died?'

'That kind of detail I can't give you yet,' Croghan said. 'Sadly I haven't yet perfected the old x-ray vision. I'll let you know as soon as, but meanwhile,' Croghan broke off what he was doing, 'go and find baby Jessica. Aren't you due a phone call?'

* * *

The atmosphere in the incident room felt ready to explode as the minutes and hours passed, waiting for Zion's next call, and Mariner had to remind everyone to continue pursuing other lines of enquiry. 'Somebody must have seen something.'

Then at five past four in the afternoon, the phone rang and Zion identified himself. As before, Mariner pressed the button and lifted the receiver.

'Have you got the money?' Zion asked immediately.

No reference to the findings at the Lickeys, Mariner noticed. He didn't know. 'We haven't had enough time,' he said, reasonably. 'It's the weekend. Mr Klinnemann can't put his hands on that amount of money instantly.'

'Then he's not trying hard enough,' said the distorted voice. 'If he wants his daughter back he'll find it. I'll call back tomorrow morning with the location.'

'I need some kind of proof that you have Jessica and that she is safe and well. She has a birthmark. Can you tell me where it is?'

'I'm not playing games. You'll just have to trust me.' And the line went dead. There was an audible echo around the room as everyone seemed to collectively sigh, the tension temporarily relieved.

'What about the voice?' Mariner asked. 'Have we had the analysis report on the first recording yet?'

Tony Knox had the paperwork. 'It's definitely a man's voice, but it's been disguised, muffled somehow.'

'Professionally?'

'No, according to this there's no distortion device. More likely that he's covering the receiver with something. It'll disguise the sound of his voice but the vocal pattern will stay the same.' Knox finished reading. 'All we need now is someone to compare it with.'

'Christie said the woman had a northern accent.'

'That isn't obvious, though again it could have been deliberately disguised.'

'I don't like this,' Mariner paced in front of the white board. 'We have no proof that he's even holding Jessica. I think we should stall him for longer.'

'It's a big risk, boss.'

'What choice do we have?'

Knox's mobile rang and he went outside to take it.

'Sergeant Knox, it's Christie. I thought you should know. Jimmy just phoned me and asked a really weird question. He wanted to know if baby Jessica had a birthmark. I didn't know and he started getting angry,' her voice went up an octave and she began to whimper. 'Why would he ask me something like that? I don't understand.'

'You've done the right thing, Christie. Where is he? This is important.'

'I think he's still at the garage.'

'Stay where you are, and don't contact him again,' said Knox. 'If he tries to ring you again, don't answer. Do you understand?'

'Okay.'

He'd save the bad news for later. Ending the call Knox pushed open the door of the incident room. 'Boss? We've got Zion.'

'You're sure about this?' Mariner said as they bounded down the stairs.

'Why else would Bond want to know about birthmark?'

'He clearly doesn't have Jessica then.'

'Unless he's keeping her somewhere else. But no, I don't think he's that bright. He hasn't got it in him.'

* * *

Bond's showroom was all locked up as it had been when Knox had called there earlier in the day, but this time when he raced up the fire escape and kicked open the door the love nest was empty, too. By now it was dusk and when they went back onto the street Mariner saw the faintest sliver of light escaping from below a door at the back of the showroom. They hammered on the outer door, fully prepared to break it down. But they didn't have to. Jimmy Bond appeared, looking amazingly cool, even smiling. He had absolutely no idea that he'd been caught. 'What can I do for—' The smile left his face as Knox interrupted to read him his rights, and in one smooth move cuffed his wrists behind his back.

'I don't understand, you've got the wrong—' But it was another sentence he didn't complete. He knew he'd been had.

Bond protested his innocence all the way to Granville Lane. Knowing that he wasn't holding Jessica, they had the luxury of letting him stew overnight in a cell. Free of that particular false trail there were more important things to do. But Knox did make a further call to Christie, to let her know what had happened. 'It's your choice, love, of course, but we'll be keeping him in at least overnight, probably twenty-four hours. Might be a good time to make yourself scarce. We haven't told him what you told us but he'll probably work it out for himself.' He considered telling her what else he'd learned about Bond that day but decided against it. She'd been hurt enough already. 'Have you got somewhere you can go?'

'Yes.'

Almost all the vehicles leaving the hospital car park at around the time of Jessica's abduction had been accounted for. The only ones that had not been claimed were a dark saloon, possibly a Renault, with a partial index, and a white or silver four-wheel drive. The CCTV enhancement team had provided clearer footage, which they had studied, straining to see who was in the cars. But in both cases the driver's features were indistinct. It was possible that there could be a passenger in the back, or a child in a child seat, but the vehicles flashed by too fast for them to see. Nonetheless, the grainy photographs of both vehicles were shown on the next national news bulletin, along with all the other details.

By the following morning they'd had two breakthroughs that would help seal the fate of Jimmy Bond. The mobile number had been traced to a pay-as-you-go handset registered in his name some months previously, and the two PCs sent back to do a more thorough search of his house had come across the computer game *Urban Warrior*, which included a character called Zion. Alongside it were numerous *CSI* DVDs, among them one that featured a kidnapping for ransom. It was circumstantial evidence and by no means conclusive, but it was a start, and Mariner had one more trick up his sleeve for Jimmy Bond.

Inside the interview room Mariner put two tapes into the machine and set the scene.

'Where is she?' Mariner demanded.

'I don't know what you're talking about.' After his overnight stay, Bond was looking less relaxed, and fear was making him belligerent and defensive.

'Of course you do,' said Mariner. 'It's in all the papers. Only we think you know more than they're reporting. What have you been up to the last few days, apart from shagging your receptionist?'

'All sorts of things, I'm a busy man.'

Mariner had the phone log in front of him. 'Let me refresh your memory. Yesterday morning at eleven fifteen you made a phone call to this station, demanding money in exchange for the safe return of Jessica.'

'That's rubbish.'

'Two hundred and fifty thousand euros to be precise.'

'What are you on about? Two hundred and fifty thousand euros. You're yanking my chain.'

'Not at all,' said Mariner allowing himself a brief smile of satisfaction. 'The call was traced to a mobile that's registered to you.' Mariner recited the number. 'Recognise it?'

'I lost that phone ages ago.' Bond was dismissive.

'When exactly?'

'I don't remember. Couple of months or so.'

The bad news for Mariner was that the phone hadn't yet been found. The probability was that Bond had ditched it. But Mariner didn't really care, because in the last minute or so Jimmy Bond had as good as sentenced himself. The tape machine gave off a high-pitched whine and clunked loudly. His brow furrowing, Mariner reached out, removed one of the tapes and examined it. 'Faulty tape,' he concluded. 'I'll get a replacement. And we'll take a break for a while.'

'But you've only just—' Bond's solicitor started to protest.

'I'm a busy man too,' said Mariner. Informing the remaining tape of what was going on he suspended the interview and stepped outside, where Tony Knox was waiting with a second tape. Mariner exchanged it for the 'broken' one. 'Get this to the forensic service,' he told Knox. 'And let me know as soon as we have some results.'

Later that morning Mariner was able to return to the interview room armed with two sheets of A4. Switching on the tape, he slapped the two computer printouts on the table in front of Jimmy Bond. The rows of coloured, jagged lines were, to the naked eye, identical. 'Know what these are, Jimmy?' he asked pleasantly, not expecting a reply. 'They're voice analysis printouts. We've got a man in our lab who's an expert in voice prints.' He indicated the sheet on the right. 'This one is what your voice looks like.

It's the sample taken from the recording we made in here this morning. Pretty isn't it?' said Mariner. 'Here, for instance, is what your voice looks like when you say the words *two hundred and fifty thousand*. It's different from the way anyone else's voice looks when it says those words. You might say it's unique. And yet here,' he tapped the left-hand page, 'are the words *two hundred and fifty thousand* as spoken by Zion, the person who made the ransom demand in exchange for the safe return of baby Jessica. Can you spot any differences? No, you can't because they're exactly the same, and they prove that you made those calls. And the best part is, they're admissible in court. Jimmy Bond, I'm charging you with the abduction of Jessica Klinnemann, and if you want to make it easy on yourself you'd better start off by telling us where she—'

'No, *no*!' Bond cut in, his face pure panic now. 'I admit. I did make the phone call. But I haven't got the baby. I swear. That's nothing to do with me. I just saw an . . . opportunity.'

'*Opportunity*?' Anger boiled up inside Mariner.

Bond shrugged, as if it was the kind of decision he made every day. 'I needed the money. And no one else was asking for it. I thought I might as well.'

'You stupid, self-serving bastard.' It took all of Mariner's willpower to stop himself from lunging at Bond and squeezing the life out of him. 'Do you know what you've done, wasting valuable time when we could have been out looking for that baby? If anything happens to her you'll have to live with it being your fault.' Mariner wanted to smash Bond's gormless face against the wall. Instead he just pushed back his chair, with such force that it toppled with a crash, and walked out.

'What do you want us to do with him?' The duty sergeant asked.

'Charge him with wasting police time. He hasn't got Jessica. He hasn't got the balls or the brains for it.' Mariner hesitated. 'It'll be a CPS decision, but with a bit of luck we can have him for perverting the course of justice, and he'll end up with a custodial sentence.'

Mariner told Knox what had happened.

'Did you have to drop Christie in it?' he asked.

Mariner shook his head. 'No need. The voiceprint gave us a way in and he confessed to making the calls. We're charging him but we'll have to let him go for now. You might want to let Christie know.'

'I already have. But I'll have a little chat with Bond before he leaves us.'

Bond was in custody signing for his belongings when Knox caught up with him.

'I'll see Mr Bond out,' he told the duty sergeant.

Following at a discreet distance Knox waited until Bond was almost at the exit door before darting past him and blocking the way. Stepping forward he put his face up so close to Bond's that he could feel his breath. 'I know about you,' he said. 'And I know what you do to your girlfriend. If she's got any sense she'll have gone by the time you get back, but if I find out that you've so much as touched her again, your life won't be worth living.'

* * *

With Bond out of the frame the enquiry had ground once again to a halt. It had been three days now. Three days for the abductor to get Jessica far away. Three days for another adult to form a relationship with the child. Every day lessened the chances of finding her safe.

Mariner had to keep Emma O'Brien and Peter Klinnemann up to speed with the latest developments. When he got to the hotel, there was a young woman with them.

'This is my daughter, Lisbet,' said Klinnemann.

With white blonde hair and eyes the colour of cornflowers, Lisbet Klinnemann had a model's good looks and spoke with the kind of precise diction that could only be bought with an expensive private education. 'You have some news?'

'Not the best, I'm afraid,' said Mariner. 'We'll be charging a man with wasting police time. He made the ransom demands but we've no reason to think that he's connected to the abduction. He just saw it as a money-making opportunity.'

Emma O'Brien was disgusted. 'That's sick,' she said. She was pale and shaking.

'Yes, it is. I'm sorry. It goes without saying that we're continuing to follow up other leads, and if we get anything new . . .' He left it at that.

Lisbet Klinnemann walked Mariner out. 'Dad asked me to bring this,' she passed him an envelope. When Mariner looked inside he found several fine blonde hairs. 'I hope you don't need it.'

'So do I.' He didn't like to say that the chances were becoming greater by the hour. 'Does your mother know you're here?' he asked her.

She smiled. 'No. She'd be annoyed. But what am I supposed to do? Don't misunderstand me, I'm mad about what Dad has done to us, to Mum and to our family, but he's still my dad, and right now he needs some support. I know he'd do the same for any of us if we needed it. He's done something foolish but that doesn't make him a bad man. And it's not entirely his fault.'

'Oh?'

'The last few years Mum has put him under incredible pressure about his job.'

'Concerned for his and your safety, I suppose.'

'As if Dad didn't care?' she said. 'Dad knew — has known for years — that there's always a risk from animal rights fanatics, but his is important work and it would be ethically wrong to give in to these people. Mum just doesn't get it.'

'It must have been difficult for you.'

'The atmosphere in the house was sometimes awful. By the time Emma came along, Mum and Dad were virtually leading separate lives anyway. But it was still a shock when it all happened. And Jessica — I mean, it was bad enough to find out that Dad was seeing someone else, but a baby makes everything so much more explicit, don't you think?'

'It must have been a tough time,' said Mariner. 'I understand your mother didn't take the separation very well.'

'I suppose you've been checking up on her.'

'We talked to colleagues in the area.'

'Mum was devastated. Who wouldn't be? She hadn't a clue what was going on until Dad blurted out that Emma was pregnant and he was the father.'

'You knew Emma?'

'She was one of his research assistants. We'd met her once or twice, but none of us had a clue. Mum reacted badly, that's all. She was angry.'

'How does she feel now?'

'You mean, would she do something like this? Of course not. She's a mother too. She knows how cruel it would be.'

'Even to Emma?'

'Even to Emma.'

'How do you get on with your . . .?'

'My father's bit on the side?' Her smile was wry. 'I have to work hard at being civil towards her, if you must know. But it's not entirely her fault either, is it? It was hardly an immaculate conception.'

'And what about your brother?'

'Paul's taken it much harder than me. He really wanted to kill Dad. It's exacerbated his problems.'

'His drug problems?'

'Oh, you know about that. Paul had been getting clean but he went back to heroin when it all happened.'

'And now?'

'He has it under control again.' She said it with absolute confidence.

'When did you last see him?' asked Mariner.

'A couple of weeks ago. He was home for the vacation. He's doing well.'

'Does he still want to kill your father?'

'Metaphorically, maybe. He sees what effect it's had on Mum on a daily basis. He has to live with her.'

'And do you know where Paul is now?'

'No, he's not answering his phone. But that isn't unusual,' she added hastily. 'Paul's what you might call a free spirit. It's my guess that he knows nothing about all this.'

Mariner wasn't so sure and the conversation prompted him to phone Ruth Tunstall in Cambridge as soon as he got back to the station. 'Has Paul Klinnemann turned up yet?'

'Not yet.'

'His sister describes him as a free spirit.'

'That's one way of putting it,' said Tunstall. 'I've had officers speaking to his close friends — the ones we can track down — but no one seems to have seen him since last Thursday evening.' The day before Jessica went missing.

'How about the animal rights sympathisers?'

'We've done a series of raids, but of the likely contenders we've picked up, so far they all either have sound alibis or can be placed away from the scene at the time of Jessica's abduction,' she told him. 'However, three of our repeat offenders are unaccounted for, two men and a woman. Again, they haven't been seen since the end of the week. We're trying to establish their whereabouts. I'll let you know as soon as we have anything.'

'Could you send us through their mugshots that we can run by our witnesses?' Mariner asked.

'I'll fax them through.' Finally they might have the glimmer of a lead.

Mariner took this news with him back to the incident room, where there was a message waiting for him from Stuart Croghan.

'News regarding the infant remains,' said Croghan. 'It's a male, two to four weeks old. I'd say he died from a non-accidental injury. The skull appears to have been crushed, as if he was dropped from a height or banged against a hard surface.' The thought made Mariner feel sick. So now they had an infanticide on their hands too. 'Oh, and something else that might help with identification; the baby had a cleft palate.'

'How long had the body been there?'

'It's hard to be precise, but my first guess was pretty close to the mark. The etymology and decay would indicate anything from nine to about fourteen months.'

So it was old news, but Mariner passed it to the press office, regardless. In the furore stirred up by the abduction the discovery of the remains would be reported and they needed to hear from anyone who may have seen anything suspicious at around that time, or from anyone who knew of a four-week-old baby who'd disappeared between September and December last year. Chances were the mother would turn out to be some teenage kid who'd gone through it all on her own.

* * *

In the early hours of the following morning Mariner gathered everyone together for a further briefing. The investigation was beginning to lose momentum and that was the last thing that he wanted. Scanning his co-workers' faces he saw exhaustion written all over them but somehow he had to find it within himself to fire up their enthusiasm and confidence. 'We need to make another appeal, but this time, if we can persuade her, I'd like Emma O'Brien to make a statement. Do you think she's up to it?'

His question was directed at Millie, who nodded thoughtfully. 'She's pretty fragile but she'll pull herself together if it means getting Jessica back.'

'We're back to not knowing why Jessica's been taken, but the animal rights angle is looking stronger. Cambridge police have three possible suspects who have gone AWOL, along with Paul Klinnemann. They're faxing through photographs. Tony, we'll need to get Christie to have a look.'

There was a knock on the door. It was PC Mann, who was grinning like an idiot.

'I'm really not in the mood for jokes,' said Mariner.

'You'll like this one, sir,' Mann said, with confidence. 'There's a guy from Lincolnshire police on the phone. A local vicar contacted them twenty minutes ago. He's got baby Jessica, alive and well.'

Chapter Eight

'What?' The word echoed around the room, a perfectly synchronised chorus.

'Apparently the vicar got a phone call a couple of hours ago to say that he should go and look in the church porch. He did as suggested and there she was. The description of her clothes, the car seat and everything matches and the vicar's confirmed that she's got a small port wine stain in the nape of her neck, just under the hairline. They're saying she looks clean and well-cared-for. They're faxing over a picture.'

By the time the printout chugged through painfully slowly, to reveal a digital photograph of a bemused looking baby, everyone in the room had gathered around the fax machine, as if worshipping some strange electronic god. Mariner snatched the sheet the instant it stopped printing. It certainly looked pretty similar to the photograph of Jessica they'd been circulating. There were yelps of delight around the room which Mariner quashed immediately. 'Let's stay calm, folks, until we know this is really it. Don't get carried away. Millie, call Ms O'Brien and Mr Klinnemann. Tell them we'll pick them up in fifteen minutes to drive them over there. Say a baby has been found who *may* be Jessica. And remind the Lincolnshire plods to preserve the drop-off point as a crime scene. We'll want to give it a going over.'

Mariner had experienced tension many times before but rarely as thickly as that inside the car as they travelled the miles to Stamford. Emma O'Brien and Peter Klinnemann sat in the back seat, their hands gripped tightly between them, Emma intermittently tearful.

'Do you have any connection with Stamford?' Mariner asked as they drove.

'None,' said Peter Klinnemann.

'Does your son drive?'

'Yes.'

'And he has his own car?'

'Yes, but I don't understand. What are you implying?'

But now wasn't the time and Mariner let it rest. He couldn't help but think about the proximity of Stamford to Cambridge, though Klinnemann wouldn't like that. If the baby had been snatched by someone with a connection in that area, the route back was via the A1 and A14, Cambridge, Birmingham and Stamford forming their own Bermuda triangle into which baby Jessica had temporarily vanished.

It was an emotional reunion at the local police station where a crowd of local and national reporters and TV crews had gathered. Baby Jessica slept throughout, but there was no doubt from the reaction of her parents that this was their baby girl. Lifting her from the car seat, Emma O'Brien squeezed her so tight that Mariner thought she'd crush the child. The surge of relief, coupled with sheer exhaustion, brought him to the brink of tears himself. He wandered away to try and keep a manly lid on his emotions. It was such a change to have a happy ending. Peter Klinnemann and Emma O'Brien were full of gratitude, even though this outcome had very little to do with him. They'd been incredibly lucky, that was all. Either the abductor or someone close to her had been seized by conscience, or the purpose — to scare the living daylights out of Peter Klinnemann — had been served. They would still need to pursue it to find out who had instigated the abduction.

'There was a note, sir.' The officer passed Mariner the crumpled paper in the plastic sheath of an evidence bag. *Take this as a warning,* it said. But a warning for whom?

The Reverend Jonathan Sands was a modern vicar, tall and lean, in his mid-thirties, with a mop of blond hair. When they interviewed him he was in torn jeans and a Darkness T-shirt.

'Not the usual garb,' he grinned apologetically. 'I just grabbed the nearest things when I got the call.' He pushed a hand through hair that already stood on end like a shoe brush.

'I know you've already been through all this, but would you mind telling us again what happened?' Mariner said.

'No, of course not. The first thing was when the phone rang, and I checked the clock as I always do. It was shortly before 5:30 a.m. The caller said, "Go down to the church and look by the door. Baby Jessica is there."'

'You remember it word for word?'

'I always try. Occasionally we get calls from people in distress and have to notify your colleagues. The detail can be important.' What he said made sense.

'Do you remember anything distinctive about the voice?' asked Mariner.

Sands frowned. 'I've thought about that. It was quite slow and deliberate, but I assumed that it was because the caller didn't want me to miss anything. The voice was muffled too, as if an attempt was being made to disguise it. The phrasing was slightly unusual, as if—'

'What?'

'Look, I'd hate to mislead you, it's just a feeling, but it was as if the caller didn't naturally speak English.' Or had learned it from someone who didn't? 'But please, don't read too much into that.'

'Any accent?' As Christie had said.

'Not that I noticed.'

'And what did you do?'

'I told my wife — she had woken up by then. We were both a bit stunned. Then I pulled on some clothes, grabbed a torch and went down to the church, and there was Jessica, sleeping peacefully.' He beamed. A happy outcome must make a pleasant change for him, too.

'Did you notice anything else unusual?' Mariner asked.

'No. I kept my eyes and ears open, of course, in case whoever had left her was waiting around to make sure she was found. I even called out, "Is anyone there? If you want to talk you can do so in confidence." I waited a couple of minutes, but there was nothing. I thought I heard a car start up in the distance, but this is a residential area, so it could have just been someone going off early to work.'

Local officers took Mariner and Knox down to the place where the baby had been found. The Lincolnshire SOCOs had been all over the area for the last couple of hours. There was the inevitable group of bystanders watching everything and more press among them. Mariner cast his eye over the motley group, idly wondering if their kidnapper was one of them. It was not unknown for the perpetrator of a crime to get an added thrill from being so close yet undetected.

Alternatives were brought so that Jessica's clothes and car seat could be taken back for forensic testing, in the hope that they might turn up some distinctive fibres or hairs.

The note seemed to imply that they'd been correct about animal rights activists, but Mariner wasn't entirely convinced. 'There's no code,' he said. 'Don't they generally use a code?'

'So what the fuck was it about?' asked Knox. 'Why take her and then deliver her back safely?'

'Maybe they lost their nerve. Or it was simply about giving Peter Klinnemann a fright. Whatever we find out here, I want to interview his son.'

It looked as though he would get his wish sooner than expected. When Mariner checked his mobile he found a message from Ruth Tunstall. He called her back.

'Paul Klinnemann has surfaced,' Tunstall told him. 'As have the missing members of the animal rights cell.'

'Well, well. Coincidence or what? Where are they?'

'We've got them all here if you'd like to come down and talk to them. So far none of them is admitting to anything, of course, but one of them is a woman, thirty-three-year-old Tessa Caldwell.'

'Does she fit our description of the abductor?'

Tunstall was guarded. 'She could do, with a bit of work.'

Mariner went back to break the news to Klinnemann and Emma. 'Sergeant Knox and I will be travelling to Cambridge. Some members of an animal rights cell have been brought in for questioning and we will be going to talk to them as part of our investigation.' So far, so uncontroversial. 'We can offer you a lift back with us if you'd like that.' To his surprise Klinnemann accepted. 'I should say that your son Paul is among the people who've been brought in,' Mariner added.

'What on earth for?' Klinnemann demanded. 'I've told you before, Paul wouldn't do anything to hurt Jessica or me.'

No mention of Emma O'Brien, Mariner noticed. 'I'm sure you're right,' he said. 'But we need to talk to him, just to eliminate him from the enquiry.'

'I understand.' Klinnemann was content with that, but then, gazing at his baby daughter at that moment he was a very contented man indeed.

Before moving off, Peter Klinnemann issued a brief statement to the press thanking Mariner and his team for all that they'd done. 'We don't know who took our daughter, but if it's someone who has lost a child or who has been unable to have a child I urge them to seek help. For the last week we have shared your anguish. Thank you for looking after her so well. But please, if you need help, come forward. Thank you to the public and the press for all that they've done. We would now like to be left to get on with our lives.' For some reason Mariner felt like a fraud.

They drove directly to the station in Cambridge where a car had been arranged to take the Klinnemanns home. It was good to meet Ruth Tunstall in person. She turned out to be a smiley-faced woman in her late forties with cropped greying hair. She took Mariner and Knox down to the interview rooms where members of the animal rights cell were being held. 'They're all over the place, literally and figuratively,' she said. 'I don't think it'll take long to find out what they've been up to, but that's what bothers me. If they'd been involved in the abduction I'd expect them to have at least got their stories straight.'

It bothered Mariner too. 'How did you track down Paul Klinnemann?'

'Through the mother of one of the friends we went to talk to. He turned up at their house to see his mate. He was in a bit of a state.'

On the other side of the table Paul Klinnemann looked weary, but was newly washed and wearing clean clothes. He glanced up as they went in and Mariner saw the same blue eyes as his father's, but he was baby-faced, almost pretty with dark curly hair. As a professional courtesy Mariner allowed Ruth Tunstall to proceed with the interview, while he sat in as an observer. To open the conversation, she produced the front page of a national newspaper, Saturday's edition.

Klinnemann glanced over it, initially uninterested, but when he saw the content he was suddenly alert. 'What's this meant to be?'

'You didn't know?'

'No. God, is she all right?' He was trying hard to make it sound as if he cared.

'She was found safe and well this morning, by a vicar.'

'Well, praise the lord.' He flashed a sarcastic grin.

'Shortly before you appeared at your friend's house, as it happens. Where have you been since last Thursday?'

'I was at a party.'

'All weekend?'

'It was a good party.' He smiled, lazily, his eyelids low. 'I crashed at a friend's house afterwards. I was out of it, you know? Still am, as a matter of fact.'

But Mariner wasn't convinced. Klinnemann's eyes looked too clear. Underneath the façade he was too alert. He needed a little prod. He caught Tunstall's eye and she gave him the go ahead. 'Did you know that your stepmother was lecturing in Birmingham last Friday?' he asked.

Klinnemann's eyes narrowed. 'She's not my stepmother, she's my dad's tart. And frankly I'm not interested in what the bitch gets up to.'

Charming. 'Have you passed on information to anyone about where Emma O'Brien would be?'

'No.'

'We'll need the address of this party and a list of the names of anyone who may have seen you there.'

'Names? Man, what sort of parties do you go to?'

A knock on the door interrupted them and the duty sergeant invited Tunstall and Mariner outside. One of the detectives interviewing another of the detainees had made a breakthrough. 'They've been up to no good, but it wasn't exactly what we hoped. Tessa Caldwell has admitted to being in Great Yarmouth for the last five days.'

'That's not a crime is it?' said Mariner.

'It's what they were doing there, sir,' the sergeant continued patiently. 'They went with the sole purpose of vandalising the greyhound track there. They stayed at a nearby caravan park, booking in on Friday afternoon at around the time Jessica was abducted. The park owner has confirmed it. We think they spent Friday night doing reconnaissance before attacking the track in the early hours of Sunday morning.'

'Can we prove that Paul Klinnemann was with them?'

Eventually they did, through CCTV footage retrieved from the caravan park. Klinnemann and his friends could be charged with criminal damage, but they were nowhere near Jack and the Beanstalk nursery on Friday afternoon. It didn't rule out the animal rights angle entirely, but now they were left with no suspects. Before returning to Birmingham, Mariner and Tony Knox went to visit Emma and Klinnemann. It wasn't strictly necessary, but Mariner felt a compulsion to see them in their home environment. They lived in a village in the flat countryside outside the city, in the kind of chocolate-box stone cottage that must have cost a small fortune. Inside was a cosy domestic scene, Emma O'Brien playing on the carpet with her daughter and Peter Klinnemann hovering over them, the attentive father. Knox immediately squatted down beside the baby and began playing with her, while Mariner stayed at a safe distance.

'How is she?' he asked.

'She seems fine.' Emma sounded amazed. 'Absolutely no ill effects that we can see. Thank you so much for everything you did.'

'We'll continue to follow all lines of enquiry,' Mariner assured them. 'It's important that we find out who was responsible.'

'But surely there's no need,' Emma O'Brien exchanged a glance with her partner. 'We have Jessica back and she really seems none the worse for her ordeal. We don't want to take up any more of your time. I'm sure you have other more important things to do.'

'It remains that a criminal offence has been committed,' Mariner reminded her, a little taken aback by the response. 'It's still our job to find out who it was and how exactly it happened.'

'No really. We insist, don't we, Peter?' She looked to Klinnemann for support. 'We don't want to bring charges or anything. This was probably a cry for help by some desperate woman, and the last thing we would want to do is make life worse for her.'

Mariner didn't like to point out that all the evidence was to the contrary, but he was tired and it seemed a futile argument to have when everything had worked out as it had. Instead he said: 'There was the note, remember? It would be a mistake to become complacent.'

'We've made a decision about that,' Emma O'Brien smiled triumphantly. 'Peter is going to look for another job.' Klinnemann didn't look altogether thrilled about it.

'Well, if anything turns up, we'll be in touch,' Mariner said. It was time to go.

'Christ, how's Mary Klinnemann going to feel when she hears about that?' Mariner said, when they were safely in the car and driving away. 'She'd been pressuring him for years to leave his job.'

'It makes it pretty obvious who he thinks is responsible, with or without the help of his son.'

* * *

Mariner and Knox arrived back in the Granville Lane incident room to heroes' welcomes and celebrations. DCI Sharp had got in cases of beer and she made a short speech of congratulation. But the overwhelming feeling was one of relief. They had been so very lucky. Mariner helped himself to a beer and made the effort to join in, though he was itching to go.

'Wasn't there something about annual leave before all this started?' DS Sharp came over to where he lingered on the periphery.

'The paperwork won't do itself, ma'am.'

'Oh, I'm sure I can get off my pedestal for a few days to help with that. Go on, clear off.'

As always after a case as intense as this one had been, exhaustion overtook Mariner on the short drive home. Part of him hoped that Anna might be out, but her car was there on the drive when he pulled in. Ominously there were a couple of packed bags sitting in the hall too, but Mariner chose to ignore them. She was out in the garden doing some early autumn pruning, tidying up the garden in preparation for the new residents, but she came into the kitchen as soon as she saw him. Pulling off her gardening gloves she came over and gave him a hug.

'I heard the news,' she smiled. 'Well done, you.'

Mariner picked a twig out of her hair. She smelled lightly of damp soil and the outdoors. 'Didn't have much to do with me as it turned out. We were blessed with some excellent luck.'

'Nobody cares about that, so take the credit. You got her back safe, that's the most important thing. Her parents must be ecstatic.'

'It was an emotional reunion.'

'I'll bet. And now you're on holiday?' She was wondering about the paperwork.

Mariner squeezed her tighter. 'I'm on holiday. The boss practically threw me out.'

'That's wonderful,' she beamed. 'I told Becks we'd be down first thing in the morning.'

'Tomorrow?' Mariner took a step back, holding her at arm's length.

'Well, we've already missed three days and I'm going nuts here. Look at me — I'm tending the garden of a house I'm about to leave.'

'Anna, I haven't had any sleep for three nights. I feel like a zombie. I can't possibly drive—'

'You won't have to. I'll drive and you can sleep.'

Mariner shook his head. 'I need my bed, for more than just a few hours. And you know what it's like after something like this. I need a bit of down time. I can't face meeting a whole bunch of new people straight away. I'd make a very poor impression. But listen, if you've told Becky we're going, why don't you go anyway and I'll join you in a couple of days. Some time on my own is probably the best thing for everyone.'

'I wanted us to go together,' she said, mildly.

'I know, but I'm sure they'll understand. It's not as if they won't know what kind of a weekend I've had, is it?'

'I suppose I could go down tomorrow and call in and see Jamie on the way.' She was coming round. This was easier than he'd expected.

'Good idea. And now I need a shower.'

'Hm, me too.'

'Well that sounds like a very agreeable start to my holiday.'

But when it came to it he was too tired to do anything but fall into bed and a deep and catatonic sleep. When he woke the following day it was late morning and Anna had gone.

Feeling jet-lagged Mariner got up and for a while simply savoured the quiet, but after a while the euphoria of the previous day began to wear off and niggling doubts began to encroach on his thoughts. There were too many loose ends; something about the case that they'd all missed, and which he was certain would come back to haunt them. Who the hell had been responsible for Jessica's abduction, and if that really was just a warning, what else were they in for? And while the investigation had provided a useful distraction from it, Mariner was suddenly aware that 17 October, Kenneth McCrae's trial date now loomed large, with only a few days' holiday in between then and now. Slowly and by stealth Mariner felt a melancholy creeping over him, the inevitable anti-climax that followed a weekend of high stress. He dealt with it in the only way he knew, by going to the garage and getting out his walking boots. It was a grey and drizzly afternoon, but this was the best way he knew of spending it.

* * *

Tony Knox arrived home expecting to be greeted by the usual noisy flurry of paws and fur. Instead all he got was empty silence. Then he saw the note by the phone. *Mr Knox, I've took Nelson home to my house, from Michael.*

Knox crossed the road to a semi that was a mirror image of his own and rang the bell. Michael's mum came to the door. Jean, if he remembered rightly, though they'd never formally been introduced. The puzzled look of partial recognition when she opened the door made him feel marginally better about his own cloudy memory.

'Tony Knox,' he reminded her, turning to indicate his house across the road. 'I think you've got my dog?'

'Oh, of course, Tony. I'm sorry.' She was younger than he'd thought from a distance, early forties probably, her hair cut boyishly short and turning prematurely grey.

'Don't worry about it. It's Jean, isn't it?'

'Yes, that's right. I hope you don't mind Michael bringing Nelson over here. It seemed a shame to shut him back in the house when he could be running free in our garden. Michael's getting quite attached to him and he can be very persuasive.'

'No, it's great. I really appreciate it, thanks.'

'They're in the garden. Why don't you come through?'

Knox followed her along the hall and into the kitchen, and couldn't help noticing the muddy paw prints on the otherwise pristine tiled floor. 'It's good of you to do this,' he said.

'Not at all. Michael loves it. He's wanted a dog for years, but I've always used the working mother excuse. This arrangement is perfect. It takes the heat off me.'

Through the window they could see the lad kicking a ball about and Nelson chasing after it barking with excitement. It made Knox feel knackered just watching them.

'He's a lovely animal,' Jean said.

'Quite an aristocrat, too,' Knox told her. 'He used to belong to Sir Geoffrey Ryland.'

'The MP who—? You knew him?'

'Friend of a friend,' said Knox. It was too long a story for now.

A pine table in the centre of the kitchen was piled high with stacks of exercise books, alongside them a bottle and glass of white wine. She saw Knox take in the wine. 'Something to get me through the marking,' she smiled. 'Year nine essays are a challenge to anyone's staying power. Would you like a glass, or a beer perhaps?' She misread Knox's hesitation. 'Sorry, you're tired of course. You'll want to get back. Shaun worked nights. I know what it's like.'

'No, it's just that I'm keeping you from your work,' Knox said, indicating the books. 'I don't want to interrupt.'

'Oh, I *love* interruptions, believe me.' She spoke with feeling. 'I thought it would be a good idea to get it out of the way, but I'm really not in the right frame of mind this evening.'

'Well if you're sure, a beer would go down well. Although I might not be the best of company,' Knox admitted.

'Don't take this the wrong way, but for me these days, any company is good company. Pull up a pew.'

While Knox sat at the table, she fetched a bottle of German lager and a bottle opener. 'I'll let you do the honours. I was always hopeless with those things.' She watched as Knox expertly flipped the lid. 'I heard on the news that the baby's been found. That's fantastic.'

'It's a relief,' said Knox, truthfully.

'You must be exhausted.'

'It's been a long week.'

'Have you eaten?'

'Oh, I'll settle for a takeaway tonight.'

'Could you eat some chicken casserole? We had a lot left over.'

Hearing the words made Knox salivate, but manners prevailed. 'I couldn't—' he started to protest.

'Honestly, I've got a freezer full too, so it'll only go to waste. Shaun had a hearty appetite and I can't seem to get the hang of cooking for just the two of us, somehow.'

So it was a serious offer. 'All right then. Thanks very much.' Knox watched as she retrieved an earthenware casserole dish from the fridge and transferred it to the microwave, putting a plate to warm in the oven. She had a good figure, in jeans and a plain white T-shirt and Knox suddenly became aware of how he must look in a shirt that was three days old. 'Is there somewhere I could just, er, wash my hands?' he asked, pushing back his chair.

'Of course. There's a cloakroom just by the front door where you came in.'

In the tiny washroom Knox washed his hands and face. It woke him up a bit but made not a scrap of difference to his appearance. 'You still look like shite,' he told his reflection.

'You're a teacher then,' Knox said, settling himself back at the kitchen table, now with a place setting for one.

'Only part-time, up at Kingsmead Comp,' said Jean. 'I'm not sure that it does much for Michael's street-cred having his mum at the school, but it's a stop-gap until something else comes along.' The microwave pinged and she tipped steaming chicken and vegetables onto the plate, passing it to Knox along with cutlery. It smelled delicious and Knox tucked in.

'What subject?' he asked.

'Maths and physics.'

'Wow.'

'Why are men always surprised by that? And you, I know, are a detective,' she confirmed. 'Mrs Burrows at number forty-three filled me in. Actually she probably let slip more about your personal life than you would have liked, too. But don't worry, I'm the soul of discretion.'

Knox demolished the food within minutes. 'I can't tell you how good this is after three days of butties and takeaways.'

She laughed. 'It's nice to get some appreciation. Ten-year-old boys tend not to notice the difference between one meal and the next.'

'How long have you been—?'

'Widowed?' She helped him out. 'Long enough to have got used to saying it out loud. Four years and three months, not that I'm counting. How about you?'

'I've been separated a couple of years.'

'Occupational hazard, I suppose, if all the TV cop shows are to be believed.'

'Something like that.' It was probably a bit too soon to admit to the serial infidelity.

Knox sat back, replete. 'That was delicious,' he said, truthfully.

She took the plate from him as he stifled a massive yawn. 'And now you must go and get some rest.'

Knox pushed his chair back from the table. 'And let you get back to your marking.'

'Sadly, yes.'

'Thanks again.'

'You're very welcome. Did you want to take Nelson with you, or shall we keep him here tonight? Michael can bring him back in the morning and let you have a lie in.'

'Who are you really?' Knox asked with mock suspicion. 'Mother Teresa? The morning would be great, thanks.'

* * *

In the normal course of things, after an investigation with the intensity of baby Jessica's abduction, it would have taken at least two or three days for Mariner to adjust to being back in the real world again, and to make up for the sleep deprivation. The prospect of being sociable with a bunch of strangers was the last thing that he needed. But at the same time, he recognised how important this trip was to Anna. Something about their conversation yesterday had unsettled him. So often these days he seemed to disappoint her. Becky and Mark were her best friends. They'd been brilliantly supportive after the miscarriage, when Anna had spent time at their house recuperating. He should make the effort. So on Wednesday morning Mariner roused himself from what felt like another drug-induced sleep and by ten thirty he was driving south on the M5, the Malverns looming ahead of him on the skyline.

He'd been unable to get in touch with Anna, but had left messages on her phone and Becky and Mark's answer machine to let them know his ETA. It was a crystal clear autumn day, but he didn't even have the energy to appreciate the bright sunshine highlighting the colours of the turning trees.

Mariner had never been to the village of Upper Burwell before, so Anna had left him detailed instructions on how to find Becky and Mark's house, and as he got nearer, he couldn't help but soak up some of her enthusiasm for the area. Initially he'd been against the whole idea of this move to the countryside, but maybe it would be good after all. Perhaps a change of location was exactly what he needed. Making good time, he was there a little after twelve but when he bumped along the track to Becky and Mark's house, although Anna's car was parked on the driveway next to Becky's, there was no one at home. Mariner got out of his car and strolled around the sprawling garden, which was rampant with bird life. It was in a lovely spot, with no background noise except the chirping of the birds, and he found it surprisingly easy to picture himself living here.

Having explored every inch of the garden and with still no sign of anyone returning, Mariner recalled the village pub he'd driven past and decided to walk back the half-mile or so for a pint. This was the kind of picturesque village that American tourists would go nuts for, and the Farmers Arms was a black and white half-timbered building straight from the guide books. He walked into the bar, the prospect of a quiet pint suddenly hugely inviting. It wasn't to be. The half-empty car park had fooled him and the bar was packed with people and loud with conversation. As he stood at the bar waiting to be served he scanned the room seeking a quiet seat tucked away somewhere, and that was when, in the far corner, at the centre of the group that seemed to be making all the noise, he saw Anna. She was surrounded by about half a dozen people, none of whom Mariner recognised. And she looked happier than she had done in months. Abandoning his place in the queue, he wove a path through the crowd to where she sat.

'Tom! You made it!' She greeted him heartily, though more like a long lost friend than as her partner, allowing him just a peck on the cheek, and seemed more concerned with her empty glass '—and just in time to get in a round. What are you drinking, folks?' Her eyes gleamed and there was a flush to her cheeks that left Mariner wondering how long she'd been in here.

Once he was back from the bar, bearing what, to him, seemed like an extortionately priced round, Anna made introductions, though with all the noise Mariner could barely hear the names, let alone commit them to memory.

'Didn't you get my message?' he asked her, raising his voice above the din.

'Yes, but I knew you'd find us in here.'

'Where are Becky and Mark?' he asked.

'Oh, they had to go into Hereford to buy Megan's christening outfit. I didn't feel like going.'

'Well, it doesn't look as if you're stuck for company,' Mariner observed.

'That's exactly it!' She grinned, the irony in his words lost on her. 'Everyone's so friendly here. Great, isn't it?'

'Yes,' Mariner smiled, his hopes for a peaceful afternoon in just Anna's company shattered, but she was having such a good time he couldn't ruin it for her the minute he arrived. 'How was Jamie?'

'He's on form.' The only thing going right for them at the moment was Jamie, Anna's severely autistic younger brother, who had settled well into his new home, a rural farm community in Herefordshire. 'We went for a walk and had a drink at the teashop in the village. He was out in the garden when I got there, with a girl called Julie, or "Dooley" as he calls her. They've got quite close so the staff said.'

'A girlfriend? That's a turn up.'

'Isn't it?' Aged thirty-four, Jamie had never had a friendship in his life.

'How close are they?' Mariner asked.

'Oh, the staff are keeping a watchful eye on things. Julie likes to look after Jamie, which mostly involves bossing him around, but Jamie likes being looked after. Simple as that. There's such a difference in him, you wouldn't believe. He's thriving on the outdoor life. He looks so fit and strong, and he actually smiled when he saw me. We did the right thing.'

Yes, for Jamie at least, they had.

'It was such a nice time. I wish I could do it more often,' Anna said.

Mariner knew what she was thinking. It was part of the rationale behind moving to this area and they'd been over it before, many times. 'Jamie doesn't mind,' he said.

'We don't know that. He can't tell us.'

They stayed in the pub until the middle of the afternoon, when Mariner was finally able to tear Anna away. Mostly he had sat back and let the conversation wash over him, especially as for much of the time he had no idea about the people or places being talked about. But the Marston's was slipping down nicely and after a while he began to relax.

Walking back along the lane, Mariner slipped a hand into Anna's, but she pulled it out again to find a tissue to blow her nose. 'So what do you think of this place?' she asked.

'It's very nice. I can see what you mean.'

Back at the house, Becky, Mark and Megan had returned from their shopping trip. Becky and Mark greeted Mariner warmly, but within seconds the focus was on toddler Megan, clearly used to being the centre of attention. The Indian summer made it balmy enough for them to sit outside on the terrace and for some reason Megan took a shine to Mariner, delivering toys to him every few minutes and saying 'Ta,' to which Mariner was obliged to reciprocate each time. Perhaps if he hadn't been so tired he wouldn't have found it so wearing.

'Thanks so much for coming down,' said Becky.

'It must seem crazy to be having her christened at this late stage,' said Mark. 'We always meant to, but never quite got round to it. And now there's a bit more urgency,' he looked across at Becky and smiled knowingly. 'We wanted to wait until you were both here before telling you. We're having another.'

Anna didn't miss a beat, although the news must have crushed her. 'Wow, that's fantastic, isn't it Tom?' She leaned across and put a protective arm around Becky, but she was avoiding his gaze.

'You're pregnant?' Mariner said, with surprise. It hadn't escaped him that Becky had already poured herself a generous glass of Chablis.

'Not exactly,' Becky was enigmatic. 'We've decided that we've already done our bit adding to the world population, so we're adopting a baby from China, giving a home to a little girl who doesn't have one. There are thousands abandoned there every year. We're going through the adoption process at the moment, though it's taking forever.'

'Well, that's very er, commendable,' said Mariner, unable to think of anything more appropriate.

'And it gives you some catching up to do,' Becky said throwing him a meaningful glance.

'We're doing our best,' said Mariner, neutrally, but he wasn't close enough to Anna to reach out to her. There was a cry from across the patio as Megan stumbled over the sill, coming out of the house with yet another offering for Mariner, and went down on her hands and knees. The howling built to a crescendo.

'Right,' said Becky. 'I think a young lady needs to have her bath now. I want to get her settled before supper. We've invited a couple of local friends round Tom, so that you can start getting to know people.'

Mariner groaned inwardly, his social skills already stretched to their limits.

Chapter Nine

Becky and Anna went to bathe Megan leaving Mariner and Mark alone out in the garden.

'You must be delighted with the way things have worked out,' Mark said, conversationally.

'Sorry?'

'The safe return of baby Jessica. You're quite a hero.'

'We were just fortunate,' Mariner said. 'It could have gone either way.'

'Did you find out who was behind it?'

'We have some ideas about that, but we're still following them through. At the moment the main suspects are animal rights activists. We think they were trying to give the father, Peter Klinnemann, a scare.'

'And no doubt succeeded. He works for Hamilton Sciences, doesn't he?'

'Yes, though I'm not sure for how much longer. His partner seems to have finally persuaded him to quit his job.'

'I can understand that reaction, of course, but that's a crying shame. If we didn't have companies like Hamilton, I'd be stuffed as a GP. Still, I can't say I blame him.' He shuddered. 'Throughout that whole episode I kept trying to imagine how I'd feel if anything like that happened to Megan. Thank God we've never had to resort to leaving her in a place like that.'

'It wasn't the nursery's fault,' Mariner said, sounding more defensive than he'd intended. 'It could have happened anywhere.' But even as he said it he wasn't so sure.

'And how are you?' Mark asked, changing the subject, his tone implying that the enquiry was more professional than personal.

'I'm fine,' said Mariner.

'You're still seeing a counsellor?'

'Yes.' Mariner was astonished that Mark should be aware of that arrangement and he felt uncomfortable discussing it with a man he hardly knew. He certainly wasn't about to admit that after the first couple of appointments he'd found a convenient reason to cancel whenever his counsellor had tried to schedule a follow-up.

'I know from what Becky says that Anna's been very concerned about you.'

'Yes.' Mariner didn't know what else to say.

'She still seems a bit low,' Mark went on.

'Well, things are not exactly going to plan.' Mariner wondered how much Mark knew. He probably thought Mariner was referring to the miscarriage, but it was more than that. Fortunately he was saved from further explanation by the distant ringing of the front doorbell, signalling the arrival of the first of the guests.

Gareth, also a GP, was one of Mark's partners in the medical practice and was already known to Mariner. He'd been instrumental in getting Jamie into his new home, and when she came down again Anna greeted him warmly, their embrace lasting, in Mariner's opinion, just a few seconds too long.

'Jamie's doing brilliantly,' Anna enthused. 'We're so indebted to Gareth, aren't we, Tom?'

'Indeed we are.' Mariner shook Gareth's hand.

'Hello again, Tom. How are you?' And Mariner was disturbed to see the same look in his eyes as he'd seen earlier in Mark's. Christ, they didn't even live here yet but everyone knew all about them. How much had Anna told him about what he'd gone through? Mariner didn't like the thought of that.

Completing the party were near neighbours Jolyon, who was 'in business,' and his wife Lavinia, 'call me Vinnie.' There was lots of air-kissing and faux hugging before they settled around the vast dining table in the conservatory overlooking the garden.

'We're so looking forward to having you guys down here, especially you, Tom,' Jolyon said. 'The local plods are a complete waste of space. Had my workshop broken into a few months back and apart from a visit to find out what happened, we haven't heard a whisper from them.'

'I'm sure they're doing a good job.' Mariner felt himself bristling slightly. 'They'll be in touch when they have something.'

'And it's hardly the crime of the century, darling, is it?' Vinnie added tactfully.

'Well, you should try and get down here in time for Christmas,' said Jolyon. 'There's so much going on. Do you hunt?'

Anna giggled. 'Tom's more of a dominoes man.' That prompted laughter all round, which needled Mariner.

'Well, I don't suppose Birmingham's much of a hunting sort of place,' said Gareth. 'But that will all change down here. What do you think about the job?' There was an awkward pause.

Anna reached over for some bread. 'He's only just got here,' she said. 'I haven't had the chance to tell him about it yet.'

'What job is that?' Mariner asked, making an effort to stay casual.

'Our practice receptionist is due to retire,' said Mark. 'Gareth and I have been trying to persuade Anna that it would be perfect for her.'

'But you haven't got any medical experience,' Mariner pointed out.

Mark laughed. 'It's not rocket science, as they say. Anna's got what it takes; excellent communication skills, professionalism—'

'We know we can trust her,' added Gareth. 'And she'd bring a bit of glamour to the practice.'

'Not that we don't have that already.' Mark fluttered his eyelashes, coyly.

'And when does your receptionist retire?' Mariner asked.

'At the end of this month.'

Blimey. That was only a couple of weeks away. They didn't hang about.

'And if you're looking for a place to live, I see that Heron's Nest is on the market,' Jolyon chipped in.

'Really?' Suddenly all eyes were on him.

'Yes, John Latham's taken a position in the States, so they're selling up.'

'Oh, wow. That would be perfect,' Becky gushed. 'You should go and see it. It's a gorgeous converted mill in about three acres, with views across the whole valley.'

'Do you know the asking price?' Mark saved Mariner from having to ask.

'That's the best thing,' said Jolyon. 'They want a quick sale so it's up for six hundred and fifty thou'.'

Mariner nearly choked on his fettuccini. 'That's a bit beyond our price range,' he said.

'I'm sure you'd be able to knock them down a bit.' Jolyon spoke with the easy confidence of a man for whom money is no object.

'We're not really in a position to move yet anyway,' said Mariner. 'Anna's accepted the offer on her house, but mine seems to be taking a little longer.'

'That's basically because no one wants to buy it, at least, not at the asking price,' Anna's tone was aggrieved, resentful even. 'They all want a reduction because of . . . well, you know, its notoriety.'

'Really?' said Vinnie. 'Given the morbid curiosity of the great British public, I'd have thought people would be queuing up for it.' So they all knew about that, too.

'Oh, plenty want to look round it, of course, but so far no one's interested in buying.'

'But you were only held there,' said Mark. 'No one came to any harm, did they?' said Mark.

Mariner controlled an involuntary shudder. Even just talking about the episode brought back vivid memories of his three days incarcerated in the cellar while Kenneth McCrae held him captive.

'It has connections with a killer though, doesn't it?' Jolyon lowered his voice for dramatic effect.

'Yes, and a killer who might well get away with it,' murmured Mariner before he could stop himself.

'What do you mean?' Anna demanded, leaving Mariner little choice but to explain the latest development to them, though deep down he had no desire to discuss the case with people who couldn't understand.

'McCrae's pleading not guilty,' he said.

'What?'

'He's going for diminished responsibility. If the jury accepts it, it'll reduce the charge to manslaughter and get his sentence reduced by half.'

Mark shook his head slowly, in disbelief. 'The good old British criminal justice system.'

'But that's crazy!' Anna was outraged.

'That's how it is,' said Mariner. 'It has a certain symmetry, doesn't it? Sir Geoffrey was the chair of the government body examining miscarriages of justice. And now the outcome of the investigation into his murder is likely to be just that.'

'But that's appalling. Surely the prosecution can do something.'

'Put me on the witness stand,' Mariner said. 'Ironically I've got to stand up and say that Kenneth McCrae was behaving rationally at the time when it all happened.'

'When does it come to court?' asked Jolyon.

'Next week,' Anna put in. 'It's what Tom's got to look forward to when we go back.'

'That's tough.'

'He's only being charged with murder, too,' said Anna. 'Not enough evidence to get him for abduction or false imprisonment.'

'As long as he's convicted he'll be going away for long enough to satisfy me,' said Mariner. It wasn't quite true but he'd had enough of talking about it.

'And meanwhile we can't sell the house,' said Anna brightly.

'Well, I think you should have a look at Heron's Nest anyway,' Becky was undeterred. 'You could always come and stay with us and do a weekly commute until Tom's place is sold. With the hours he works he'd hardly miss you anyway, would you, Tom?'

Mariner smiled through gritted teeth.

As the conversation rambled on, Mariner found himself drinking steadily, more than he'd drunk in weeks and gradually faded out of it, until suddenly Jolyon and Lavinia were on their feet and saying their goodbyes.

'Let's have another drink,' said Gareth, when they'd gone.

'Haven't you had enough?' Becky teased him.

Gareth looked pointedly at Mariner. 'Don't worry, officer. I've only got to stagger a few yards up the road.'

'You live quite close by then,' Mariner surmised.

'Gareth's got a barn conversion on the edge of the village,' Anna chipped in. 'He's got fabulous views, too.'

Mariner didn't like to ask how it was that she knew that. He was desperate for his bed, now, but for some reason he didn't want to leave the party until Gareth had gone. He wasn't sure that Anna would have come with him. They finally made it up the stairs well after midnight. 'You didn't tell me about this job,' Mariner said as they were getting undressed.

'I didn't know about it myself until yesterday. It sounds wonderful though, doesn't it?'

'It sounds like the kind of thing you could do with your eyes shut.'

'That's what I mean.'

'But you'd be bored to death. What happened to your career progression?'

'I wouldn't have to be there for ever. While I'm doing that, I can be on the lookout for other opportunities.'

Despite his fatigue, when he got into bed and felt Anna beside him, Mariner's body began to respond. He reached out for her, but she pushed him playfully away. 'We might disturb Megan,' she giggled, sleepily.

'She's at the other end of the house,' said Mariner, now very much awake. 'And we don't make that much noise, at least, we don't have to.'

'It just feels weird, that's all. I can't.'

'You can,' Mariner insisted, but she rolled away from him.

'Maybe in the morning.'

But when Mariner next opened his eyes to light and sunshine, Anna was already out of bed and sitting peering through a gap in the curtains, her chin propped on her hand. 'Becky and Mark are so lucky,' she said, seeing that he was awake. 'They've got it all.'

'I'm sure it's not as perfect as it looks,' said Mariner. 'No one's life is perfect. Come back to bed.'

'But what more could anyone want? A gorgeous house with stunning views, a healthy lifestyle, great friends and their own little family—'

Mariner wondered if she'd listed them in order of importance. 'We'll have that soon enough. It just takes time.'

'I bet I'd get pregnant quicker living down here,' she was thinking aloud. 'The air is healthier.'

'Why don't we test the theory,' Mariner said. 'Come on.' He patted the mattress beside him. 'I'm as horny as hell.'

But Anna just rolled her eyes. 'Becky and Mark are down in the kitchen, they'll wonder where we are.'

'They're grown-ups. I think they'll be able to work it out.'

'I don't want them to. Come on, we're guests in their house.' The next three days seemed, to Mariner, to go on interminably. They did find time to go and look at Heron's Nest, which was certainly impressive, and Anna was in raptures about it. But it was way beyond their means and she wasn't being at all realistic about it. A little further along the lane they came across a more modest dwelling.

'That would be more within our budget,' Mariner said, but Anna wrinkled her nose.

'Yes and I bet it's got an outside toilet and no central heating either.'

On the day of the christening Mariner joined Mark for breakfast. 'You've made the Sunday papers, Tom,' said Mark, holding up the relevant section. 'They've run a piece on Sir Geoffrey Ryland prior to next week's trial.' Mark read: '*—and after the killing spree, McCrae was finally caught when he abducted Ryland's estranged son, Detective Inspector Tom Mariner.* Infamy, infamy, they've all got it in-for-me!'

Mariner smiled politely.

'Sorry,' Mark was contrite. 'Tactless of me. Are you very worried about the trial?'

'No reason for me to be,' said Mariner casually. 'It'll hardly be the first time I've given evidence in court.' He shouldn't have been surprised that it would be covered on the national news, as a man on trial for the murder of a prominent politician, Kenneth McCrae was unique, but it had caught him off guard.

'But this is different,' Mark observed. 'It's personal.'

With a capital P. 'I'll be fine.'

Megan's baptism was held in the village church, a small private ceremony in which the star turn, perilously dressed in pure white silk, had to be caught and held under protest so that she could be anointed as required. Afterwards there was a reception back at Mark and Becky's house, to which the whole village appeared to have been invited. After a couple of hours of making small talk Mariner wanted to scream. All those empty hills and fields out there, and nothing he could do to get away. Instead he lurked on the fringes as he generally did, nursing his drink and marvelling yet again at how very much at home Anna was with all these people.

They finally escaped in the early evening, but on the drive north Mariner's temper deteriorated by the moment. 'It seems to me that everyone else is doing a great job of planning my life for me,' he grumbled. 'Was I going to be consulted on any of this? We don't even live there yet and everyone seems to know all about me. It's all so bloody incestuous; looking for a house for us, finding you a job, even membership of the hunt, of all things. Do I get a say at all?'

'Don't be ridiculous, Tom,' Anna retorted. 'They're only trying to make us feel welcome and involved. The job is something that just happens to have cropped up, and they're concerned that by the time you've got your transfer and sold your house it'll be gone. Maybe I should do what Becky suggested and move down there anyway. How long does it take for you to get a transfer?'

'It varies.'

She eyed him suspiciously. 'You haven't even applied for it, have you?'

'When have I had time? I'll do it soon.'

‘Of course, if you’d accepted what was rightfully yours from your father’s estate, we wouldn’t have to wait for your house to be sold, we could have put in an offer for Heron’s Nest right away.’

‘Don’t drag that up again. The money was not mine and I couldn’t accept it.’ It had been a sore point that Mariner had rejected the inheritance from his estranged father’s will. And he couldn’t fully explain, even to himself, why he’d had to do it.

‘Most people would have taken the money and been gracious about it.’

‘I’m not most people.’

‘You can say that again.’

The air was still tense when they arrived home and Mariner was restless. ‘I think I’ll go down to the Boatman for an hour.’

‘Fine.’

But when he got there he was disappointed to find that the pub was closed for refurbishment. He should have known. For years now it had been caught in a time warp, untouched for decades with its numerous little snugs and bars offering the only things that, in Mariner’s view, a good pub should offer: excellent beer, a quiet, comfortable place in which to drink it and facilities for the occasional game of cards, chess or dominoes. He could go to the off-licence and back to Anna’s house, but he also knew where there were half a dozen free bottles of Theakston’s stashed, waiting to be consumed. Leaving his car in the pub car park he wandered along the service road and back to the cottage on the canal that he had, until not long ago, called home. He hadn’t been back since that night when he was found, filthy and starving in the cellar; he hadn’t had the nerve. The estate agents had undertaken to show prospective buyers around.

But looking at the place now, even in the dusk, it didn’t seem so threatening. A flutter of apprehension tickled at Mariner’s stomach as he walked up the path, growing into full-blown fear by the time he was standing on the step in the darkness. He had a powerful sense of déjà vu and his heart seemed to be bouncing off the inside of his ribcage. This was the last place he'd stood before coming round, incarcerated in the cellar.

It embarrassed him, this level of fear he was feeling, and he was glad there was no one around to witness it. He almost couldn't go through with it. But turning the key in the latch and letting himself in, he switched on the hall light and the feeling of nausea passed. The place was clean and tidy with no hint of what had gone on here. Someone must have seen to it. He knew that, among others, Tony Knox had been back and collected some of his things for him. Mariner moved cautiously from room to room, surprisingly comforted by the familiarity.

The place had a musty, unlived-in smell and the first thing he did was go into the kitchen and open up the back door onto the canal. On this side of the house the air was chilly and damp, tangy with autumn. Crane flies danced around in the glow cast by the outside light. Back in the lounge he put on some music: Janis Ian, soulful and reassuring, the sound of a different era. Then, taking a bottle from under the sink, he sat down on the stone bench outside the house swigging his beer and allowed the remaining feelings of unease to wear off.

There was just one more thing he had to do, but it took another bottle of Old Peculier before he had the courage to do it. In the cupboard under the stairs stuff had been thrown back in any old how. Dragging out a couple of boxes to make way, he shone a torch on the small crooked door at the rear. Bending low he pulled open the door, and, as the cool darkness appeared and that familiar smell hit his nostrils, he retched, his whole body alive with adrenaline. He forced himself forward until the torch-beam sliced into the cavern of the cellar. It was completely bare, the stone floor swept cleaner than it had ever been. The chain that McCrae had tethered him to was gone and someone had even filled in the hole in the wall. It occurred to Mariner that if he installed proper lighting and painted the walls, the room could be a useful storage space, and with that in mind he closed the door on it once more. He'd reclaimed his territory. This was his home, and he felt as comfortable here now as he ever had. Right now, selling it seemed to symbolise something else; the loss of freedom. He thought back over the last couple of days. Not much doubt now in his mind about where he'd rather be.

Back in the lounge, Mariner's eye was caught by the autobiography of the father he'd never known, and alongside it his collection of *Wainwright* guides to the long distance footpaths and the long shelf of Ordnance Survey maps; some of the few things he'd left behind because they were not part of his life with Anna. Her idea of a good walk was covering the distance between the Bullring and the Mail Box. He tried to remember the last time he'd had a decent walk but couldn't. All at once it seemed to matter, a great deal. Closing the door behind him he acknowledged that he'd overcome one of his demons. The other one he'd confront in just a couple of days. His therapist would be proud of him.

Chapter Ten

Mariner hadn't intended going to the trial right from the beginning, he wouldn't be needed right away, but something drew him to it. Packing an overnight bag, he drove down to Reading first thing on the Monday morning and checked into a small and modest hotel close to the city centre. From there he could walk to the court. The murder of a Member of Parliament was always going to be a high-profile case, and the law courts, modern and sleek as most were these days, were throbbing when he arrived, and security was painstaking.

'Tom?' The first familiar person Mariner saw on his way in was Felicity Fitzgibbon, his aunt, by marriage anyway. As Mariner wouldn't be required on the first day, he joined her in the gallery. 'How's Nelson doing?' she wanted to know. It was she who had talked Mariner into taking on the animal.

'He's keeping my sergeant out of trouble,' Mariner told her.

Mariner wasn't sure how he'd react to seeing McCrae again, the man who'd had such a devastating impact on his life, but he felt nothing. It was as if it had all happened to someone else. It was a disappointing experience.

McCrae, Mariner noted, was wearing just the right appearance for a man pleading diminished responsibility. His skin was pallid and his eyes carried a haunted look as he gazed straight ahead throughout. His ginger hair had grown longer and unruly, and his neck was scrawny in a shirt that looked a couple of sizes too big. The grandeur of the court room, combined with months on remand, had diminished him, so that it was hard to imagine him as the man who could have wreaked havoc on so many lives. The defeated exterior would do nothing to harm his case. It was likely that the jury would find some sympathy for a man who had served his country and visibly paid the price. Even he, Mariner, sometimes found it hard to reconcile what had happened and could imagine falling for McCrae's charms all over again. Louise Byrne would have a tough job on her hands.

In her opening speech, she was impressive. 'As the evidence will show, there is little doubt that Kenneth McCrae killed four innocent people in cold blood; Sir Geoffrey and Lady Diana Ryland, their chauffeur, Joseph O'Connor, and Lady Eleanor Ryland. He also attempted to murder his own stepbrother, Detective Inspector Tom Mariner, whom he believed was competing against him to inherit his mother's estate. His defence lawyers will tell you that Mr McCrae was a man suffering from mental illness as a direct result of serving his country in the armed forces. They will tell you that when he committed these heinous crimes he was not of sound mind.

'But these crimes were planned and executed with such attention to detail, and with such care — so as to leave behind no trace of evidence — that they could only have been committed by a man who was thinking clearly and rationally. The only reason Kenneth McCrae was found out was because he believed that he'd got away with it. That wasn't mental illness, it was arrogance — pure and simple. And the motive for these murders was greed — plain and simple. Kenneth McCrae had recently learned the identity of his birth mother, a woman who, in contrast to him, lived a privileged life of comfort and wealth. McCrae wanted that life for himself. A scheme of extortion foundered so he used the other option, to kill his birth mother and her loved ones in order to contest the will and profit from their deaths. Had he succeeded in his plan, Kenneth McCrae would have been a wealthy man. And that was his sole motivation. Kenneth McCrae knew what he wanted and saw an opportunity to get it. His plan was logical and straightforward— complex only in its execution and attention to detail. It took a man of sound mind and strong nerve to carry out his plan so faultlessly and I assert that Kenneth McCrae was entirely rational throughout.'

The first few witnesses were almost routine, presenting the incontrovertible forensic proof that linked Kenneth McCrae to the murders, and proving beyond reasonable doubt that he was culpable. There then followed a procession of prosecution psychiatrists whose reports demonstrated, in their opinions, that Kenneth McCrae was entirely sane.

Roy Shipley, the man who had handled the letting of Mariner's cottage to McCrae turned out to be a surprisingly convincing witness. It was the first time Mariner could ever remember being impressed by an estate agent. He'd met McCrae on three occasions while he was implementing his plan, one of which was in Mariner's presence. He recalled the conversations during which McCrae had behaved perfectly normally, taking information and using it as part of his scheme.

'Was there anything about Kenneth McCrae's behaviour that would have led you to think he was suffering from some kind of mental disturbance?' was Louise's final question, and the answer was a resounding, 'No.'

Mariner was gratified too that the defence barristers seemed to let Shipley off the hook quite lightly. A prediction, he hoped, of what was to come.

Mariner, when his turn came, cited the snippets of information that he had unwittingly made known to McCrae, such as the times when murder victim Eleanor Ryland would be alone in her isolated house. Byrne also referred to Mariner's statement to police describing the conversation he'd had with McCrae in the cellar. When he'd recovered from the initial trauma of the event Mariner had been able to remember the whole conversation with surprising clarity, and could describe McCrae's intentions and actions in the greatest detail. It all made perfect sense.

Byrne ended on the same question she'd put to Roy Shipley, and Mariner was more than happy to elaborate. 'On the contrary,' Mariner said. 'Kenneth McCrae had thought about every contingency and had a plan that accounted for them all. He was able to adapt to new circumstances as they arose.'

The court adjourned until the following morning, so Mariner was able to prepare himself for the defence onslaught. 'It went well,' was Louise's verdict. But they both knew that the worst was to come. 'Where are you staying?'

'A little hotel just down the road. I thought I'd get something to eat before going back there though. You wouldn't like to keep me company would you?'

'I'd love to.' Her smile was apologetic. 'Unfortunately I need to get back. My fourteen-year-old is on her own and much as she'd like me to leave her that way for the entire evening, I need to check that she's doing something more productive than texting her friends.'

In the end it was Felicity who joined him for dinner and Mariner found himself telling her about moving to the country.

'It's not me who wants to go, it's Anna.'

'It sounds as if you're having second thoughts,' she said.

'We've been trying for a baby.'

'So you've come round to the idea?'

'Anna miscarried a few months ago.'

'That must have been devastating. For both of you.'

'Yes. It's affected Anna more than I'd thought. She seems afraid of trying again.'

'These things take time. You just need to be patient.'

'Yes.'

When he left Felicity, Mariner went alone to a small bar where the atmosphere was depressing. Too many kids there with the sole purpose of getting drunk. He left before ten, resigned to an early night.

* * *

The following morning the defence cross-examination began by taking the same line with Mariner as they had with Shipley.

'On how many occasions did you meet Kenneth McCrae?'

'Five times,' Mariner replied.

'And how long did each of these meetings last?'

'I didn't time them,' Mariner said, reasonably.

'But you must have a rough idea. Was it five minutes, half an hour, an hour? What about the first meeting?'

'About twenty minutes.'

'And the second?'

'About ten.'

After this tedious process had been completed, the defence barrister concluded: 'So in total you met with Kenneth McCrae for around two hours.' Mariner confirmed it. 'And at the time of your last conversation with Mr McCrae you'd been held by him in the cellar for how long?'

'Three days.'

'During which time you'd had no food or water and were in temperatures of minus eight degrees, in complete and utter darkness. Do you think you were in a fit state to judge the frame of mind of another person?'

'Possibly not, but—'

'I understand that you've recently been receiving counselling yourself, Inspector.'

'Yes.' In theory.

'What for?'

'Post-traumatic stress disorder.' Mariner felt a pinch of unease in the pit of his stomach.

'And when was this condition diagnosed?'

'About nine months ago.'

'Shortly after the night when you were involved in the bomb explosion in Birmingham city centre. Is that correct?'

'Yes.'

'So you've been on sick leave for the last nine months?'

'Not all of it, no.'

'Indeed, we have all been reading in the papers about the success of your investigation into the abduction of Jessica Klinnemann, is that correct?'

'Yes.'

'So how much time have you had off work during the last nine months, as a result of this diagnosis?'

'I had a couple of weeks off.'

'A couple of weeks? That doesn't sound like much. So, for all but a couple of weeks of the last nine months, while you've been suffering from post-traumatic stress disorder, you've been back at work, and some of that time working on an extremely high-profile case.'

'Yes.'

'You're a detective inspector. It must be a difficult job at times.'

'It has its challenges.'

'And yet, as we saw from the happy outcome of the abduction of baby Jessica, you have been able to function perfectly well in that job, despite having a diagnosis of PTSD. Isn't it true that the very nature of PTSD is that it affects every individual differently, that it comes and goes, and that with the right kind of treatment it can be controlled?' The question was apparently rhetorical. 'You have, by your own admission, been behaving in a perfectly rational way while battling this condition, so isn't it possible that in the brief times at which you had contact with Kenneth McCrae, he was merely doing the same thing?'

Mariner stalled. He could think of no comeback.

'Mr Mariner?'

'Possible, I suppose. Yes.'

Next came the expert defence witnesses; a couple of specialists in post-traumatic stress disorder and its effects, followed by the specialist McCrae had been seeing, who also introduced the stark facts about his early life and the effects of deprivation and the trauma of Tumbledown.

Somehow the defence had also persuaded Kenneth McCrae's reticent brother to appear as a witness for the defence. During the final, dramatic hunt for Kenneth McCrae, Tony Knox and Jack Coleman had interviewed the man in the garden of his home in a remote Scottish community. Mariner had read the notes. Here he looked uncomfortable, scrubbed up and in a suit and tie. He described, as he had to Knox and Coleman, the extreme maltreatment and physical abuse he and his brother had received during their childhoods with a brutal adoptive father, providing a further layer of reasoning for the jury to feel sorry for McCrae. Louise's cross-examination, though competent, would have barely dented the jury's sympathy.

'Could you tell us what you do for a living?' she asked.

'I'm a storeman.'

'Did you suffer abuse at the hands of your adoptive parents?'

'Yes, but—'

'And have you ever killed, or felt the urge to kill, another human being?'

'No.'

A couple of McCrae's army colleagues were wheeled out to describe the horrors of Tumbledown. They probably left the jury feeling amazed that it had taken McCrae another ten years to commit murder.

As a final flourish the defence insisted that once Kenneth McCrae had realised the enormity of his crimes, he was penitent. Mariner looked across at the defendant. He didn't look especially remorseful and as the jury was sent out, Mariner left the courtroom feeling empty.

Almost inevitably, it seemed to Mariner, Kenneth McCrae was found not guilty of murder, but guilty of manslaughter on the grounds of diminished responsibility. Sentencing was deferred and would be based on the outcome of further medical assessments.

'How do you feel?' Felicity asked Mariner.

'Cheated, I suppose,' Mariner said, wryly. 'McCrae had a tough life, there's no doubt about that, and I'm sorry for him that he did. But so do lots of people and they don't end up going on killing sprees.'

She gave him a hug. 'Give my love to Nelson.'

'I will.'

* * *

Nelson was enjoying an early morning walk on a dull and drizzly Saturday with Tony Knox. Since the abduction case had finished things had quietened down considerably and Knox's morning strolls were becoming routine again. The woman Knox had hoped to bump into still wasn't around. Unless . . . he wondered if this was her, just crossing the far end of the playing field. Hard to tell the make of dog from here, but it was bounding around all over the place, as hers had. Knox stepped up his pace to try and catch up with her, but then his mobile rang.

Cursing the fact that he'd left it in his pocket, he nonetheless took the call.

'Sergeant Knox? It's Christie, from Jack and the Beanstalk nursery. You said I could call you?' She sounded distant, but it might just have been the line.

'Are you all right? Has he hurt you?' Knox was immediately alert and back in professional mode.

There was a pause, and noises in the background. 'I can't talk about this on the phone. Can you meet me, tonight?' She sounded strung out, breathless even, but maybe she was walking fast.

'It'll keep until then?' Knox had one eye back on the woman who had changed direction and was now walking away from him again.

'Yeah, it's okay.' She sounded calmer. 'Do you know the Golden Cross?'

Knox remembered seeing the pub a little way down from the nursery, though it wasn't one he'd ever been into. He agreed to meet her there at eight o'clock. Switching off his phone, he was in time to see the woman exiting the park and disappearing from view.

Walking back up the street towards his house, Knox saw a car pulling away from the kerb, his neighbour, Jean, waving to the passengers inside. The driver was an elderly man.

'I'm afraid you'll have to manage without your dog-walker for a couple of days,' Jean said, as Knox approached. 'Michael's gone to stay with his grandparents tonight.'

'That's okay. Things have eased off at work now and it's about time I got some exercise again. Does this mean you've got a weekend of freedom?'

She grinned. 'I don't know what I'll do with myself.'

'How about a drink tonight?' said Knox.

'Oh,' now she was embarrassed. 'I wasn't dropping hints.'

Knox laughed. 'You don't have to. I'd have asked anyway. What do you think?'

'I think it sounds great, thanks.'

'I'll call for you at about eight.'

'Okay,' she said, though she was distracted, biting her lower lip as she watched the car proceed painfully slowly, Knox thought, to the end of the road.

'Everything all right?' he asked, casting his eyes in the same direction.

'Yes. It's just . . . I worry about Dad driving at his age. I offered to take Michael over but they wouldn't hear of it.'

'How far have they got to go?' asked Knox.

'Only up to Lichfield. I'd normally put Michael on the train, but there's nothing running this weekend. "Essential maintenance," so they say.'

As she spoke the car reached the end of the close, signalled and disappeared around the corner. She sighed.

'I'm sure they'll be fine,' said Knox. 'He's driving slowly, which is better than going too fast.'

She gave an apologetic smile. 'I'm neurotic about car accidents,' she said. 'It's how Shaun died.'

'I'm sorry.'

'Thanks.'

'Well, enjoy your first hours of freedom and I'll see you later.'

'I look forward to it.'

Only as he was unlocking the door did Knox remember his appointment with Christie. Still, it was he who had named the time. If he called her back and made it earlier, say seven, he could undertake both commitments. Christie shouldn't take long. If she was having trouble with Bond and wanted to make a complaint, she'd need to come in to the station to make a statement anyway, and if things were more desperate than that, he could recommend a couple of women's refuges, and deliver her there if necessary. It would be awkward to cancel the date with Jean, given that he'd only just arranged it and the truth was, he didn't want to. He'd even, for a split second, allowed himself to speculate on whether they might end up in bed. Unlikely, he thought on balance, but if they did, he wouldn't object.

He called Christie straight away on her mobile but got only her voicemail. He left a message saying he would meet her at the earlier time. It was the best he could do.

* * *

Knox felt like a dirty old man when he went that evening to meet Christie. All he was missing was the raincoat. It was just that sort of pub too, loud and brash, what passed these days for a typical city pub. He got there ahead of time and bought a coke from a lad who himself barely looked old enough to drink. Seven o'clock came and went, as did half past. Knox heard the same music come round on the sound system, but Christie didn't show. He found it hard to believe that she hadn't got his message. Knox really hoped that Bond hadn't got to her first. Or, maybe it was simpler than that; she'd changed her mind about coming at all. He went for a pee, and out in the corridor tried her mobile again but this time it was switched off altogether. By now it was seven forty-five and he was pushing it to get back in time to pick up Jean. Casting a last look around the bar he walked out.

'I feel like I'm on my first date,' Knox admitted, half an hour later as he and Jean were driving out to a very different establishment, the Peacock at Wetheroak, a leafy corner of Worcestershire. He realised what he'd said. 'Not that I'm treating this like—'

She laughed easily. 'You mean you can actually remember your first date?'

'Oh yes. Tracey McAllister. We were sixteen and I thought I was the dog's boll— I mean, the bees knees in me Sta-Prest and Ben Sherman shirt, monkey boots all polished up.'

'Where did you take her?'

'The end of term school disco. It was dire. Girls dancing round their handbags, lads standing round the edges being cool, and the teachers desperately trying to look like they're having fun.'

'Thank God we don't do that anymore. Things have got a bit more sophisticated.'

'How about you?'

'Dates? Oh, I was a late starter. Shaun was my first boyfriend. He was working for a big construction firm, only as the tea boy I think at that point, and asked me to rather a grand work's function at the Botanical Gardens. The thing I remember most was the dress. For some reason I was determined to go looking like Mary Quant. We've got some photos somewhere.'

The evening passed, it seemed to Knox, in no time at all and before long he was pulling back onto his drive.

'Thank you for that. I had a really good time.' As she leaned across and kissed his cheek, a hand dropped onto Knox's thigh. 'You'll come in?'

'I'd like to.' A thought occurred. 'I should just go and let Nelson out for five minutes though, then I'll come over.'

'Don't be long.'

It was with some relief that Knox found a couple of condoms in the bathroom cabinet. He didn't know what made him check his mobile. There was a message from Christie, left at eight thirty-nine. She must have picked up his earlier message after it was too late. There was a lot of noise in the background. 'I do need to talk to you. I'm at the Golden Cross now and I'll stay here till eleven o'clock. Please meet me here.'

The time by Knox's watch was just after eleven. Even breaking the speed limits he wouldn't be able to get to the Golden Cross in less than fifteen minutes, by which time she'd have decided he wasn't coming and left again. He turned one of the condoms over in his fingers. He could phone her, of course, but if she answered and was prepared to wait for him, he'd be committed to going and would have to let Jean down. He listened to the message again. Christie didn't sound panicked or upset. She seemed calm. In fact from the racket in the background it sounded as if she was having a party. And she couldn't necessarily expect him to get her message tonight. He'd call her first thing in the morning and arrange to meet her tomorrow.

Jean had left the door on the latch. 'In here,' she called as Knox closed it behind him. He went through to the kitchen.

'Coffee or something stronger?' she asked.

'Coffee's fine.'

'Go and make yourself comfortable.'

Knox sat on the sofa, and when she brought the coffee through she came and sat beside him. Still uncertain about whether it would be welcomed, Knox was considering how and when to make his move. He needn't have bothered. Quite suddenly she turned and kissed him full on the mouth, her tongue pushing apart his teeth, while at the same time she reached down a hand, aggressively exploring between his legs. In seconds his zip was open and her hand inside. 'That will do nicely.' She smiled mischievously. The next morning when the post-coital elation had waned, Knox was consumed with guilt. He tried calling Christie's number several times, but each time was cut off. He tried not to think about what that might mean. Late in the afternoon he watched out of the window as Michael's grandparents dropped him safely off again.

* * *

On Monday morning Knox went into the office as usual. In place of Mariner, DCI Sharp took the usual Monday morning briefing meeting.

'Have we heard from the boss?' someone asked.

'He's a few more days' leave due. After that verdict it wouldn't surprise me if he stays away a little longer,' Sharp said. 'Right, now to work. Over the weekend we've had the usual spate of burglaries, TDAs and Saturday night brawls.'

'Any domestics?' Knox asked tentatively.

Sharp frowned at her notes. 'Not that I'm aware. Most of this stuff is pretty routine and we're still following up on Ocean Blue and the abduction case . . .'

Knox tuned himself out of what the DCI was saying. When the briefing was over he'd go across to the nursery to see Christie, apologise for Saturday night and find out what it was that she'd wanted—

'Tony, I'd like you to handle it.'

At the mention of his name, Knox came round, realising that he'd no idea what Sharp was talking about. 'Sorry, ma'am?'

'Wake up, DS Knox. I want you to talk to Mrs Wrigley. She's convinced that her holiday cottage was used as a bolt hole by baby Jessica's kidnappers. She's coming in to make a statement,' Sharp glanced up at the wall clock, 'about now.'

'It's a bit of a long shot, isn't it?' said Knox.

'Probably,' agreed Sharp. 'But she's driven quite a long way to report it, so I think the least we can do is talk to her.'

'Yes, ma'am.' *Shit.* He'd have to phone the nursery instead. But when he did the line was engaged and he couldn't get through. Christie's phone was switched off.

Betty Wrigley seemed to Knox to be a busybody. The owner of a holiday cottage near Bakewell in Derbyshire, it wasn't long before he had her pegged as the kind of hostess who requires all the intricate details of her guests' lives, and takes offence when they don't oblige. When this particular couple who had stayed at her holiday cottage weren't forthcoming, she was irked. 'They barely communicated with me and then they left abruptly, abandoning the cottage part way through the week and returning the key, without so much as a goodbye. Very strange behaviour, I thought.'

'Perhaps they had a family emergency,' Knox offered.

'So why didn't they just say?'

'What were their names?' asked Knox patiently, thinking he probably should at least write some of this down.

'Mr and Mrs Jones. I mean, that makes you think straight away, doesn't it?'

'It makes me think that maybe their name was Jones,' said Knox, drily, making a note of it.

Betty Wrigley glared. She wasn't warming to him, Knox could tell. 'Mr Jones booked the cottage over the telephone for the week. He sent me a cash deposit and paid the rest in cash when they arrived.'

'There's no crime in that, said Knox. 'What was it that made you suspicious of them?'

'Well, it was the secrecy to begin with. They kept themselves to themselves, even the baby. I mean, normally couples are proud of a new baby, and want to show it off, but not these two. In fact, I hadn't even realised that they had a baby when they arrived, but suddenly after a couple of days there were baby clothes on the washing line. And when I went to tidy up the cottage after they'd gone I found nappies in the bin.'

'Perhaps there was something wrong with the baby.'

'Perhaps.' But she was sceptical. 'Then on the Tuesday I thought I'd drop by to see how they were getting along and they'd gone, door locked and keys pushed back through the letterbox. They'd left a note saying that Mrs Jones wasn't feeling well so they had decided to go home early.'

It seemed to Knox like a perfectly sound explanation. 'Have you still got the note?' he asked.

'Yes, it's here somewhere. I kept it because I thought you'd want to see it.' She rummaged through a capacious handbag for several minutes, finally producing a carefully folded piece of paper. Like the note that had been left with baby Jessica it was handwritten in block capitals but, to

Knox's untrained eye, there was no further similarity. Nonetheless he would send it to the lab for comparison.

He showed her the e-fit of the kidnapper. 'Does she look like Mrs Jones?'

'I didn't see her, well, at least, only at a distance. As I said, my dealings were with Mr Jones. It could have been her,' she added hopefully.

But the description of Mr Jones didn't fit anyone they'd had in the frame, and Betty Wrigley was unable to pick him out in any of the photographs of the male animal rights activists Knox showed her. Most of them were, she said, too young. 'And Mr Jones had a beard. They were a more mature couple.'

'I thought you said you didn't really see Mrs Jones.'

'Well the man was, and I got a sense—'

A *sense*? What was the woman now, clairvoyant? 'Well, thank you very much for coming in Mrs Wrigley,' Knox stood up, concluding the interview.

She looked crestfallen. 'Is that all? I could do one of those identity parades for you.'

'We'll call you back if we need that,' said Knox, pretty sure that they wouldn't.

After that, Knox needed a cuppa and went up to the canteen. He joined a lengthy queue behind two uniforms, deep in conversation, and the word 'suicide' caught his attention.

'What suicide?' he asked.

It was PC Mick Crawford who'd mentioned it. 'BTP reported it first thing this morning. They found the body of an unidentified young woman on the railway line between Kingsmead and Bournville stations over the weekend, a probable suicide. Bit grim so they said.'

'A young woman?' Knox echoed, his stomach bubbling a little. 'Where exactly?'

'Back of Cottesbrooke Park.' So, miles away from the Golden Cross, Knox thought with relief.

'It looks straightforward so we're leaving it to them,' Crawford said. It was standard procedure for the Transport Police to handle any deaths on the railways. The only exceptions being when the death happened to be connected with an ongoing police investigation. Knox hoped this wasn't going to be one of those exceptions. 'They wanted to know if we'd had any mispers reported over the weekend, but we've got none that fit their profile.'

'You've got a description?' asked Knox.

'Sure.'

'Can I see?'

Knox followed Crawford back to his desk. He didn't know why he was compelled to look at the description, and afterwards he half-wished he hadn't. An involuntary groan escaped his lips. The girl had a fading bruise running the length of her face.

'You all right?' Crawford asked.

Chapter Eleven

Back at his desk, a phone call determined the exact location of the body and Knox grabbed his coat. As he crossed the office he almost collided with DCI Sharp. 'Where are you off to in such a rush?'

'Transport Police have found a body on the railway track.'

'It's a suicide,' said Sharp. 'It's not one for us.'

'I think it could be Christie Walker, the girl who gave us the description of baby Jessica's abductor.'

'How the hell did you come up with that?'

'She called me on Saturday morning and wanted to meet with me. I . . . er, couldn't make it at the time she wanted and I haven't been able to get hold of her since. Her boyfriend used to knock her about.'

'That doesn't necessarily mean—'

'I know. I just want to be certain, ma'am.'

'All right then, follow it through, but unless it's definitely her, you leave it to BTP.'

'Yes, ma'am. It's just for my own peace of mind.'

'Well I admire your thoroughness, DC Knox.'

Could Christie have been that desperate? Knox had assumed when she called that she'd wanted practical help, the name of a hostel or a women's refuge, but what if she'd got beyond that? He wished now that he'd saved her message so that he could listen to it again.

The body had been found at a point along the main Bristol to Birmingham railway line below a footbridge that lay at the entrance to Cottesbrooke Park, an area of tamed green lawns and rough woodland. Though wide enough to take a vehicle the bridge was blocked off at one end by three concrete bollards, making it a footway leading into the park. It came at the right-angled junction of two roads of terraced houses, the nearest of which was thirty metres away. The railway bridge from which the young woman had jumped was now jammed with emergency vehicles and a small group of onlookers, all illuminated by flickering blue strobes.

Identifying himself, Knox was allowed access through a gate in the steel perimeter fencing that would normally be kept locked. He cut through brambles and nettles before slithering down the muddy, grass covered embankment onto the clinker, and walked across the sleepers towards the white tent that had been constructed just the other side of the line. Just being on the track, with the smell of the railway, prompted a gruesome rush of memories from twenty years ago.

The Transport Police investigation team had begun its work. Approaching the nearest officer Knox was directed on to the man leading the investigation, Andy Olsen. He introduced himself.

'And how can I help you, DC Knox?' Olsen asked.

'I think I might know the victim. Can I take a look?'

'Be my guest.'

With some reluctance Knox pulled back the flimsy flap that provided some privacy from the inquisitive world. Some deaths are unreal, neat and clean, leaving the victim's body almost unscathed, but Christie Walker's death had been the opposite. Her limbs were angled in grotesque and improbable positions, the flesh on one side of her face, torn open and bloodied. After a moment, Knox became aware that someone was speaking to him.

'Is it her?' Olsen was asking.

Knox nodded, dully, his gut turned to lead. 'Her name is Christie Walker,' he said.

'I've heard that name before,' Olsen said, trying to figure it out.

'She was a key witness during the baby abduction case. She worked at the nursery that Jessica was taken from.'

'Of course.'

'She was also the girl who gave us the most detailed description of the abductor.'

'That's a coincidence,' said Olsen. 'You never did find the abductor, did you? Do you think someone might have wanted her out of the way?'

'She was in an abusive relationship,' Knox told him. 'And the guy who was beating her up was the same guy who made the hoax ransom demand. He's been charged with PCJ.'

'And probably thinks she grassed him up. She wouldn't be the first person to take this way out. Either way it looks as if this is one for you after all. I'll let you have everything we've got so far.'

'Thanks. Who found her?' asked Knox.

'One of our goods drivers. He managed to stop in time, but they've taken him to Selly Oak to be treated for shock.'

'So if he stopped in time how come she's in such a bad way?'

'We think she must have been hit by an earlier train. The high speed one during the night may not have even noticed. If he did feel it, the driver would have thought he'd hit a fox or something. There's not much blood in the area where she was found so she could have been dragged a little way. Hard to tell which side of the bridge she jumped off.'

'There's no ID on her?' Knox was thinking particularly of Christie's phone.

Olsen shook his head. It wasn't unusual. Suicides often didn't want to be identified. Olsen nodded down towards her feet. 'She's lost one of her shoes, too. Our guys are out there looking, but as far as I know, they haven't found it yet. It's possible it could have been carried some distance by the train that hit her of course.'

* * *

The train driver who'd made the discovery was in accident and emergency in a curtained cubicle waiting to be attended to. In late middle age, his complexion had a greyish pallor. 'I was coming out of Kingsmead station, just building up a bit of speed when I saw her,' he told Knox, the image clearly still very much on his mind. 'Whenever you see something big and bulky like that up ahead you always think, and hope — you hear stories all the time. I could see what it was when I was about twenty yards away so I had time to stop. She was just to the side of the track, sort of half on, half off, if you know what I mean. She must have been hit by an earlier train, but I managed to stop before I ran over her. I got out and had a look.' He gulped hard and Knox cast around for a receptacle in case he was about to throw up. 'God, I wish I hadn't, though . . .'

'It was the right thing to do,' Knox said. 'Thanks.' As he got up to go the driver gripped his arm so hard it was painful. 'Do you think I'll ever forget it?' he wanted to know.

'It'll fade in time,' Knox told him, reminding himself of the same thing.

By the time Knox got to the mortuary, Stuart Croghan was beginning his preliminary examination. Knox scrubbed up, put on greens and lurked in the background. He hated this aspect of the job. It was one of those things you almost, but never quite, got used to. For a while the only sounds were the clink of surgical instruments and Croghan's commentary murmured into the Dictaphone as he and his assistant, a medical student, worked. In the end Knox couldn't bear the tension any longer. 'Has Bond knocked her about recently, in the last couple of days?' he wanted to know, the uncertainty eating into him.

'Not in the last day,' said Croghan. 'She's been dead more than twenty-four hours. It looks as if she died sometime in the early hours of Sunday morning. There must have been other trains that drove past without seeing her. And she's a mess, so it may be impossible to tell whether she'd recently been subjected to a beating. As well as the broken neck that I'm assuming caused her death, there are a whole range of impact injuries from the fall and from being struck by the train.'

Knox had fallen silent.

'Are you all right?' Croghan sounded curious. It wasn't as if Knox hadn't been through all this before.

'She rang me on Saturday night and I was supposed to meet her. I think she was going to turn him in, or maybe she just needed help to find somewhere safe she could go. I had other arrangements so I put her off.'

Croghan picked up on his tone of voice. 'Not your fault, Tony,' he said, lightly. 'If she wanted to do it she'd have done it anyway. You think she killed herself because you stood her up? There were other reasons.'

'I'll never know now though, will I? Cause of death?'

'I need to do more work, but at first glance, a broken neck and impact injuries, multiple fractures, would be enough to do the job. But you're right, there are other, older injuries.'

'Like I said, she'd been subjected to physical abuse over time.' Knox clenched and unclenched his fists. Before he left Knox asked: 'Would she have known anything about it?'

'I doubt it. The break in her neck is clean and the initial impact of it would have knocked her unconscious straight away. She wouldn't have felt anything.'

It was small comfort. Knox still left the mortuary feeling sick. It was a horrible way to choose to die, and now he would have to live with the thought that he might have prevented it. A couple of weeks ago he'd offered Christie a way out, a lifeline. But then when the time had come he'd snatched it away from her, and all for the sake of a shag.

* * *

By the time Knox had driven to the garage that Jimmy Bond owned, the guilt had been displaced by anger and his blood was up. He pulled on to the forecourt, tyres protesting at the abrupt halt.

'Where's Bond?' Bursting onto the forecourt, Knox yelled at an overall-clad youth who trained a jet-wash on the forecourt cars. He gestured towards the glass-fronted showroom. Shoving open the swing door, Knox picked out Bond immediately; smooth and oily today in his designer suit, doing the hard-sell on a second-hand Ford Focus to a young couple. He was bigger than Knox, but the sergeant was stronger and angrier, and Bond barely had time to glance round before he'd been grabbed by the shoulders, spun round and slammed against the wall, an elbow across his throat.

'What was it this time?' Knox breathed menacingly, his face inches from Bond's. 'Didn't she cook your steak the way you like it? Or did you get it into your stupid skull that she shopped you? You wouldn't know loyalty if it jumped up and bit you on the arse, would you? You might think you've got away with this, you bastard, but I know the history and one way or another I'll trace it back to you.'

For several seconds Bond was afraid, but there was something else in his eyes; he was perplexed, too. 'What's going on?' he managed.

'We've found Christie's body,' said Knox. 'That's what's going on.'

Bond went slack and the colour drained from his face. 'What?'

Caught off guard by the reaction, Knox released his grip and Bond slid down against the wall. The young car-buyers had backed away and were making a discreet exit through the swing doors.

'Bit of a stunner, eh, Jimmy?' Knox went on, gasping for breath. 'See what you did to her.'

'I don't know what you're talking about. Christie and me broke up.'

'When?'

'Couple of weeks ago.'

'Who ended it?'

'She did. She did a runner while I was being held by you lot. That's how loyal she was. Before you interfered, I'd proposed to her. I wanted us to get married, have a family and that before we both got past it.'

'She was going to marry you?'

'She turned me down.'

'I can't imagine why,' said Knox, his voice dripping sarcasm. 'Upset you, did it? Thought she'd always be there for you, your own personal punch bag.'

Bond didn't deny it. 'She might have said yes if—'

'If you'd extorted two hundred and fifty grand out of Peter Klinnemann? She'd have put up with you knocking her around for the sake of the money, would she? You're kidding yourself. Christie had too much common sense and too much integrity to waste her life on a loser like you. She didn't grass you up, you know, she didn't have to. We already had you.'

'I know that.'

Bond was defiant, but Knox could see that it was bravado. He was shaken. Maybe in spite of it all, he really had loved Christie. 'What were you doing on Saturday night?' Knox demanded.

'I was in Blackpool, getting pissed.'

'Why?'

'It was my mate's stag night.' Bond's expression suddenly changed. 'This is your fault,' he said, turning on Knox. 'You did this.'

'How do you work that out?' Knox said uneasily.

'If it hadn't been for you giving her ideas, Christie would still be with me. She needed me.'

'Like a hole in the fucking head. That's crap and you know it. You might not have pushed her off that bridge but one way or another you were responsible. I'll be back for you.'

'You don't know what you're on about. If it wasn't for you she'd still be alive.'

And those were the words that rang in Tony Knox's ears as he walked back across the forecourt.

* * *

Last time Mariner had been at Granville Lane it had been a night of celebration, with everyone in high spirits. Today it couldn't have felt more different, and when Mariner walked in, CID was practically deserted, everyone out catching up on the backlog of cases that had been put on hold for the duration of baby Jessica's abduction. One of the few officers remaining at his desk was Charlie Glover. He looked up when Mariner walked in. 'Crap verdict, sir,' he sympathised.

So news had got around. 'You could say that.'

'Still, with luck they'll stick him somewhere like Broadmoor.'

'We can but hope. Where's Tony Knox?'

Glover seemed to choose his words carefully. 'He's out. You remember that girl we interviewed when the

Klinnemann baby went missing: Christie Walker? There's been a suicide. Knox thinks it could be her.'

'Christ. How?'

'Jumped in front of a train.'

'Poor kid,' said Mariner. 'What's happening with the boyfriend, Bond?'

Glover shook his head. 'He's out on bail, but if Tony Knox gets hold of him I wouldn't say much for his chances.' He said it just as Tony Knox walked in the door.

'So?' Mariner said.

'It's her all right.'

'No.' Mariner grimaced. 'And Bond?'

'I've just paid him a visit. To his credit he seemed pretty shocked.'

'Does he think she shopped him?'

Knox considered this for a moment. 'No. I really don't think he does. He claims they'd split up.'

'That puts a convenient distance between them,' said Mariner. 'Did you believe him?'

'I didn't want to, but I suppose I did. And he's been away all weekend on a stag do in Blackpool, so he says.'

'Well, that will be easy enough to check out.'

Knox had gone a funny colour. 'I was meant to meet Christie on Saturday night, you know. Then I had a better offer, so I tried to rearrange it and it all got messed up. I let her down. She'd probably still be alive if it wasn't for me.'

Mariner shook his head. 'Come on, you know better than that. Christie was a responsible adult, old enough to make her own decisions. Do you think she'd made up her mind to bring charges against Bond for what he did to her?'

'Maybe, though the evidence has faded. Croghan said as much. It was only going to stick if she did it straight away. I don't think she did make up her mind about that. It's what she said. When I asked if Bond had hurt her, she said: "I can't talk about it on the phone."'

'Maybe she didn't feel comfortable telling you about it over the phone. Maybe she just preferred face to face contact.'

'But if that was it, why not just say "yes?" She knew I knew all about it.'

'So what are you thinking?'

'That it was something else.'

'Something else that Bond was into?'

'It wouldn't surprise me.'

'But we turned over his place and his garage when he was brought in and we didn't find anything. So all we can really do is watch him.' Mariner could sense Knox's frustration.

'He's a dodgy piece of work, and look at the history. He's got a previous conviction, and he made the ransom demand.'

'You're still certain that Christie had nothing to do with that?'

Knox was unequivocal. 'She was too straight. She hated him for it. It prompted her to leave him. And he didn't make any attempt to incriminate her, did he? No, that was all him. I think it has to be something else.'

'So if there was something she needed to tell you, why kill herself?'

'I don't know. I can't make it fit,' Knox said. 'There was something in her voice on the phone. She didn't sound like someone at the end of her tether. She sounded resolved, eager even — like she was ready to move on.' He broke off. 'Nah, I'm just making excuses because I fucked up.'

'No,' said Mariner. 'If she'd sounded that desperate, you'd have done something about it. Your "better offer" work out?'

'Yeah.'

'So maybe you're feeling bad about that too.'

Knox shot him a look. 'You've been in therapy too long.' He shook his head, as if freeing it from some restraint. 'No.'

'Have you told the parents yet?'

'It's the next job. I've already got her address.'

'I'll come with you.'

'It's a bummer about McCrae, boss,' Knox said when they were in the car.

'He had a good defence team and they did a sound job,' said Mariner, evenly. 'And who knows, maybe they're right.'

Knox was surprised. 'You think he really is nuts?'

'Truthfully? Maybe. It still doesn't give him the right to kill.'

'No.'

* * *

The address they had for Christie Walker was a modest ex-council property in Weoley Castle. Knox rang the bell and after some delay, a woman in her mid-sixties came to the door. She regarded them warily, prepared to ward off their sales pitch. Knox raised his warrant card so that she could see it.

'Police?' The old woman said, looking past them onto the street. 'I haven't called the police.'

'No. You're Mrs Walker?'

'No, I'm Phyllis Gates.'

'Are you Christie Walker's—?'

'I'm her nan.'

'I'm Detective Inspector Mariner and this is Detective Sergeant Knox. We need to speak to you. Could we come in?'

Phyllis Gates was quick on the uptake and her suspicion grew. 'What's happened?'

'Why don't we go in and sit down?' Mariner indicated the living room.

Leaving Knox to close the door, she led the way into a neat sixties-style lounge, complete with a glass display cabinet of china ornaments, like the one Mariner remembered from his own grandparents' house. There was a big framed photograph of Christie on the mantelpiece. Mariner saw Knox flinch away from it. Inviting them to sit in the armchairs of a brown velour three piece, Phyllis Gates perched uncomfortably on the edge on the sofa opposite. Mariner couldn't help noticing a pile of *Watchtower* magazines stacked in a corner of the room, still bound in their plastic packaging and awaiting distribution. No wonder she was cautious about door-steppers. She was probably an expert. By the time they had all settled the air was filled with tension.

'We were hoping to speak to Christie's parents?' Mariner said.

'Christie's mum died when she was little,' Phyllis Gates nervously told him. 'Her dad's never been around. I take care of her.'

'Well, then it's you we need to speak to.'

'About what?' She was making an effort to keep her voice steady.

'I'm very sorry,' Mariner said. 'But the body of a young woman was found on the Bristol to Birmingham railway line, early this morning. We have reason to believe that it's Christie.'

Her sharp intake of breath resounded around the room, then silence. She dropped her head, and after a moment when Mariner glanced across, he saw her shoulders heaving as she wept silent tears. They should have brought a female officer with them. He reached out and placed a comforting arm on hers as they waited for the shock to subside. 'Do you keep any brandy in the house?' Mariner asked, trying to remember if Jehovah's witnesses were teetotallers, and when the response was in the negative he said, 'Go and stick the kettle on,' quietly, to Knox.

Five minutes later when Knox returned with tea in a china cup, no saucer, her sobbing had diminished and she took the cup from him with shaking hands. 'I can't believe it. How did she end up there?' Her voice was a whisper.

'We're not altogether sure yet.' Mariner spoke slowly. 'When was the last time you saw Christie?'

'On Saturday afternoon. She'd finished with her boyfriend a couple of weeks ago, and she was moving her things back here.' Mariner and Knox exchanged a look. It corroborated Bond's story.

'How did Christie seem?'

'She was okay.'

'Was she upset about the split?'

'She was sad,' said Phyllis, wiping her eyes. 'But she thought it was the right thing to do.'

'So she didn't seem depressed about it?' Mariner asked.

'No. Not at all.' She was struggling to comprehend.

'How did you feel about it?' Mariner asked.

'It was a nightmare.' said Phyllis, misunderstanding the question. 'She'd got so much stuff to move back into her tiny little room we didn't know where to put it all. She's had to leave some of it at his house.'

Mariner tried again. 'I meant, how did you feel about her splitting up with Jimmy Bond?'

'I was glad really. I always thought he was a bit too old for her—' no mention of the physical violence '—and when he made those phone calls about the baby — Christie was so upset about that.'

So had Christie finally stood up to Bond? He wouldn't have taken it well. 'Did Jimmy help to move her things back?'

'Oh no, she got her uncle to help. He's got a van.'

'And you didn't see Bond at all?'

'No. Christie said he wasn't there. But it was Saturday. He was probably at work. Moving back here was only temporary, like. She was going to get a place of her own, a flat. She'd already seen one that she fancied on that new development on the Bristol Road, by the college.'

Mariner had seen that development. It was all luxury jobs. How on earth could Christie have afforded that? 'They're expensive properties,' he said.

'I know. But she'd won some money on one of those scratch cards, and she was going to get a pay rise,' said Phyllis confidently.

It'd have to be one hell of a pay rise, Mariner thought. 'Then what?' he asked.

'When we'd put her things in her room we had some tea. I went down the road and got fish and chips, and we had it in front of the telly, then she went out about half past six.'

'Did she say where she was going?'

'She's twenty-four years old,' Phyllis reminded him. 'She doesn't have to tell me everything. I suppose I thought it was the girls from the nursery.'

'And that's the last time you saw her. You didn't report her missing. Why was that?'

'I thought she must be staying with friends. She often did. She's not a child.'

'Would she have taken anything with her?' Mariner asked. 'A handbag, for example.'

'Oh yes, she always had her bag with her, and her mobile.'

Mariner glanced up at Knox who gave a slight shake of the head. They were both thinking the same thing. 'It wasn't with her when she was found,' Mariner said. 'It would help if you could describe it for us.'

'It was one of those Morgan bags,' Phyllis said, which didn't help either man in the slightest. 'It was white leather, with lots of little pockets. She was very proud of it. She got it on eBay. It was a bargain.'

'Mrs Gates, this may be uncomfortable, but we have to consider the possibility that Christie took her own life . .

. this is hard, but can you think of any reason why she might have wanted to do that?'

'Suicide? Oh no, Christie wouldn't. She knows what we think of that.' A glimmer of hope crossed her face. 'Are you sure it's her?'

'As sure as we can be,' Knox said, gently. 'I spoke to Christie during our investigation into baby Jessica's disappearance.'

Phyllis Gates fixed him with a bright-eyed gaze. 'You're Tony. She told me about you, about how kind you were. She liked you.'

Knox squirmed. 'She contacted me on Saturday,' he went on. 'She said she wanted to talk to me. Do you have any idea what it might have been about?'

For a moment she stared off into the middle distance, the cup in her hand tilting precariously. 'No,' she said, vaguely. 'I can't think of anything.'

'Did you know that Jimmy Bond hit Christie?'

'Jimmy?' It brought her back to them, but she couldn't meet Mariner's eye. Instead she smoothed an imaginary wrinkle on the arm of the sofa. 'Oh, I don't think so. Christie was accident-prone, that was all. She always was quite a clumsy child. She and Jimmy had their differences at the end, but she loved him and he was good to her.'

Mariner saw the look on Knox's face. Hard to tell if she really hadn't seen what was going on, or if she was in denial. Either way it had got to him. 'Do you think Christie might have been more upset about splitting up from Jimmy than she let you see?' Mariner asked.

Phyllis considered this for a moment. 'They'd been together a long time,' she said.

Mariner gestured to the photograph propped up on the fireplace. 'Could we borrow that picture to take a copy?'

'Help yourself.'

'This is hard, Mrs Gates, but we'll need someone to formally identify Christie.'

'I can do that,' she said, without hesitation.

'Are you sure?'

'Yes. I want to see her, to say goodbye. And to make sure.'

She was still hoping it wouldn't be Christie, Mariner thought. She wouldn't be the first. 'Before we go, would it be possible to just have a quick look at Christie's room?'

Christie may have moved her possessions in but she hadn't got as far as unpacking, and the room was so crammed with boxes and black bin bags that they could hardly open the door to get in. The components of a personal computer stood unconnected on top of a dressing table. If Christie had left a note, she'd made no effort to draw attention to it.

'This is too big a job,' said Mariner. 'We'll do it later.'

An hour later, after identifying her granddaughter's body, Phyllis collapsed, sobbing with distress and turned to clutch at Mariner. 'What am I going to do without her?'

He couldn't give her an answer.

Chapter Twelve

A new sign was being erected outside Jack and the Beanstalk nursery renaming it *ABC Nursery*.

'That was quick,' observed Mariner. 'The kidnap must have left its mark.' The doorbell had also been replaced by a more sophisticated affair and, unlike the last time, summoned an immediate response. It was Trudy Barratt who let them in and she didn't seem particularly pleased to see them. The alterations it seemed were cosmetic and nothing had visibly altered inside. She returned immediately to her desk in the office, leaving them to follow.

'What could you possibly want now?' she asked, already attending to the papers in front of her.

'How's business?' Mariner asked, pointedly.

'Most of the sensible parents have stayed with us. A handful have chosen to place their children elsewhere.'

'Any "elsewhere" in particular?' Mariner couldn't help wondering again about rival nurseries.

'Not as far as I know. The reasons have been varied, but all quite diplomatic,' she said with a wry smile.

'And the staff?'

'They've been more erratic than ever, which is why I'm rather busy just now. Three of them haven't turned up today—'

'Including Christie Walker.'

'Yes.' That had come out of the blue, and she finally looked up from what she was doing. 'How did you know—?'

'Christie's body was found on the main Birmingham to Bristol line early this morning.'

'What? Oh God. No.' Now they had her full attention and for a couple of seconds she gripped the edge of the desk, swaying slightly. Mariner crossed the room to the tiny high window, pushing it open as far as it would go. 'Let's get some air in here. Would you like some water?'

'Yes, thank you.' Knox filled a plastic cup from the water cooler in the corner and passed it to her. She swallowed it in three gulps. 'How? What happened?' she asked, finally. 'Was it — an accident?'

'At the moment we're treating it as suicide,' said Mariner.

Her eyes widened. 'I can't believe it. Poor girl.' Her voice grew stronger. 'It's a terrible shock, of course, but in some ways I'm not surprised. I've always thought Christie was a little fragile.'

'Fragile enough to want to end her life?'

'Well . . . I wouldn't know about that. But she had good reason to want to get away from that bully of a boyfriend of hers.'

'Her relationship with Jimmy Bond had finished,' Knox told her.

'Had it?'

'Last weekend. She didn't say?'

'Christie didn't share much of her personal life with me. She might have told some of the other girls. I'm sure, despite what Bond was like, that must have upset her. They'd been together quite a while. She did take the kidnapping to heart too. I think she felt that it was her fault, even though we all know it wasn't, of course. And then that awful man making the ransom demand. I think Christie is — I mean, she was — accustomed to taking the blame for things. It had got to be a habit.' It all spilled out, one conscious train of thought, the nervous reaction to bad news.

'When did you last see her?' asked Mariner.

Trudy Barratt thought for a moment. 'Sometime during Friday afternoon. I had to go into the baby room.'

'Christie wasn't in the crèche?'

'The crèche has been suspended indefinitely.'

'Oh.' Mariner allowed himself a glance in Knox's direction. 'Whose decision was that?'

'It was a decision mutually agreed by myself and the hospital,' she said, tightly.

They'd look into that later. 'And how did Christie seem when you saw her on Friday?'

'Well, she did seem quiet, I suppose, as if she had a lot on her mind.'

'We'll need to talk to her friends,' Mariner said.

'Now?'

'As soon as possible.'

The rest of the staff were naturally engaged with the children so interviewing them was a slow and painful process. Again they used the staff room, but this time the young women were called in one at a time for Mariner and Knox to break the news. Without exception, they took it emotionally. As well as being valued, Christie had been a popular member of staff. Once over the initial shock, and clutching a glass of water, it was a girl named Joy who seemed able to provide them with the most information.

'When did you last see Christie?' Mariner asked her, as he had the other girls.

'She came to Frankie & Benny's for Rachel's leaving-do on Friday night, but that was it. She was going to spend Saturday moving her stuff back into her nan's house.'

'So you were aware of the split from Jimmy?'

Joy nodded.

'And how did she feel about that?'

'It was hard, but deep down she knew she'd done the right thing. I was glad. We'd all been trying to tell her for months what a loser he was.'

'You knew that he hit her?'

'How could we not? She always had some excuse about the bruises, but we saw right through it. I think when he made that bogus ransom demand, she saw him for what he really was, so it seemed like at least one good thing came out of the kidnapping. But now . . .'

'How did Christie seem on Friday night?'

'To tell you the truth we all got pretty bladdered, but I remember thinking how much happier she seemed. She'd been sort of edgy earlier in the week and I know she nearly didn't come, but then I think she'd realised she'd done the right thing leaving Jimmy and she started to relax. It even crossed my mind that there could be someone else on the scene.'

'What makes you say that?' asked Mariner.

'I made some comment about enjoying her freedom, but she said it might not last long anyway. I asked her what she meant and she said something like "plenty more fish in the sea, and some of them a bit more grown up than Jimmy."'

'What do you think she meant by that exactly?'

'I can't be certain, but it sounded like she had her eye on another older guy. Christie always seemed to go for older men. Then later when we were talking about Rachel leaving — there have been a few people who've gone since baby Jessica — Christie said, "Could be me next."'

'Those were her exact words?'

'Yes. I asked her what she meant but she just sort of laughed.'

So what was Christie so cheerful about? Leaving Jimmy Bond, or because she'd thought of another way out? As Mariner and Knox left the building, they acknowledged a couple of the auxiliary staff who sat on the outside wall smoking. 'You've been asking about Christie, haven't you, poor girl,' called out the older of the two; a woman in her fifties Mariner would have guessed.

'We have,' said Mariner.

'Mrs Barratt tell you about the ding dong?'

'The ding dong?'

The woman glanced knowingly at her friend. 'What did I tell you?' She turned back to Mariner. 'Friday night when everyone else had gone home, I'd just finished up and needed to put the keys back in the cupboard in the office, but I couldn't go in because Christie was in there with Mrs Barratt and they were at it hammer and tongs.'

'They were having an argument?'

'A right old slanging match. I thought world war three was about to start.'

'How long did this go on for?'

'Well, I came out here and had another ciggie. I was putting it out when Christie came out the door.'

'Was she upset?' asked Knox.

'No. She was grinning, like the cat that got the cream. She looked well pleased with herself.'

With an impatient sigh, Mariner led the way back into the nursery, annoyed that their time was being wasted. He confronted Trudy Barratt. 'You didn't tell us that Christie came to see you before she went home on Friday.'

'Oh, was that Friday?' She was all innocence. 'I could have sworn it was earlier in the week. The time just goes, doesn't it?'

Genuine mistake or not? 'We've just been told quite definitively that it was Friday,' said Mariner. 'What was the discussion about?'

'Christie was talking about leaving. I tried to dissuade her. She was a good nursery nurse, reliable. There aren't too many of those around at present. And if I'm honest, I've invested a lot in her in terms of training. I was disappointed that she'd be going before I got a return on that.'

'Did she tell you why she wanted to leave?'

'Not specifically, but she'd had her name in all the papers, I expect she thought she could get a better job at another nursery. That's what usually happens. It's frustrating. You train up members of staff and then they move on.'

'So you didn't part on the best of terms?' Mariner surmised.

'It wasn't like that.' She spoke quickly. 'We resolved the matter.'

'How?'

'I persuaded her to stay.'

'Did you offer her a sweetener, an incentive? A pay rise, for example?' Mariner thought back to what Christie had told her nan.

'Not exactly. But I might have implied that one would be forthcoming. Samantha will be going on maternity leave soon, so the deputy cover will be available.'

'Isn't that a risky precedent, to give in to that kind of pressure from a member of staff?'

Mrs Barratt gave a nervous laugh. 'That's putting it rather strongly. But no, I don't usually respond to threats of any kind, but Christie wasn't really that sort of girl, and she was a valued member of staff. I genuinely didn't want to lose her.'

* * *

'Doesn't make any sense at all,' Knox reiterated, when they were outside on the street again. 'The promise of a future promotion and a pay rise, even if it's only temporary, would surely have made her happy. So why kill herself twenty-four hours later? Where to now, boss?' he wondered aloud.

'The last place we know Christie was before she died. The Golden Cross. We can walk it from here. What about this other man?' Mariner said, as they walked.

'Yeah, where did he come from? No one else has said anything about him.'

'An older man, possibly not available—' Mariner stopped. 'You don't think—?'

'What?'

'Christie helps us with the abduction investigation which, you said, she seemed really keen on. She builds a bit of a rapport with you, even mentioning you to her nan. As you say, you had something in common; you understood her circumstances. Then, on your advice, she leaves her boyfriend. Do you think she could have developed a crush on you? She wanted to meet up with you to tell you that she's left Jimmy and that she's available?'

'And then throws herself in front of a train because I'm not? Thanks a lot. That makes me feel a whole lot better.'

'Yeah, sorry, you're right,' Mariner conceded. 'It's a big conclusion to arrive at.'

They'd also arrived at the pub, one of those that had begun opening all day and now, in the middle of the afternoon, held a smattering of customers watching Sky News on the giant flat-screen TV. Mariner could remember a time when people went to the pub to socialise. Not anymore. Instead a dozen pairs of dead eyes gazed at the screen. There was one barmaid, of about Christie's age, in jeans and the traditional low-cut T-shirt. Knox showed her the picture of Christie.

'Yes, I do remember her,' the girl affirmed. 'She's been in a few times, usually with her mates. I think she's one of the girls from the nursery up the road. She sat here, at the bar, and kept asking me the time. I got the impression she was waiting for someone and that he'd stood her up. Git. They'd arranged to meet at eleven.'

'Is that what she told you?'

The girl shook her head. 'I guessed, because up until that point she was on soft drinks, but after that, she was knocking back Bacardi Breezers like there was no tomorrow and she stopped the clock-watching. By the time she left she'd had a skin full — could hardly stand up.'

'What time did she leave?' asked Knox.

'About midnight. I wanted to call a cab for her because I could see what a state she was in, but she wouldn't let me. She'd spent all her money and couldn't pay for it. I offered to lend it her but she didn't want to know.'

'Did she seem upset that she'd been stood up?'

'She wasn't in tears if that's what you mean, but nobody happy gets hammered alone, do they? I'll bet it was one of those internet dates. We get that all the time these days. Still, maybe he was a psychopath and she was better off without him.'

'She's dead,' said Mariner, bluntly.

'Oh, God. That's awful, I'm so sorry . . .'

Outside the pub Knox and Mariner studied the map. 'She should have been going back to her nan's house,' said Mariner. 'So the most logical way for her to go would have been this way.'

'—which makes no sense at all because the railway bridge where she was found is beyond that,' Knox pointed out.

'And a hell of a long way too. What is it? About three miles?'

'She was pissed. Maybe she started out and lost her bearings.'

'Where does Jimmy Bond live?'

'That's more like the direction I suppose.'

'Maybe she forgot herself and was walking back to Bond's house,' suggested Mariner.

'Is that the kind of thing you forget?'

'If she was that far gone . . . wait though, her nan's a Jehovah's witness, isn't she? She wouldn't think much of Christie arriving home drunk.'

'So?'

'What I'm saying is, maybe Christie knew she'd be in the doghouse if she went back to her nan's, and if she knew that Bond was away, his house was a safer bet. She probably still had keys.' But all they could do was speculate. 'Let's go and have another look at the scene.'

* * *

A light rain had begun to fall and it was the kind of dull late afternoon that would merge seamlessly into dusk and then night. The SOCOs were finishing off when Knox and Mariner arrived at the bridge. The distinctive tape had been wound round the wall, but despite the presence of a bored-looking uniform standing guard, the damp weather had seen off any onlookers.

Making himself known to the constable, Mariner walked to the middle of the bridge and peered over the stone parapet, down onto the track. It was a long way down. Amid the green of the surrounding trees, with the intermittent sound of birdsong, it didn't look like the scene of a grisly death. A little further down the track were signalling lights. The line had been reopened now and as they stood there a train approached, slowing and squealing to a halt as it reached the lights. After a ten-second pause it creaked into life again gradually gathering speed as it disappeared under their feet, but even then it would only have been doing about ten or fifteen miles an hour. That was how the driver had spotted her, slowing at the lights.

'This is the approach to Kingsmead station,' said Mariner as Knox walked over to where he stood.

'So?'

'The trains would be slowing down or starting to gather speed. Not the best place if you want it to be quick.'

'That's what the driver said. But she wouldn't have thought about that, would she?' Knox said. 'If she was in enough of a state to take her own life, I doubt she would have considered that detail, even if she knew it. To most people a railway line is a railway line.'

Mariner couldn't help thinking about Kenneth McCrae's attention to detail, even though a jury had concluded he was mentally ill. 'But what I'm saying is; a train wouldn't have killed her going at that speed.' Moments later there was a deep rumbling and the high speed express train roared by beneath them.

'That would do the trick though,' said Knox. 'Question is, was it an accident or intentional?'

Mariner stood back to survey the wall. The brickwork of the bridge was smooth, with nothing in the way of hand- or footholds. 'How tall d'you think she was?'

'Bit shorter than me,' said Knox, who stood at five foot nine. 'About five six or seven?'

The top of the wall was level with Mariner's chest. Stretching out his arms he heaved himself up to look over onto the line below. He was just about able to get the leverage to pull the upper half of his body on to the top of the wall, and from there he would have been able to scramble over, but it wasn't easy. Staring down at the receding track thirty feet below gave him slight vertigo. How desperate must Christie have been feeling to bring such a violent end to her life? He shuddered, before jumping back down, catching his breath. 'The wall's too high for it to be an accident,' he concluded, knowing that it wasn't what Tony Knox wanted to hear.

'So you're saying that it's suicide, even though she had things to look forward to and even though she was making plans?'

'She was a mixed up kid,' Mariner reminded him. 'She'd been knocked about over time, just split with her boyfriend and finished up back living with her nan. She blamed herself for Jessica's abduction—'

'That turned out all right though.'

'Alcohol distorts things too, doesn't it? It can leave you on a real downer. Maybe leaving Bond had more of an emotional impact than anyone thought, and spending the evening alone in — let's face it — what's a pretty bloody awful pub made her realise what she'd given up. It could be why she was headed back to Bond's house.'

'She'd walked quite a distance to get to here, though. Wouldn't she have sobered up a bit?' Knox was morose. 'Christ, if only I'd met her as planned—'

'You never did tell me what the better offer was.'

Knox told him.

'Ah.' It wouldn't have been the first time Knox had been led by the trousers.

'I suppose I saw it as an unmissable opportunity,' said Knox. 'Her ten-year-old son was—' he broke off.

'Was what?'

'There's something wrong here, boss. Christie can't have been hit by a train on this line in the early hours of Sunday morning. There were no trains running. The line was closed for essential maintenance.'

'You're sure about that?' said Mariner.

Knox told him about the conversation with Michael's mother. 'We'll have to verify it, of course, but Jean was pretty anxious about her dad's driving. If she could have put Michael on the train she would have done.'

'And the Transport Police didn't mention it?'

'Why would they? We didn't have a time of death when I spoke to them. They would have assumed that Christie was killed during Sunday night after the trains had restarted. It was Croghan who told me she'd been dead more than twenty-four hours. It's not the sort of thing he gets wrong.'

Back at Granville Lane, Knox phoned the Transport Police who were able to confirm what he already knew: that the line had been closed from ten o'clock on Friday night until ten on Sunday night. It took them back to

Stuart Croghan. 'We now know that there were no trains running at that time. Is it possible that Christie was dead before she was hit by the train?'

Croghan was doubtful. 'I can't see how. The impact injuries have to have been made when she was alive, because of the extent and nature of the haemorrhaging.'

'Could the fall onto the track have caused that?'

Croghan shook his head. 'Not a big enough drop.'

'The SOCOs didn't find much blood at the scene,' Knox remembered Olsen telling him.

'And therefore reached the conclusion that she'd been carried some distance by the train and that they were looking in the wrong place.'

'There is another alternative, of course,' said Mariner. 'That she wasn't hit by a train at all, but by a car.'

'Well, that's possible,' Croghan agreed. 'She died from impact injuries and because she was found on the railway track the natural conclusion is that a train caused them, but it's not certain. In any case we'll find out before long. There were paint flecks in her clothing and hair that I've sent off for analysis. Those will be able to tell us what kind of vehicle struck her.'

'Is there anything else?'

'Well, there are no signs of sexual assault, but as you already knew, she had very high levels of alcohol in her blood.'

'She was pretty drunk when she left the pub,' said Knox.

'As the proverbial newt, I'd say. And there are traces of gastric juices in her mouth, while her stomach is nigh on empty. I'd say she threw up somewhere along the way. We haven't had any rain to speak of since the weekend, so if you're trying to trace her last movements you could do worse than look for a pool of vomit.'

'Lovely.' Mariner grimaced.

'There's also the missing shoe,' said Croghan. 'If she was that drunk it's possible that she lost it before she got as far as the railway track.'

'Along with her handbag and phone.' Mariner added. The immediate area around the bridge and that end of the park had also been searched without a result. 'We can put out an appeal for them.'

He and Knox adjourned to his office, where Mariner pinned up the photo of Christie next to the photo of Madeleine. Two young lives ended for no clear reason.

'If Christie was hit by a car we can probably rule out suicide. It's not the most obvious or effective method.'

'—unless she deliberately stepped out in front of a vehicle.'

'It's messy though and by no means certain death. If you're serious about killing yourself that way you choose a busy road, something like a motorway. If she'd done that, even during the night it would have caused chaos and we'd have known about it. It makes it more likely to have been an accident, doesn't it? She could just have been the victim of a hit and run. She's drunk, staggers out into the road and is hit by a car or lorry. The driver panics, bundles her into his car or van, drives to a quiet spot on the railway line and throws her over the bridge to cover it up.'

'In which case, it could have happened anywhere in the area between the pub and the railway line.'

'Any reports of RTAs on Saturday night?' Mariner wondered.

'Don't remember seeing anything,' said Knox. 'But I'll check again.'

Mariner put together a press release including an appeal for anyone to come forward who may have witnessed or been involved in a hit and run. He put with it descriptions of Christie's handbag, phone and missing shoe.

'A witness is more likely. If someone went to the trouble of disposing of a body, I don't think we can count on them giving themselves up any time soon. Now we sit back and wait.'

* * *

Anna was 'out with friends' according to the note left on the kitchen table when Mariner got home that evening, so he made himself beans on toast and was enjoying the quiet when he heard the unmistakable twang of a text message arriving. It wasn't the sound of Mariner's alert, so it could only mean that Anna had left her phone behind. He should and could reasonably have ignored it, but something compelled him to look. He found the phone in the pocket of one of her many jackets and didn't much like what he saw. The message was from Gareth of all people, urging her to have a good time tonight. Did he know where she'd gone? It was more than Mariner did. He'd signed off with four kisses.

Mariner felt the first tickle of unease. He should have stopped there, but curiosity dictated that he check Anna's inbox as well. Opening and deciphering the messages was a laborious process, as he'd never really got used to text-talk, but what he found turned his stomach. Since they'd come back from Herefordshire only yesterday, there were half a dozen more messages from Gareth that Anna hadn't bothered to delete, all flirtatious to varying degrees and with kisses all over the place. Anna had replied to them all in the same tone. A lot of them referred to the planned move to Herefordshire that she seemed to be discussing in far more depth with Gareth than she ever had with Mariner. The last in particular caught his eye because of the enigmatic title: *Progress?* Anna's response shredded his heart. *No chance 2 talk yet Bp8tient 2gethersoonxxx.*

2gethersoon? What the hell did that mean? Mariner went to bed thinking that he wouldn't sleep. He'd lie awake and question Anna about it when she got home, and she'd have a perfectly rational explanation. But he remembered nothing until he woke the following morning, Anna curled up beside him in their bed, but facing away from him, as far as she could get. He had work to do, so he let her sleep on.

* * *

First thing, Mariner and Knox returned to Phyllis Gates' house to do a more methodical search of Christie's room. There was a monster of a four-wheel drive standing outside. The door was opened to them by a small black woman with a head of grey, tight curls. 'Who are you?' she demanded, eyeing them with suspicion.

Mariner produced his warrant card and made the necessary introductions. 'We're from the police.'

'Phyllis is very upset,' the woman told them, as if scolding a couple of inconsiderate little boys. 'She's not seeing visitors.'

'This isn't a social call. We need to have another look at Christie's room,' Mariner explained.

'I've seen you on the TV, haven't I?'

'Yes, you probably have.' It was enough to get them over the threshold at least. Considering she wasn't seeing visitors, there seemed to be a large number of voices emanating from Phyllis Gates' living room. A glimpse of the age, profile and dress code as the lounge door opened and closed told Mariner that they were probably church women, come to offer solace. The black woman disappeared and after what seemed like a lengthy consultation returned and allowed them up to Christie's room.

As they reached the landing, they met Trudy Barratt on her way down. She was clearly startled to see them, but then hadn't, as they had, been forewarned. 'Inspector, I didn't expect to see you here. I brought some flowers for Christie's grandmother, and had to "use the facilities."' It appeared she cared more about her staff than Mariner had first thought. 'Must be getting on though.' And she continued on down without another word.

‘What was she doing here?’ Knox wondered when they reached the landing.

‘Such a suspicious mind,’ said Mariner.

* * *

Undisturbed now for several days, the atmosphere inside Christie’s bedroom was stale and heavy, with the cloying smell of old makeup and perfume. On investigation, most of the black bin bags were found to contain clothing. ‘Christ, how many pairs of jeans does one girl need?’ Mariner said pulling out pair after pair in various shades of denim. But having gone through all the bags they were no nearer to finding Christie’s white handbag. Stacked plastic boxes contained scraps of multi-coloured paper, card and fabrics, clearly used for making children’s craft items for the nursery, and a cardboard carton held dozens of magazines of the celebrity variety, some of them with pictures and articles cut out.

They had almost come to the end before they actually found something of use — a box file containing a handful of personal documents, including cheque and paying in booklets. Among the papers were half a dozen recent bank statements, a couple of them complete with ringed stains from coffee mugs. There was never much in the account, though the regular monthly credits probably indicated her salary.

‘Is that all she gets?’ Mariner was astonished. ‘It only adds up to about ten thousand a year. It’s barely more than the minimum wage.’

‘Like Mrs Barratt said, I don’t suppose hers is considered a skilled job,’ said Knox.

‘No wonder these girls can’t wait to leave and have their own families.’

Also contained in the folder was a sales brochure for the flat that Christie had talked to her nan about buying. Side by side, the two items just didn’t add up.

'This is way out of her league,' said Mariner, reading the description of the luxury apartment. 'I could barely afford a place like this on my salary.'

'Kids these days have such unrealistic expectations,' Knox said. 'Our Gary thought he was going to move straight into his penthouse flat after uni.'

It wasn't only the kids, thought Mariner, remembering Heron's Nest. Even a grown and rational adult could have her head turned by the right temptation. He shelved the unwelcome distraction.

There was one other payment into Christie's bank account only three weeks ago. It corresponded with the scratch card win her nan had talked about, and was for the princely sum of five hundred pounds. 'That won't get her very far either,' Mariner observed. 'It wouldn't even make the deposit. And any pay rise she might have negotiated with Mrs Barratt wouldn't be that much. So where the hell did she think she was going to get the money for this flat?'

'Don't you think it's strange that none of the other girls at the nursery mentioned her win? Most people would want to celebrate something like that with their friends. They wouldn't keep it a secret.'

Mariner pulled a face, the significance of that lost on him for the moment. Downstairs the doorbell rang again and Mariner peered out of the window. 'Phyllis certainly has her support network in place,' he said, expecting to see more blue rinses. But he was wrong. 'Marcella Turner. Christ. What on earth is she doing here?'

Mariner descended the stairs to see Ms Turner standing on the doorstep, her mouth agape in a rare moment of speechlessness. Phyllis Gates' white-haired minder must have broken the news. Beside her was another younger woman, with pink spiky hair and wide black-framed glasses. The silence didn't last long.

'Oh, I'm so terribly sorry,' Turner was saying. 'We didn't know. Of course we wouldn't dream of intrud—'

But the younger woman had her notebook out at the ready and was not so easily deterred. 'Can you tell us what's happened?'

It was time for Mariner to intervene. In one swift and easy movement he leapt the remaining few stairs, swept past the minder and out into the garden, ushering the two visitors along with him as he went. 'As you can see,' he said, giving spiky hair a cold glare. 'This is not the right time. What are you doing here anyway?'

Marcella Turner was defensive. 'We came to talk to Christie.'

'About what?'

Spiky hair shrugged. 'About her experiences.'

'And you are—?' Mariner asked.

Spiky hair smiled broadly to reveal pearly white teeth, encircled by a vivid aubergine lipstick, oblivious to the contempt in his voice. 'Jez Barclay, assistant producer for Angelwood TV.'

'You're a television producer?' Mariner said with disbelief, ignoring the outstretched hand.

'That's right.' The woman fished in her pocket and came out with a business card, which Mariner pocketed without a glance. 'And you are—?' she asked, the smile remaining nonetheless.

'Detective Inspector Mariner. What did you want with Christie?' He was careful to use the past tense.

The look on Jez Barclay's face said that he'd already been a topic of discussion, but it was Marcella Turner who spoke up. 'During the kidnapping I got to know Christie a little. I found that she was sympathetic to my concerns about the government's childcare agenda. Jez's company specialises in fly-on-the-wall documentaries. Christie seemed willing. We were here to discuss terms.'

'And the story was baby Jessica?'

'In the first instance.'

'I trust you've got the parents' permission.'

'Oh, yes. Initially Miss O'Brien was going to take part, though she changed her mind about that, but she has given us her blessing. We've also spoken to your boss about the police viewpoint.'

'Have you really?' Mariner couldn't imagine Davina Sharp wanting to get involved, but he resisted asking what her reaction had been.

'Mrs Barratt at the nursery declined to contribute, and that was why we approached Christie.'

'You said "in the first instance,"' Mariner said.

'We were planning a follow-up, too. Christie offered to help us with an undercover exposé of what really goes on in the day-care sector.' The two women swapped glances, but not so fleetingly that Mariner didn't notice.

'But?' he prompted.

'At first we weren't really all that interested, because it's already been done. But then Christie called me back to say that she had a story we definitely would be interested in.'

'About what?'

'That's what we were here to find out. All she would tell me on the phone was that it was "a cracking good story." Unfortunately at the time we spoke, my diary was pretty full. The first time I had a window was today. Christie was going to fill me in.'

'How much pressure were you putting her under?'

'None at all. We were in preliminary negotiations — that was all. But she seemed very keen.'

'Had you discussed fees?'

'Only in general terms. Christie did seem pathetically excited by the initial offer and I did wonder if this "other story" might be her attempt to squeeze more money out of it. People do have a tendency to get greedy in these sorts of situations. And it seemed like a last-ditch thing. She left a message on my mobile late on Saturday night of all times.'

'Do you remember exactly what time?'

She thought for a moment. 'Let me see, we were still at Gill and Bill's. Must've been around eleven thirty. There was a lot of noise in the background, as if she was in a club or bar or something, and her speech was slurred, as if she'd been drinking. Celebrating in advance perhaps.' The pearly toothed smile flashed again.

'But you hadn't paid her anything at that stage?' said Mariner.

'Not a bean. It was way too soon for that. You can't pitch a project until you know exactly what you're getting, and even then it doesn't necessarily get the green light.'

'Did Mrs Barratt know about any of this?'

'Given her attitude towards me, I can't imagine that Christie would have told her,' said Marcella Turner. 'We weren't made to feel terribly welcome. I mean the whole kidnapping thing didn't exactly do the nursery any favours, did it? It wouldn't have gone down very well.'

'And there's no way she can have found out about what Christie was planning?'

'Not from our side.' Jez couldn't resist. 'How *did* she—?'

'Her body was found on the railway track, below a footbridge.'

'She threw herself under a train?' She gaped with horror.

Mariner took the official line. 'It's how it looks.'

'Go-d.' It was said slowly and pensively and Mariner could almost hear the cogs turning as she weighed up whether this in itself might be enough of a story. 'Do you think any of the other girls would be up for it?' Jez asked. She was staring into the middle distance and the question could have been directed at anyone.

'I think it's time you went,' Mariner said.

Jez smiled artfully. 'Your boss wasn't interested, but if you felt like giving us an interview, on or off the record—'

'Just go,' said Mariner.

Chapter Thirteen

Back in Christie's room Knox was continuing to work his way systematically through her things. He'd gathered together a small collection of evidence bags, containing anything he thought may be significant, but he had still uncovered no handbag, purse or mobile phone.

'We'll take what we've got with us,' said Mariner. As he went to pull the door closed behind them, he noticed pinned to the back, a month-to-view calendar with a photograph of some cute-looking puppies and space below to record any engagements.

'Springers,' said Knox, recognising the dog belonging to the lady in the park.

But Mariner was staring at the single entry made on the previous Tuesday, which said simply, *4:00 p.m. clinic.*

'What sort of clinic?' he wondered aloud.

'Could be anything,' said Knox, helpfully.

'She'd have been at work on Tuesday.' Mariner took out his phone and called Jack and the Beanstalk. He asked to speak to Joy. 'Christie had an appointment last Tuesday afternoon,' he said, when she finally came on.

'Oh yes, I remember, she left work early.'

'Do you know what it was for?'

'It was a doctor's appointment, I think.'

'She told you she was seeing a doctor?'

'I don't remember if she actually said that. She may have just told me it was an appointment and I assumed—'

'Thank you.' Mariner ended the call. 'That's not what she wrote though,' he said to Knox. He was thinking about the calendar at home in Anna's kitchen. 'If it's a doctor's appointment, that's what you write — "doctor." If it's a dentist's appointment she'd have written "dentist." Either Joy made an assumption or Christie told her that, to cover up what it really was. What clinics are there?'

'All sorts. Family planning?'

'But Christie had just finished with Jimmy Bond, so it wouldn't seem a particularly appropriate time for that. We'll ask her nan on our way out. Have we got everything?'

Even taking the processor of Christie's computer didn't amount to much. On their way out of the house Mariner managed to breach Phyllis Gates' security for long enough to question her about the appointment but, like Joy, she knew nothing about it. She was however, able to give them details of Christie's GP.

In the car Mariner reported back to Knox on his conversation with the two unwelcome visitors. 'Never mind that a girl has just died,' said Mariner in disgust. 'All they're interested in is a story.'

The health centre where Christie's GP was based held a waiting room full of people, many of whom were curious yet not impressed when Mariner flashed his warrant card and got almost immediate access to Dr Samirayah. He didn't side-track the doctor for long. As far as Dr Samirayah was concerned Christie had no health problems, nor any need to attend a clinic. He had made no referrals for her in the recent past, in fact, she hadn't been to the doctor in months.

'The only prescription I wrote in recent years was for the contraceptive pill, but she hasn't renewed for about eight months.'

Mariner escaped just a few minutes later past the glares of the waiting patients.

* * *

Back at Granville Lane there was a pile of phone messages requiring Mariner's response. He returned Louise Byrne's call straight away.

'Kenneth McCrae has been committed to Rampton secure psychiatric unit indefinitely. He won't have much fun there.'

'No, he won't,' said Mariner. It wasn't a prison sentence but they both knew it was the next best thing. 'Thanks for everything you did.'

'My pleasure, Tom. There is something else. McCrae's written you a letter of apology expressing remorse for what he's done. I need your permission to forward it.'

Mariner's gut lurched. 'Sure, why not?'

Next up Mariner got back to Stuart Croghan. 'You've got some results on the paint flecks?' he said.

'No. Something else I thought might interest you though. The baby remains from the Lickeys. When we ran tests on them the DNA profile jogged something in my memory. I checked back over recent cases and found a match.'

'You can identify the baby?'

'We're a step nearer,' said Croghan. 'Its mother was the woman you found in the sewer last Christmas.'

'Madeleine? Christ, you're sure?'

'As sure as I can be.'

'Wow. We knew at the time that she'd recently given birth.'

'And now you've found her baby, although sadly, it still doesn't tell us who she was.'

Still astonished. Mariner took the news over to where Charlie Glover was ploughing through the paperwork on his desk. He seized upon it. 'This gives us a new lead,' he said, eagerly. 'The baby had a cleft palate. Somebody would surely remember that?'

'But we don't know if she had the baby here or in Albania,' Mariner cautioned him. 'If she had him over there we haven't any idea of the extent of the medical care available. It wouldn't necessarily be recorded anywhere, so you'd be relying on someone to remember it, and where the hell would we start with that?' Glover was crestfallen. 'It might be worth checking round local health centres and hospitals here though. It's possible she had the baby here, though it will also of course depend on whether she was here legally.'

'How old was the baby?' Glover asked.

'Around four to six weeks according to Croghan, and he died at about the same time as Madeleine, so you're looking at him being born sometime in October or November of last year.'

'What I don't understand is, if Madeleine and her baby were killed at the same time, why not dispose of them both in the same way and put them both down the sewer?' queried Glover. 'Why go to the trouble of burying the baby in a different spot?'

'Perhaps whoever did it was squeamish about doing that with a baby.'

'Can I follow this up, boss?' Glover was already starting to stack papers, tidying his desk to leave it for a while. 'I could do a house-to-house in the row opposite the woodland, too. Someone may have seen whoever it was dumping the baby's body.'

Mariner hated to dampen his enthusiasm. 'Nine or ten months ago? It's asking a lot for anyone to remember that far back. And I can't imagine it was done in broad daylight either.'

'I know but . . .' Charlie hated loose ends too.

'All right then. It won't do any harm, I suppose.'

Croghan had given Mariner the number for the paint lab, and the technician there had come up with a positive result. Mariner couldn't think what would possess anyone to opt for a career that involved spending all day in a lab, examining bits of paint, but he was bloody grateful that someone had.

'The flecks of paint found in Christie Walker's clothing are without a doubt from a car, not a train,' said the technician at the end of the phone. 'I've compared it with the manufacturer's database and it's a DuPont Cayman green, a paint used on Ford Escorts up at Halewood from the early 1990s.'

'That's a long time span,' said Mariner.

'The last car rolled off the production line up there in July 2000, so you're looking for a car more than six years old. That should narrow it down for you. Also the top layer of paint was more loosely bound on some of the samples, so you're looking for a car that's had a partial re-spray.'

'But basically we're looking for a green, six-year-old Ford Escort.'

'That's about it.'

'Thanks.' It was a starting point. At last something tangible to look for.

Mariner contacted the DVLA for a list of Ford Escorts registered in the Birmingham area, though it was only going to help them if the driver believed in tax and insurance, and there were plenty who didn't. And the CCTV cameras in the car park of the Golden Cross were no help at all as they were out of commission.

'It would help if we could pinpoint exactly where Christie was struck,' Mariner said to Tony Knox. 'To have killed her it must have been quite an impact. There must have been damage to the car so there must be some evidence of it. At least if we could establish what route she might have taken—'

'And how do you propose we do that?'

'By taking Croghan's advice and looking for anything connected with Christie.'

'Like—?' The penny dropped and Knox screwed up his face in distaste. 'You mean the vomit.'

'It's all we've got.'

Assembling a small team, they began working outwards from the pub, but in a short time it became clear that it was going to take a long time. Even aiming for the direction that Christie would have taken to get to Jimmy Bond's house, they were very quickly presented with numerous alternative routes and each pavement was dappled with possible stains. The enormity of the task was just hitting home when Mariner's mobile rang. It was CID. 'We've had a call from a man who's seen Christie Walker's shoe.'

'Seen it? What does that mean?' It seemed an odd way of phrasing it.

'So he says, and it's kind of in the area you're looking at, between the Golden Cross and Jimmy Bond's house. I said you'd go and talk to him.'

Knox and Mariner went immediately down to Grange Road where Andrew Sawyer lived. Bordering on the university campus and once the home of manufacturing industries, in recent years the old factories had been torn down and student halls of residence erected in their place. Sawyer, it transpired, was a mature student, an academic renting a flat in the university's post-graduate accommodation. Even though his face said early thirties, he dressed like a middle-aged man in dark trousers, collar and tie, with a sleeveless pullover on top. Nor was his flat anything like any student accommodation Mariner had ever been into before, everything tidy and spotlessly clean. 'Would you like a cup of tea? I was just making one.'

It was hours since they'd had a drink and Mariner's throat was parched. 'Thanks.' Knox declined the offer. Sawyer disappeared into the kitchen.

As they'd driven up, the street outside had been deserted, Sawyer seemingly the only resident in the block, a point that Mariner remarked on now.

'Yes, most of the other students aren't back yet after the summer break,' Sawyer explained, disappearing into the kitchen area. 'Give it a couple of weeks and it'll be quite different.'

'You must feel quite isolated here,' Mariner called after him.

'Not really, I quite like the peace. I'm working on my doctorate,' came the disembodied voice in reply. 'It demands a high level of concentration.'

'What's your subject?'

'The impact of electro-magnetic fields on planetary orbits.'

'Oh.' It was a real conversation killer.

Sawyer reappeared moments later carrying a tray with two mugs and a plate of chocolate digestives.

'So, the shoe?' Mariner asked, thanking him and taking one of the mugs.

'I saw it lying on the pavement when I went to the library. I remembered thinking "how strange," because it was a nice shoe and quite new. It's quite amazing, isn't it? The number of times you see just an odd shoe lying in the road, but they're usually old and worn through. During term time I'd have simply assumed that one of the undergraduates had lost it on the way home after a drunken night out. Then I saw the appeal on TV and recognised it; a blue and white striped canvas ballet shoe, with a buckle trim.'

Mariner was impressed with the level of detail. 'And where is it now?' he asked.

'I don't know. When I realised it was the same shoe, I went out to fetch it, but it was gone.'

'When was this?'

'First thing this morning. I caught it on the breakfast news.'

But the first appeal had gone out yesterday evening, meaning that someone else could have seen it then, and returned to the scene to retrieve the shoe. Either that or they were dealing not with a genuine witness, but an attention-seeker, with a possible shoe fetish.

'Can you take us to where you saw it?' Mariner asked.

'Of course.' On their way out Sawyer lifted an anorak off the hook in the hall. Mariner wouldn't have expected anything else.

Sawyer took them back out onto the road, still eerily quiet, walking back towards the Bristol Road until they were about equidistant between a sharp right-hand bend at one end and the main road at the other. He looked in both directions to judge the distances, then concluded: 'It was around here.'

'You're certain?'

'I have a photographic memory. That was how I recognised the shoe when I saw it on TV.'

Debris crunched underfoot. It was glass, the thick glass that shields car headlights. It might be just enough to make Sawyer a credible witness. Mariner scooped some of it up into an evidence bag and he and Knox scoured the road for any traces of paint. SOCO would need to come and make a more thorough search.

'And you saw only the shoe here? There was nothing else?'

'Like what?'

Mariner shrugged. 'Any other personal belongings?' He didn't want to make any suggestions.

'No, there was nothing like that.'

'Have you been aware of any disturbances out here during the past few days?' Mariner was careful not to lead Sawyer.

'A couple of nights ago I must have dozed off in the chair, because I woke suddenly in the early hours. I thought I'd heard a noise but then realised it was just a car door slamming.'

'A door or a boot?' asked Mariner.

'Hm, I thought door, but I suppose it could have been the boot. It's hard to tell the difference, isn't it? It was pretty late, after midnight, so I did get up and have a look, but the car was just pulling off as I got to the window. It would have been about here, I suppose.'

'Did you see what make the car was, or what colour?'

'I'm not very good with cars, but it was quite a smallish one and a dark colour. I think it might have been a hatchback.'

'You didn't happen to see the number plate?'

'I'm afraid not, I expect it was shadowed.'

So much for the photographic memory. 'Any idea which night this was?'

Sawyer thought hard. 'It must have been Saturday, well, early Sunday morning really.'

'Have you seen the same car back here since then, say, yesterday evening?'

'No, but then I wasn't really looking.'

'Do you drive, Mr Sawyer?'

'No. I ride a bicycle.' No big surprise there either.

Before leaving Grange Road, Mariner walked again to the spot where Sawyer claimed the shoe had been.

'The timing would be about right,' Knox said. 'The barmaid at the Golden Cross said Christie left at about midnight. The accident woke Sawyer up first, driver jumps out of the car slams the door and/or the boot. By the time Sawyer gets to the window the car's pulling away.'

'I have a problem with the hit and run accident scenario though,' Mariner was frowning.

'Which is?'

'Look at the width of this pavement. There's no need for Christie to even have been in the road.'

'Unless she'd chosen to walk there. She was drunk, remember.'

'But approaching this spot from either end a driver would have had to slow down, either to turn the corner into the street, or to round a sharp bend, and he wouldn't by this point have picked up much speed. The street lights are new and there are plenty of them. It's so well lit, he must clearly have seen any pedestrian and would have had the time and space to swerve and avoid them.'

'Unless he'd been drinking too, or worse,' said Knox.

'But who would need to drive along here at night anyway? Sawyer seems to be the only person living here. For Christie on foot it was an obvious shortcut through from the university campus to get up to Jimmy Bond's house, but it's not a through road for drivers. It doesn't go anywhere.'

'Joyriders?'

'That's a possibility,' agreed Mariner. 'Or if someone wanted to hurt Christie deliberately, it'd be a good place to do it.'

'You think someone was following her?' said Knox.

'The route between the pub and the university is all public roads and would have been fairly busy late on a Saturday night, so too risky. But if the driver knew where Christie was going, he could have watched her walk onto the campus then driven round and waited for her to emerge on this side. With the students away, this area's like a ghost town. He could have reasonably expected no witnesses at all.'

'He?'

'Okay,' conceded Mariner, 'it could have been "she," but whoever it was would need to be strong enough to lift Christie's body and heave it over the bridge parapet.'

'So why bother to move the body?'

'Because eventually it would be found, along with the broken glass from his headlights and any other forensic evidence that might lead us to the killer. Having knocked her down, the first thing he'd want to do is dump the body away from the scene of the accident. It's what, about a mile from here to the railway bridge? The only thing he failed to notice was that her shoe had come off.

Fortunately for him, we tipped him off with last night's TV appeal, giving him time to come back and retrieve it.'

'So what's the motive?' asked Knox, as they got back in the car.

'Where do we start? We come back to Jimmy Bond for a start off. Did he believe that Christie had shopped him, or is he just pissed off because she left him?'

'He's got a pretty firm alibi.'

'I'll bet he's got some interesting contacts too, though; said Mariner. 'And what about this TV documentary Christie was going to do? I bet Trudy Barratt wouldn't have been very happy about that. She wasn't going to admit it to us, but the nursery has clearly suffered as a result of the abduction. A documentary rehashing and sensationalising Jessica's abduction would have opened up old wounds and brought back all the adverse publicity for the nursery, especially if Marcella Turner's involved. She'd make sure of it.'

'How would Trudy Barratt have found out?'

'She already knew a documentary had been proposed, and Christie could have been using it to force a pay rise. Trudy Barratt told us that the heated meeting with Christie was about trying to keep her, and involved offering her more money. Perhaps she was being economical with the truth. Was Christie trying to blackmail the manager? It would explain why she was smiling when she came out of the office, and why she thought she would be able to afford a flat on the Bristol Road development.'

'Yeah, but people like Trudy Barratt don't go around killing, do they?'

'She might if she's desperate enough. We both know it happens. Jack and the Beanstalk is Trudy Barratt's livelihood, and she's already taken a battering. Then there's this "other story" that Christie told the TV producer she had. We don't know what that was. Maybe it's something else going on in the nursery.'

'—if it was anything at all. As the producer said, it could have been just a cynical ploy to screw more money out of the TV company.'

'Christie didn't call Jez Barclay about it until very late on Saturday night, after you stood her up,' said Mariner.

'Thanks for the reminder.'

'What I mean is, perhaps Christie had uncovered something illegal, something she thought you'd want to know about. When she couldn't tell you about it she decided to go public instead.'

'Or maybe this has nothing to do with me,' Knox said. He preferred it that way.

'We could do with talking to her friends again and finding out if anyone else knew about her discussions with the TV company.'

* * *

Back at Granville Lane they were greeted by Charlie Glover who was almost beside himself.

'You won't believe this, boss. I went back to finish the house-to-house last night, and I've found a guy who remembers seeing a man going into the woods late one night last year. He says it was definitely around November 5 because it was the fireworks that had kept him awake. He thought the bloke had gone into the woods for a slash but he went right into the woods and was gone for ages. He's sure he was carrying a bag of some sort too.'

'That's great,' said Mariner, wondering how soon it would be before Charlie realised how thin that was.

'Yeah, only thing is, the description doesn't match Alecsander Lucca. Lucca was short and stocky. According to this witness, the man going into the woods was tall and slim.'

'But it's something.'

'Yeah, something . . .'

Mariner and Knox returned to his office to look again through Christie's meagre belongings. 'Shame she didn't keep a diary,' he said, taking out the bank statements. Something fell out, a bright orange flyer that fluttered to the floor by Knox's feet.

Knox picked it up. 'What about this?' he held up the flyer for Mariner to see. *Fertility. New hope for childless couples. Telephone confidentially . . .*'

'What do you make of that?' he asked.

Mariner read it. 'Bond talked about wanting to settle down and start a family, but according to him, Christie wasn't interested.'

'And yet she came off the pill eight months ago,' said Knox, taking back the leaflet. He scanned it again. 'Perhaps Bond was lying. If they'd been trying unsuccessfully for a baby it's not something he'd want to own up to. It'd put a nice big dent in his macho image, wouldn't it?'

'But Christie was how old, twenty-four? Isn't that young for fertility treatment?'

'Unless she or Bond had some specific problem that they knew would affect their chances. It would explain that clinic appointment last Tuesday.'

'Given what Christie's GP said it must have been Bond's problem; his little swimmers not doing the business. He's quite a bit older than she was. It might explain why he let her go without a fight, too.'

'Yeah, I doubt that Bond would be the type to want to dwell on that particular failing.'

'It wouldn't be something that he'd want broadcast either. Does that give him a further motive?'

'To kill her?'

'It'd be quite a humiliation, 'specially as he's playing away as well. His bit on the side probably doesn't know.'

But Mariner wasn't so sure. 'It's a bit flimsy.'

Knox tried the number on the flyer. It was unobtainable.

'Let's see what else Christie was interested in.' Mariner put a call through to IT, who were examining her computer. 'You yanking my chain?' said Max, cheerfully. 'Give us five minutes at least.' It was a further hour before they had a call back.

'Is there anything?' Mariner tried not to sound too impatient.

'Well it's a pretty new machine,' Max told him. 'So there's not much on it, but if it's any use, the internet history list shows that she'd been looking at the local property market, some stuff about childcare and adoption agencies, here and abroad.'

Knox tapped a finger on the flyer still sitting in Mariner's desk. 'It's consistent at least. It's all stuff you do if you want a baby and can't conceive. If Christie was looking into adoption, it would confirm difficulties in that area too.'

'Madonna and Angelina have done their bit to make overseas adoption fashionable and we saw how much Christie liked her celebrity magazines. They're full of that kind of stuff.'

Mariner was pensive. 'It might be worth checking if Christie and Bond were known to the fertility unit up at the QE. I think I'll have a wander up there.'

'Okay.'

* * *

The north car park at the hospital looked oddly familiar, giving Mariner an unpleasant sense of déjà vu on two counts. It was the car park he and Anna had come to after the miscarriage when Anna had visited the consultant. It was also identical to the south car park, viewed in the hours of CCTV footage that had been running in the incident room just a couple of weeks before. Outside the multi-storey, he followed the pedestrian signs to the fertility department.

Decorated in subtle tones of grey and blue, it was like any other hospital division. Mariner approached the young woman behind the open reception desk and, after identifying himself, asked if they had any record of James Bond and/or Christie Walker. 'Miss Walker may have had an appointment here last Tuesday at four o'clock,' he added.

The girl checked her computer. 'There's no record of a Miss Walker or Mr Bond for last Tuesday,' she said. 'I think I'd probably remember the name too. I'll go and see if we have them on the system at all. I won't keep you a moment.'

While he waited Mariner perused the notice boards, hoping, though without reward, that he might see the orange flyer.

'Hello. It's Chief Inspector Mariner, isn't it?' The woman who approached Mariner, inadvertently promoted him. Mariner returned her gaze without recognition, though there was something about the smile.

'Sheila Fry,' she reminded him.

Of course. Mentally retracing his steps he realised that he must be practically next door to the office responsible for administering the crèche.

'You work in this department?' he asked.

'I'm a counsellor,' said Sheila. 'But don't worry, discretion is our watch word.' She smiled knowingly and it occurred to Mariner that she thought he was here for personal reasons. He decided not to disabuse her.

She glanced across at the empty reception desk. 'Is someone taking care of you?'

'Yes, thank you.'

'It was wonderful, wasn't it, that baby Jessica was found safe? I cried when I heard about it. Such a relief.'

'It was,' agreed Mariner.

Happily then she took the hint that he didn't want to chat. 'Right, well, I must get on. Things to do, places to go. But nice to see you again.' And with another bright smile she was on her way.

Moments later the clerk returned. 'I'm sorry,' she told Mariner. 'We have no record of anyone with those names having had a consultation here.'

A thought occurred. 'Would anyone use a pseudonym, a false name?' Mariner asked.

The girl looked doubtful. 'It's unlikely. We'd need a full medical history. There are several private clinics in the area though. Would you like the details?'

'Yes, thank you.'

Mariner took the orange flyer out of his pocket. 'Have you ever seen one of these?'

The woman gazed at it, taking in the detail. 'It's not one that we give out, I'm sure,' she said.

'Thanks.'

Calls to the other clinics in the area revealed that Christie Walker and James Bond had not been patients at any of those either.

'I think we need to talk to Jimmy Bond again,' Mariner concluded.

Chapter Fourteen

Mariner took Tony Knox along with him to Bond's garage. 'His alibi might check out, but he has access to all kinds of cars,' he remarked as they pulled onto the edge of the forecourt. 'While I'm talking to Bond, you have a mooch round and see if he's got a pre-2000 Escort in Cayman green that may have had a re-spray. I'm sure any damage to the car will have been repaired by now.'

While Tony Knox wandered around outside, Mariner joined Bond in his tiny cramped office that smelled of engine oil and body odour. Bond was fidgety, struggling to sit still for more than a couple of seconds and reluctant to look Mariner in the eye, but then, he already had a charge of wasting police time hanging over his head, so Mariner guessed he wouldn't have been thrilled to see them back again today.

'You and Christie were thinking of settling down,' Mariner said, reiterating what Knox had told him.

'I was. She didn't want to.' Bond was belligerent, but he rubbed his eye as he said it.

'Did that include children?' asked Mariner.

Bond shrugged. 'It's what you do, isn't it? I want to have kids before I get too old to play football with them'

'So you and Christie were trying for a family?'

'What the hell's that got to do with anything?'

'Just answer the question.'

'Not really.'

'So you hadn't been experiencing any problems in that area?'

Bond's eyes narrowed. 'What area are we talking about?'

'Conceiving.'

Bond bristled. 'Like I said, we hadn't really been trying, so I wouldn't know.' He seemed so indifferent that Mariner had little choice but to believe him.

After the stale office Mariner was glad to get outside again. He met up with Knox back at the car. 'Any luck?'

Knox shook his head. 'They're all too new, and no Fords that I can see. Mr Bond prefers Japanese cars. You find out anything useful?'

'Not really,' Mariner recapped on the conversation. 'For once I think he was being straight with me.'

'It doesn't mean that Christie didn't want a baby, though,' said Knox. 'She worked in a nursery, she obviously liked kids. Maybe she just didn't want Bond's kids and after she'd ditched him she decided to go it alone. It's very fashionable these days. That's a big celebrity thing too, and she read the right magazines.'

'Taking on a new flat at the same time?' Mariner was dubious.

'She thought she was coming into some money, thought she could have it all.'

'Let's have another word with Trudy Barratt.'

But when they got to the newly re-branded ABC Nursery, Mrs Barratt wasn't there. 'She's at Little Beans,' Samantha told them.

'Little Beans?'

'It's her other nursery. Shall I phone ahead to tell her that you're coming?'

'No, thanks. That's fine.'

'How well did you know Christie?' Mariner asked Samantha.

'As well as anyone, I guess.'

'Did you know that she was to take part in a TV documentary about the kidnapping of baby Jessica?'

'No.' If she was lying, she did it convincingly. 'I know someone had approached Mrs Barratt, but she made it clear that we weren't interested. God, Mrs B would throw a fit if she knew—' Samantha broke off, suddenly aware of what the inference might be. 'I mean, that's true . . . but she wouldn't . . .'

'It's all right, Samantha,' Mariner reassured her. 'I know exactly what you mean. Did Christie ever talk to you about having children, of her own?'

'Sometimes. We all do. Like, you hear a nice name or something and think, I'd like to call mine that.'

Hopefully not Leopold, thought Mariner. 'Do you think Christie was planning on having a child any time soon?'

'She'd have a job, wouldn't she? She'd just split up from Jimmy and everything. Christie used to say that he wanted kids though.' They were back where they'd started, and in more ways than one. Little Beans turned out to be situated on the corner of Foundry Road, just a few hundred yards from where Mariner and Knox had sat a couple of weeks earlier at dawn for operation Ocean Blue. It prompted Mariner to wonder how the girls they'd brought in were making out. There was no off-road parking, consequently the street was lined with vehicles and Knox had to drive some way up before wedging the car into a meagre space between an old and battle-scarred Fiesta and a skip. 'Do you think Mrs Barratt's aware that six doors down from her nursery there's a knocking shop?' Mariner said to Knox as they got out of the car.

'Ex-knocking shop,' Knox reminded him. 'She may know, but I bet the parents don't.'

'I'll go and talk to her. Why don't you have a look for her car, give it the once over.'

The building that housed Little Beans was of the same era as ABC, and with the same cartoon characters painted on the windows. The artist had a limited repertoire. The layout inside the nursery was very similar too. Once admitted Mariner found Trudy Barratt in her office shredding paperwork. 'Data protection act,' she said, by way of an explanation. 'It's a pain in the neck.' She posted the last sheets into the machine, then gestured Mariner to a chair before sitting herself. 'How can I help?'

'Had you any idea that a TV company had been in contact with Christie about taking part in a documentary covering Jessica's abduction?' Mariner asked.

'I knew they were planning a documentary. Some obnoxious young woman accosted me outside Jack and the Beanstalk. She wanted to feature the nursery. Put up to it by Marcella Turner no doubt.'

'You weren't interested?'

Trudy Barratt regarded him coldly. 'I'm trying very hard to put the whole episode behind us, Inspector. I didn't know they had gone after Christie too.'

'So Christie didn't try to blackmail you about it?'

Her eyebrows rose half an inch. 'Certainly not.'

'The TV producer seemed to think that Christie might have something else on her mind that would be good for primetime TV,' Mariner went on. 'Any idea what that could have been?'

'Not the faintest.'

The conversation had nowhere else to go, and minutes later Mariner met Knox back at the car. 'Did you find the four-by-four?'

'Not a mark on it, boss.'

'Well, no great surprise.' Mariner looked up and down the street. 'Do you get the sense that there's something we're missing?'

'A perp?' ventured Knox.

* * *

Mariner was back at Granville Lane, reviewing the policy book and wondering where to go next with this when Charlie Glover burst into his office. 'This gets better and better, boss.'

Leaning back in his chair, Mariner rubbed a hand down his face. Hopefully this was better news. 'Go on.'

'SOCO took samples of forensic material from all the places we raided on Ocean Blue, looking for traces of drugs mainly, as well as trying to match the men we arrested with the properties the girls were taken from. They've been cross-referencing and have found an interesting match.'

'Which is?'

'They found some hairs that match with Madeleine's DNA profile. They're from the house on Foundry Road.'

Foundry Road. Why did they keep coming back there? 'So she was a sex worker?'

'She must have been.'

'Well, it would explain why no one came forward who recognised her,' Mariner said.

'I'd like to talk to the girls we brought in on Ocean Blue,' Glover said. 'Some of them have been in this country a while. They might remember her. I'm asking the DCI if I can go down to the immigration centre.'

Mariner sorted through the papers on his desk, until he came to the Ocean Blue interview notes. 'You might not need to go that far.' How long did Katarina say she had been in this country? Finding the right page, he scanned it for the relevant data. 'Katarina has been here about a year, according to this. It's possible she could have known Madeleine.'

'This means we might find out who Madeleine really was.' Glover's enthusiasm was infectious and the possibility of a breakthrough sent a ripple of anticipation through CID. Not until now had Mariner realised the impact of not knowing Madeleine's true identity — and how it had affected them all.

* * *

Most of the girls brought in on Ocean Blue had, by now, been sent to an immigration centre before being repatriated, but as Katarina had agreed to testify against her abductors, she was staying for the moment at the Daffodil Project hostel. Mariner contacted Lorelei Fielding and made an appointment to go with Charlie to meet her. The hostel was an anonymous sixties-built council house in the middle of an estate, and was a refuge for abused woman of all backgrounds. It occurred to Mariner that in different circumstances, Christie may have ended up here too.

They were shown into a sunny lounge to wait and when Katarina appeared Mariner hardly recognised her. Dressed in T-shirt and jeans she looked nothing like the wretch they had interviewed three weeks previously, but just like any other nineteen-year-old young woman. She'd put on weight and her skin looked healthier, her hair, which had hung lank to her shoulders, was fair and almost blonde and seemed to have grown thicker and glossier. The pocket of her jeans trailed the earphones of an iPod. When Mariner stepped forward to shake her hand she brushed past it and instead put her arms around him for the briefest of hugs. 'Thank you,' she said, releasing him and stepping back, 'you saved my life.'

Mariner cleared his throat, discomfited by the display of affection. 'You're being looked after?' he asked, though the evidence spoke for itself.

'The food is a little—' she held up a flattened palm, dipping it one way then the other. 'Not much oysters or caviar.' She broke into a smile that pricked at Mariner's eyes; her sense of humour had resurfaced. 'I'm very good, thank you.' It was a response to more than simply his enquiry.

They sat again around the small low table. 'We want to ask you about a girl who we believe also once lived at the house in Foundry Road, the house we took you from.'

Glover opened Madeleine's folder and took out the mocked up photograph. 'Did you know her?' he asked. They had no way of knowing how accurate the picture was, so it would be hit or miss.

Katarina studied the picture carefully and at length before looking up at Glover, a pained expression on her face. 'I don't think so. I'm sorry.'

'She had a baby,' Glover persisted, hoping to prompt something.

For his sake Katarina looked again, she wanted so much to help, but finally shook her head. 'She's gone?' she asked.

'She's dead.'

She turned back to the picture, her bottom lip quivering. Mariner knew what she was thinking: *that could have been me.*

'Will you be showing it to the other girls?' Lorelei asked.

'Yes,' said Mariner 'It means we'll have to travel down to the immigration centre.'

'You'll need an interpreter.' She glanced across at Katarina.

'Well they have access to—' Mariner began, before catching on to what Lorelei was getting at. 'Yes,' he said. 'We will. Katarina will you come and interpret for us?'

The girl's face lit up. 'Of course.'

'Thank you,' said Lorelei, showing them out. 'She worries about the other girls. It'll be good for her to see that they are okay. It will help her to move on.'

'It seems like you're doing a terrific job already,' said Mariner. 'She looks like a different person.'

'It's a job that shouldn't have to be done.'

* * *

Driving back to Granville Lane, Glover was like a dog with two tails. 'Helen will be chuffed to bits if we find out who she was,' Glover said.

'How long have you two been married now?' Mariner asked.

'Ten years last March,' Glover said.

'That's quite an achievement.'

'You said it. Specially in this job.'

'What's the most important thing, do you think?'

Charlie didn't miss a beat. 'Trust,' he said.

* * *

It had been a long day. Mariner went home hoping for a shower and an early night. He found Anna getting ready to go out with friends from work. Her greeting to him was perfunctory. 'Have you seen my phone?' she asked. 'I couldn't find it this morning.'

'It's in the pocket of your brown jacket.' Mariner knew it was a bad idea but he couldn't resist adding: 'You've had a message, from Doctor Gareth.'

'Oh.'

'In fact, you had quite a few messages from him yesterday.'

Her reaction was telling. 'What the hell were you doing, going through my messages?'

'I was curious,' said Mariner. 'You two seem to have a lot to talk about.'

She met his gaze. 'He's a nice guy, uncomplicated.'

'As opposed to—?'

She simply shot him a meaningful look.

'Thanks. What was it that you "haven't had the chance" to talk to me about?' Mariner persisted.

Suddenly it was harder for her to maintain eye contact. 'I've handed in my notice at work,' she said. 'I'm going to take the receptionist's job. It's a great opportunity and I'd be silly not to.'

'We're not discussing this?'

'Like I said to Gareth, we haven't had the chance. When are you ever here to discuss anything? Besides, we've been "discussing" moving out of the city for almost a year now and we're no further forward. If I don't take this chance soon it'll be lost.' Her words rushed out. She was hiding something.

'I've put in for a transfer but nothing has come up.' Mariner defended himself. 'These things take time.'

'Not this much time. You've been dragging your heels on this from the beginning because it's not really what you want, is it? I think it's time for a fresh start.'

'I thought that was what this is all about.'

'No. I mean a real fresh start.' Her eyes locked onto his.

It took a couple of seconds for the underlying message to hit its target. 'Without me,' Mariner said, when finally it did.

'Let's be honest, it's not the sort of life you really want, is it?' said Anna. 'You were miserable down there, like a fish out of water.'

'Because I play dominoes?'

'You know what I mean. You hardly spoke to anyone that week.'

'What did you expect?' Mariner retorted. 'I was knackered after the abduction case and had the trial coming up. I had a lot on my mind.'

'You always have a lot on your mind.'

'And Doctor Gareth doesn't?'

'Don't keep calling him that!' she snapped. 'His name is Gareth. And of course he has a lot on his mind, he's a GP. It's just that he knows where to draw the line between work and play. He's good fun.'

'Life isn't always about fun.' Mariner could feel his defences rising.

'Life is never about fun with you anymore.'

Mariner had a sudden recollection of the odd way that she had greeted him when he got to the pub in Upper Burwell, and her reluctance to engage in any intimacy with him. Realisation rendered him temporarily speechless. Finally he had to ask; 'Are you sleeping with him?' From her avoidance of eye contact he knew immediately that she was. He waited out the silence.

'Once,' she said, eventually. 'It was just before you came down for the christening. I hadn't intended to, it just sort of happened. I'm really sorry, Tom.' She reached out and stroked his arm. 'It hasn't happened again, but I want to. It feels right. I think I'm in love with him.' She glanced up, her eyes glistening.

'Bloody hell,' said Mariner. 'It's all pretty sudden, isn't it?'

'Not really. I've always liked Gareth, you know that.'

'This is about more than liking him. When did it get to be more?'

'I guess it started to develop back in April if you must know.'

'After you lost the baby, *our* baby?' Christ, it was Mariner's idea that she should go and spend some time with Becky. How stupid was that?

'Gareth was so sweet.' Anna allowed herself a smile. 'He understood. He had the time to talk to me.'

'I would have talked to you, but you didn't want to.'

'I know. I think it helped that Gareth wasn't emotionally involved.'

'It certainly helped him.'

Her eyes flashed. 'At least this isn't some sordid little one night stand.'

Wow. He wasn't expecting that. 'Millie? That was years ago, and it was completely different.' But as he said it he had to question whether it really was.

She gave a weary sigh and reached out for his hands, taking them in hers. 'Things haven't been right between us for a long time, have they, even since before the bombing. I get the idea that you're only going along with this move to please me, and that's not a good enough reason. It should be because it's what you want too. I think this is better for both of us. In a way it might not be the worst thing that we lost the baby. The time wasn't right for us and I don't think it ever will be. I'm sorry. I can't help the way I feel.'

'Obviously,' said Mariner, recognising that her decision was made. 'When are you going?'

'At the weekend probably. I'll stay with Becky and Mark until I can find a place. I've got to get ready to leave here anyway. The agents will be exchanging contracts in the next couple of weeks, and then I'll have to move out.'

'I think I'll go and stay at my house tonight,' said Mariner, after a moment.

She made no attempt to stop him.

* * *

On his way over, Mariner stopped at the off-licence and picked up some bottles of the strongest beer he could find. It felt unreal and beyond comprehension that after all he and Anna had been through in the last few years, it wasn't enough to keep them together. Sitting in an armchair in the lounge, the room around him began to get blurred around the edges. Rubbing a hand over his eyes he found that his face was wet.

Mariner woke up the following morning, still in the armchair surrounded by a collection of empty brown bottles. His mouth was dry and he had a slight headache, but the biggest pain filled up his chest, which felt as if someone had been stamping all over it all night. And as his mind replayed the previous evening his eyes began watering again. An hour later he was showered and dressed in time for Charlie Glover to pick him up, but he could tell from Glover's face that he still looked like shite and he was grateful that Charlie could read his body language well enough not to ask what was wrong.

They stopped off at the Daffodil to collect Katarina, with Lorelei as a chaperone, and after initial greetings and light conversation everyone seemed content to sit back and watch the scenery go by, such as it was on the southbound M6. At the Catthorpe interchange Glover took the A14 towards Huntingdon to the immigration compound at Oakington, a fenced in collection of boxy, temporary-looking buildings that could equally have been a prison complex or a university campus.

After passing through heavy security, Mariner and Glover were taken to wait in a small windowless room, while Lorelei and Katarina went to speak to the other girls. The two men sat for what seemed like an age, watching the minute hand of the wall clock tick slowly round. Half an hour later Katarina reappeared and for a moment Mariner thought they'd had a wasted a journey, until he spied the small, slight figure almost hidden from view behind her. 'This is Valenka,' Katarina told them. She spoke to the girl in a language that wasn't English and the girl tentatively reached out to Mariner and passed him a small snapshot. It wasn't the picture they'd given Katarina, but a real photograph, probably taken on an instant camera, of a young girl cradling a newborn.

'This is her friend Nadia, after her baby came,' Katarina told them, as Mariner and Glover stared down at a snapshot of the girl they'd all come to know as Madeleine. Her hair seemed a little darker than in the reconstruction, but other than that there was no doubt.

'Bloody hell, it's her,' breathed Glover.

'It's a baby boy?' Mariner asked.

The girl nodded assent. 'She called him Nikolai.'

From his pocket Glover retrieved a polythene packet containing the silver crucifix that they had retrieved from Madeleine's body.

'Do you recognise this?' he asked. Valenka nodded miserably in reply.

'What can she tell us about Nadia?' Mariner asked inviting the girls to sit.

Valenka spoke and Katarina translated for her, a strange halting conversation.

'Nadia was already living in the house when I came here. She was kind to me and we became friends. Nadia was already pregnant then but she hadn't told anyone. She was afraid because she wanted to keep her baby but she knows that if they find out they will make her get rid of it.'

'Who's "they?"'

'The men who brought her to the house.'

Mariner took out a picture of Alecsander Lucca. 'Is this one of them?'

But it was a moot question. He only had to see the sheer terror on her face. She gabbled something to Katarina, who repeated to Mariner, 'He's coming back?'

'It's all right,' said Glover. 'He's dead. But so is her friend Nadia.'

At the translation the girl's eyes widened and she shook her head. Katarina hadn't told her. 'No. She went home.'

'We found her body ten months ago. We recently found the body of her baby.'

The girl took the news with blank resignation, but her eyes filled up and a single tear trailed down her cheek. Suddenly the room felt hot and claustrophobic.

'What happened when Lucca found out about the baby?' Mariner asked.

'He says she can keep it if she works until one month before it will be born.'

'Dear God, she's eight months pregnant and she's turning tricks,' said Glover in disgust.

'Some men like it,' said Katarina. It was a simple observation.

'Where did Nadia have the baby?'

Valenka picked up the story. 'They take her to another house. I thought they had gone to the hospital, but when she came back she says it was another house. There was . . . a baby nurse—' Katarina, translating, groped for the right word.

'Midwife?' Glover volunteered. 'A nurse who delivers babies?'

'Yes the midwife come. She stay there for a few days and then they take the baby from Nadia. They tell her they will take it back to Albania to be cared for by her family.'

'Did she see the midwife? Can she tell us what she looked like?' asked Mariner.

'I don't see her. I only hear her in another room, talking to Nadia.'

'And afterwards Nadia came back to the house on Foundry Road, the house where we found you?'

'Yes, but only for two, maybe three days and then she left again. I ask where she is and they tell me she has gone home to be with her baby. I am surprised because I know that Nadia owes them money for bringing her here, and we are never allowed to go out of the house. And she leave the picture behind.' Valenka leaned forward and picked up the snapshot. Tears were streaming down her face by now and she brushed them away, murmuring something unintelligible to Glover and Mariner.

'Did Lucca take Nadia's baby?' Mariner asked.

'No. Lucca bring her to this country. The big man take the baby.'

'The big man? Does he have a name?'

'Zjelic, she thinks Zjelic.'

Mariner and Glover exchanged a look. 'Could it be Zjalic?' Mariner asked. They had interviewed a Serbian, Goran Zjalic, as part of the murder enquiry at the address where Lucca lived. At the time Zjalic had claimed that he and Lucca just happened to live in the same house and they'd had no reason to disbelieve him.

Katarina translated and Valenka nodded miserably. 'Maybe.' said Katarina.

'What else does she know about Nadia?' Glover asked. 'Another name, her birth date or where she is from? We want to find her family to tell them what has happened.'

Valenka was able to provide them with Nadia's family name, her age and the name of the town she came from. They hoped it would be enough.

'Will Valenka come back with us to do a formal interview — make a statement?'

Valenka agreed and Katarina went with her to collect her things.

'Have you heard of this happening before, a girl being allowed to have her baby?' Mariner asked Lorelei, as they waited for the two girls to return.

'Only in isolated cases, and usually it's by accident. Some of these girls are so young and inexperienced they don't even know they're pregnant until they go into labour. They don't know about contraception and the punters prefer sex without, so their pimps don't enlighten them and pregnancy is the inevitable result. They're undernourished anyway so they wouldn't put on much weight. If they do realise what's happening, some of the girls get rid of the babies themselves using the crudest of methods, or more commonly their pimps get it done for them.'

'It's barbaric,' said Charlie. 'What about antenatal care? Medical care before the baby is born.'

'There isn't any. They just see a midwife at the time when the child is born. Often we pick up girls who have been thrown out of the brothel they're working in and left to fend for themselves on the streets.'

'And if a baby does go to term, and survives, it is murdered in cold blood like Madeleine's baby.' It left a nasty taste in Mariner's mouth.

Lorelei was pragmatic. 'What's the alternative? The men who run the operations know that most families would reject a child born in these circumstances. It's much less trouble to just get rid of the child.'

'But why then kill Nadia too? She could still be useful to them.'

'Perhaps motherhood gave Nadia a different perspective on her way of life and she didn't want to give up her baby. The maternal bond is immensely powerful. Maybe she got too difficult to handle, so Zjalic dealt with her and her baby instead. It would be the simplest thing. There are plenty more girls to take her place, they are disposable commodities.'

'Or more accurately he had Lucca do some of the dirty work for him,' Glover reminded him. 'It was Lucca's prints all over the tape. We only have Zjalic's word that the two men didn't know one other. And the witness who saw someone dumping something in the small hours last November identified a tall man. Zjalic is certainly that.'

'We need to find Goran Zjalic.'

Chapter Fifteen

The drive back to Birmingham was mostly a silent one, punctuated by occasional murmured exchanges between Katarina and Lorelei. Mariner and Glover were lost in their own thoughts, the euphoria of identifying Madeleine replaced by the grim realisation of what the end of her life had been like. They took the two women back to the project hostel. 'When is Ocean Blue likely to come to trial?' Lorelei asked Mariner.

'It could be months, why?'

'We're running out of space. I don't know how long we'll be able to keep Katarina here. Our beds are in constant demand and she is no longer in immediate danger. It's getting hard for me to justify her presence.'

'And if you can't keep her?' said Mariner.

'We may have to consider letting her go back to Albania.'

'What will happen to her if she does?'

'It's hard to tell, but to be truthful, the prospects aren't great. I doubt she'll be going home to mum and dad. My experience is that most of the girls we send back either get caught up in the sex trade in their own country, bought again by traffickers or, worst-case scenario, will end up killing themselves. They've been through so much that they're not in a fit mental state to be reintegrated into their families.'

'When I talked to Katarina about it she said she'd feel too ashamed.'

'Wouldn't you be?' said Lorelei 'It's a common response.'

'But that means we might lose her and we might never get her captors to court in time for her to testify.'

'Regrettable though that is, it's not really my problem,' said Lorelei, candidly. 'For the moment Katarina is safe. There are other women out there whose need right now is greater.'

'How long have we got?' Mariner asked.

'I could only guarantee her a couple more nights, then an alternative will need to be found.'

* * *

First things first though. Immediately he and Glover got back to Granville Lane, Mariner called the police officer he'd made contact with in Tirana at the time when Nadia's body was discovered, and followed up by faxing through the description and photograph of Nadia. The officer seemed optimistic that they would be able to trace her family, and would arrange for one of them to fly over.

No rush, Mariner wanted to say. It was a meeting he didn't anticipate with any pleasure.

The other item low on his list of anticipated events was going back to Anna's house, but even so, what he saw on the drive came as a shock. Snuggled in behind Anna's car in Mariner's usual spot was a gleaming one-year-old silver Audi TT. The front door of the house was open, so some little way back down the road Mariner reverse parked into a row of cars from which he could observe without being seen. His worst fears were confirmed when after a few minutes, Dr Gareth appeared from the front door. He went round to the boot of the Audi and opened it up, at the same time as Anna emerged from the house carrying a cardboard box. The laughter and playful banter between them made Mariner's chest constrict and his eyes well up again. He waited until they'd retreated again into the house, pulled out of the parking space, did a three-point turn and drove back to his house.

Mariner had never been afraid of his own company, and there were times in the last few years when he'd craved solitude. But that had been from the safe position of having an alternative. Suddenly he felt very alone and the house very empty. One of the next things he'd do was let out the second-floor flat as he had done in the past, once successfully when Tony Knox was temporarily homeless, and then rather less successfully when Kenneth McCrae had taken up his unfortunate short-term occupancy. He might not feel like opening up his home to the general public quite yet, but there were plenty of trainee officers looking for cheap lodgings. He climbed the stairs to inspect the rooms. They'd need a bit of a clean, but otherwise everything was in good order. He'd get an ad put on the Intranet tomorrow. It wasn't until he was standing under the shower the following morning that he had a much better idea.

DCI Sharp's car was in the car park so Mariner went straight to her office. 'I need to talk to you about Katarina, the girl we interviewed from Ocean Blue,' he said.

'All right.' Sharp sat back in her chair.

'They need her bed at the hostel. But I'm concerned that if we let her go we run the risk of losing our star witness. Katarina is the best we've had for years and we have no way of knowing what she's going back to, or whether we'll be able to keep track of her.'

'So?'

'She came here to be a translator. She's a bright girl with skills and . . . experience. Can't we do something to help find her a job or something? We do it for offenders, why not for a victim?' He was being naïve, Mariner knew that. They couldn't possibly help every victim of every crime. But Katarina had endured so much and in the long-run they were going to need her here.

DCI Sharp must have agreed with him. 'Talk to Millie,' she said. 'See if they can't do something through the offender rehabilitation scheme.'

Millie's response was mixed. 'We could probably get Katarina interpreting work through the Brasshouse centre, but accommodation will be more difficult. She'll need somewhere to stay, an address.'

Mariner had already covered that base, though he hesitated to say it. 'She can stay at my place, in the flat upstairs.'

'Is that wise?'

'Probably not.' But, as far as Mariner was concerned, it was the only humane thing to do.

* * *

Mariner and Glover had first interviewed Goran Zjalic at 158 Wilmott Road, Stirchley, at the address where he and Alecsander Lucca lived. When there was no response today to their banging on the door, Mariner ordered it broken down. They and two uniforms burst into an empty house, but one that had until lately been lived in. There was recently bought food in the kitchen cupboards.

'We're looking for anything that might link Zjalic to Ocean Blue or to Nadia,' Mariner told them. He dispatched one of the uniforms to knock on doors and talk to the neighbours on either side.

The house was as grubby and sparsely furnished as the last time they had been here, with fixtures and fittings that were more than second hand. Furniture was minimal, but in the small box room upstairs was a cot. 'He had his sister living with him,' Glover reminded Mariner about the young woman who had come in while they were talking, cradling a baby on her hip.

'If that's who she was,' Mariner said. 'From what we now know she could have been another Nadia. I mean, we don't even know that the baby was hers—' He stopped suddenly.

'It could have been Nadia's baby,' said Glover, picking up Mariner's train of thought. 'We only know that Nadia and the child were killed at around the same.'

'Nadia's baby had a cleft lip and palate,' Mariner reminded him. 'I didn't notice that about the child.'

'It might have had a dummy in its mouth. That would have covered it up. The baby died of a crushed skull. Zjalic losing his temper when it cried too much?'

'It's possible,' Mariner had to concede. 'But I don't think this is Zjalic's normal residence. Valenka called him "the big man" but I don't think she was just talking about physical attributes. He's higher up the food chain. He could afford somewhere much smarter than this.'

The uniform returned. 'The neighbours on one side recognised the description of Zjalic, but according to them he hasn't been seen since around the time of Ocean Blue.'

'It doesn't mean he hasn't been here,' said Mariner. 'Didn't you notice the lack of post in the hall when we first came in? If Zjalic has really been off the scene for three weeks there would have been a stack of junk mail on the floor. Someone's been in and moved it. It might not have been at the time of day when anyone would see him, but Zjalic has been back. We'd do well to put this place under surveillance. Anyone else seen here?'

'They said there's sometimes a young woman with a baby, but again, not in the last two or three weeks.'

'It's always the same woman?'

'They seemed to think so.'

'Nadia's baby died at the end of last year, so maybe it really was Zjalic's sister we met,' said Glover.

'Sir.' As they were talking the second PC descended the stairs carrying a crumpled black bin liner, which he passed to Mariner. 'I found it stuffed in the back of a wardrobe.'

When Mariner opened up the neck of the bag, sitting inside were a white leather handbag with multiple pockets, a mobile phone and a blue and white striped canvas ballet shoe with a buckle trim. 'What the hell is going on?' Mariner said, staring at the items. 'Where does Christie Walker come into this?'

* * *

A pit-stop at Phyllis Gates' house verified that the bag belonged to her late granddaughter and all three items were retained for forensic examination — which Mariner hoped would provide some clue as to what they were doing in Goran Zjalic's house.

Late that afternoon Mariner fetched Katarina and her meagre belongings and took her to his house. He'd made sure that the fire was lit and that it was warm, and he had put some basic food in the fridge. She moved tentatively from room to room looking and touching. Out of the secure setting of the hostel she seemed jumpy again prompting Mariner to wonder if he'd done the right thing.

'You'll be okay?' he asked.

'Yes.' But she hugged herself uncertainly. 'It's a big house. You have to go?'

'Yes.' Her face fell a little. 'No. Wait a minute.' He went into the hall to phone Anna. If she was going to be difficult he didn't want Katarina to overhear. He needn't have worried. The phone rang and rang until eventually the answering service kicked in. Mariner didn't leave a message.

'You have a woman?' Katarina deduced when he went back into the living room. When Mariner paused she drew her own conclusion, raising a quizzical eyebrow. 'Or man?'

Mariner laughed. 'A woman, but it's complicated.' Not to mention finished.

'Com-pli-cated.' Her brow furrowed as she tested out the long and unfamiliar word.

'Mixed up,' Mariner helped her out with the nearest explanation he could come up with.

She nodded, understanding.

'So we'll go out for dinner,' Mariner declared.

'We go out?'

'To a pub, a restaurant.'

Her eyes filled with alarm. 'People they will look at me.'

'Yes, they will,' agreed Mariner. 'You're a pretty girl.'

'But they look at me and you—'

Mariner knew what she was getting at. 'Yes, and they'll think you're my daughter,' he said, reasonably. 'No one will know what's happened to you. You're just like any other teenage girl out for dinner. Aren't you hungry? Wouldn't you like a pizza, ice cream. . . caviar?'

That seemed to do it, and a smile brightened up her face again. 'Yes, I like that very much.'

'I'll go and change.'

'Change?'

'Change my clothes.'

Her face dropped again and she looked down at the jeans and T-shirt, the same ones she'd been wearing since Mariner had last interviewed her. 'I have only these clothes.'

'It's fine. We'll take you shopping soon for more clothes.'

'You go shopping with me?'

That made him laugh again. 'Not me. I'm very bad at shopping.' But he felt sure that Millie would be glad to help out.

'I have no money,' she pointed out.

'I've got money. You can pay me back.' Almost imperceptibly she stiffened, eye contact snatched away, and she flushed a deep red, but it took Mariner several seconds to fathom her reaction. Then it hit him like a sledge hammer. 'Not like that,' he said, quickly. 'Never like that.'

At that she seemed to shrink a little, such a fragile self-worth. 'You think I'm a bad person.' She spoke in a whisper.

'No.' Mariner was firm. 'You're a sweet girl who has had some bad things happen to her, and my job is to keep you safe. You can pay me back when you have work and you have money.' It took several seconds but she relaxed again, forced a smile. Christ, this was going to be a minefield.

Wearing his oldest, scruffiest jeans and trainers to show solidarity, Mariner took her to the Coach and Horses, a mid-range pub where he knew they wouldn't stand out. She devoured a 12oz steak that would have challenged his appetite. They used the whole experience to extend her vocabulary, Mariner naming some of the things she was less familiar with, while she introduced Mariner to some basic Albanian, though languages had never been his forte. It must have looked as if they were filming for the Open University. Mariner hammed it up to make her laugh, but towards the end of the meal she went quiet.

'Penny for them,' said Mariner, carelessly. Then, short of the voiceover translation he added, 'It's an English saying, "a penny for your thoughts." It means: what are you thinking about?'

'I think about my friends, the girls from the house.' She looked around her. 'This is so nice.' Her eyes glistened. 'I think they don't have such a nice time.'

'What will they do when they go home?' They must have talked about it when they were at the Daffodil Project.'

'They look for work.' Mariner's heart turned leaden. He didn't like to ask what kind of work. 'My friend Sonja, she go back to her little girl.'

'She has a child?'

Katarina smiled, but her eyes had filled up. 'She is very excited to see her.'

But then what? Mariner wanted to ask. What future for Sonja and her daughter? It was one of several moments through the evening when Mariner wanted to reach out and touch Katarina to reassure her, but after what she'd been through it was the last thing he could have done.

After dropping off Katarina and taking her through the security routine, Mariner drove back to Anna's house, but she wasn't there. In the lounge and the bedroom he noticed that some of her clothes and personal things had gone. Propped on the kitchen table was an envelope. Mariner opened it.

New job starts tomorrow so staying overnight with Becky and Mark. Out celebrating tonight, but give me a call after 10:30 p.m.

Anna xxx

So that was it. Their four-year relationship ended with the most cursory of notes. Mariner picked up the phone and dialled. Becky answered, but they didn't linger on small talk and she put Anna on straight away.

'Hi.'

'Hi. So you've moved out then.'

'I've started to.' Her tone was bright and pragmatic. 'I'll only be staying with Becky short-term though. They're going to need my room.'

'Oh?'

'They've been approved to adopt a baby from China. It's what we've been celebrating — along with my job, of course. Fantastic news, isn't it?'

'The best,' said Mariner without enthusiasm. 'So where will you stay?'

'Well, obviously, I'll be on the lookout for somewhere—'

'Heron's Nest?'

'Hm, I think not. But in the meantime Gareth has a spare room I can crash in.' Her words tumbled out as if she hoped he might not hear them.

'Good old Dr Gareth,' said Mariner, instantly rubbishing the spare room fairytale.

She ignored his sarcasm. 'I'll be exchanging contracts on the house next Wednesday, so I've ordered a removal van for the following Friday and will be handing over the keys and moving out the rest of my stuff, so you'll need to—'

'Sure.' Hanging up the phone Mariner felt overwhelmingly exhausted. Upstairs, he went into the room that until recently they'd shared. Lying down on Anna's side of the bed he found that it still smelled lightly of her. Her scent made him hard and the pain in his chest returned. He couldn't believe that she would never again lie here beside him and that in such a short space of time she'd so completely moved on. He had to accept that Anna wanted something different from life. She wanted what Becky and Mark had, and what apparently he couldn't give her.

He wondered about Becky and Mark. Adopting a child from abroad was dressed up as some great philanthropic gesture, but they were essentially doing it because they wanted to. Was it really in the interests of the child or simply some warped kind of fashion statement? What did Marcella Turner call it? The children-as-accessories culture. On one level what they were doing seemed not so very different from what Alecsander Lucca and Goran Zjalic were involved in. It was what the world had come to; human beings shipped around and traded like any other merchandise. Still, at least Becky and Mark's child might stand more of a chance than Sonja's baby. Mariner was still thinking about Sonja's baby when he awoke very early the following morning.

He left it until a respectable time then drove back to his house. Letting himself in he was pleased to find Katarina up and about, in the kitchen making tea. 'You want some?' she asked.

But Mariner declined. 'I want you to tell me about your friend Sonja,' he said. 'Did she leave her baby behind when she came to this country?'

'No, she have her baby here, in England.'

'The baby was a surprise? She didn't know she was pregnant?' Mariner hazarded, thinking back to what Lorelei had told him.

'Oh no,' Katarina waggled her head and smiled. 'She want her baby.'

'Like Nadia.'

'Yes.'

It was at that point that Mariner saw the faintest spark of light at the end of a very long tunnel. Christ they'd been through all this before with Valenka but didn't think to ask if there were any others. 'What happened to Sonja's baby?' he asked.

'They take it to, um, the house,' she frowned as she groped for the right words, 'the house for children have no mother, no father.'

'An orphanage,' Mariner said.

'Or-phan-age.' She hadn't come across that word before.

'Who's they?' Mariner asked. 'Who took Sonja's baby?'

But Katarina didn't know. 'Sonja tell me when we come to your police station.'

Even so, it took all Mariner's willpower to stop himself from hugging her. Now all he needed to do was run it by Knox and Glover to establish if he was anywhere near the truth.

He was prevented from doing this by Delrose, who met him on his way in to Granville Lane. 'There's an official from the Albanian Embassy here with a Mr Troshani,' she said. 'They seemed to think that you're expecting them?'

Christ, that was quick. 'Oh God,' Mariner sighed, out loud. 'Now I have to break it to a man that his daughter was a sex worker and that she and her bastard child are now dead,' he flashed Delrose a humourless smile. 'This job doesn't get any easier, does it? Is Charlie Glover in yet?'

'I saw him come in about ten minutes ago.'

Armed with the photograph of Nadia, Mariner went down to the informal interview room where Mr Troshani and his interpreter had been taken and plied with coffee. Even sitting down Mariner could see that Troshani was a big man, with his daughter's dark, intense eyes. About fifty, his hair silver-stranded at the temples, the suit he was wearing had seen better days and was straining at the seams. His expression was bleak, but Mariner couldn't begin to imagine what he must be feeling.

Introducing himself, Mariner gave Troshani the silver crucifix they had retrieved from around his daughter's neck, and the photograph that Valenka had given them. Troshani stared at the picture, touching the faces of Nadia and then her baby as if doing so might bring them back to life. Head bowed, he confirmed with a wordless nod that this was his daughter pinching his nose between finger and thumb to stem any tears. He spoke to the embassy interpreter.

'He wants to know what happened,' the interpreter translated.

It was the question Mariner had been dreading. 'Some of the detail—' he hesitated, and gave the interpreter what he hoped was a meaningful look.

'He wants to know everything,' came the reply.

As well as he could, Mariner went on to describe the gruesome discovery last Christmas, piecing it together with what they thought had happened to Nadia based on what her friend Valenka had told them so recently. When he had finished, Troshani sat in silence, no longer even trying to control his weeping.

'Does he know how she came to this country?' Mariner asked, knowing that the story would be similar to the others.

'She had an offer of work,' the translator told him when Troshani had spoken. 'I encouraged her to come. I thought it would be a better life for her. She sent a letter home telling us what a good life she had here.' Troshani went through his pockets, producing a crumpled and dirty envelope. 'She told us she was going to have a baby and that she would be coming home. And now she will be coming home in a wooden casket.' Finally, his shoulders gave way and he sobbed. 'She was my child and I should have taken care of her.'

Before Troshani left, Mariner summoned Charlie Glover. 'This is the man who was responsible for tracking down Nadia's killer, and for identifying her,' Mariner told Troshani. 'If it hadn't been for him, we may never have known.' As Mariner had expected, it was an emotional meeting.

Afterwards Mariner felt drained, his earlier momentum lost. He went back up to CID where Knox was working at his desk. The sergeant followed him into his office. 'You're looking rough,' he remarked.

'Yeah, didn't get much sleep,' said Mariner flopping into the seat behind his desk.

'Oh yeah?' Knox raised a suggestive eyebrow. 'Anything to do with Anna?'

'What? No. Anna and me, it's over.' Mariner watched the shock register on Knox's face.

'Jesus, when did that happen?'

'That's what I keep asking myself.'

'Anything to do with the Welsh medic?'

'You should be a detective.'

'Nah. Hours are crap and the pay's not much better.'

'You heard that Christie's stuff turned up at Zjalic's house,' Mariner said, not wishing to dwell on his own problems.

'Charlie told me. What the hell's going on?'

'I think I might know.'

Knox pulled up a chair. 'Cough it up then.'

'I talked to Katarina last night. She told me about her friend Sonja.'

'I interviewed Sonja,' said Knox, the memory of it forcing a grimace. 'She couldn't wait to get home to her kid.'

'That's right, and I'll bet you assumed the same thing I did; that Sonja left her child behind to come and work here.'

'I suppose I did.'

'But that's not what happened,' Mariner enlightened him. 'Sonja had her baby here, while she was working at the house on Foundry Road, in exactly the same way that Nadia did.'

'So we've got a coincidence,' said Knox, not getting it.

'But don't you think that's weird?' Mariner continued. 'I mean, as a one-off you could just about understand it, but on two occasions a pimp allows a girl to go ahead with her pregnancy? The normal thing would be an enforced termination.'

Knox thought it through for a moment. 'Except, apart from a few weeks when they can't work it's no skin off his nose, is it? Maybe it was simpler to go with the flow.'

'It's possible,' conceded Mariner. 'And it could be that the pimp has already got somewhere lined up for these babies to go. Goran Zjalic is probably pulling the strings here, too. According to Katarina, Sonja's baby was taken to an orphanage, and Nadia's baby was meant to have been sent back to her family. The woman we met at Zjalic's house could have been a courier, taking the baby back to Eastern Europe.'

'So what's the problem then?' Knox asked.

'I can't square it,' said Mariner. 'I keep asking myself, why would he bother? It's all unnecessary trouble and expense for Zjalic to go to. I mean, he's not under any obligation to these girls, it's not that kind of relationship, so why go to all that trouble, paying for a return flight to wherever for the courier, and lose several working weeks out of the girls, to boot? A man like Goran Zjalic is only interested in one thing: money. And I can think of a much more profitable way of disposing of a couple of surplus babies in this country.'

'Which is—?'

'To sell them.'

'Which would be illegal,' Knox pointed out.

Mariner's laugh was bitter with contempt. 'Oh yes, and if what we know about Zjalic is true then we all know how much he likes to stay on the right side of the law, don't we? I'm not saying he's set up a market stall in the Bullring. He'd dress it up as something much more respectable, like private adoption. But the end result is the same.'

'But if a couple wants to adopt they'd surely go down the social services route.'

'And it's a long and complicated process. Then what about the couples who are deemed unsuitable, or too old to adopt in this country, or the couples who specifically want a baby? There's a shortage over here. Couples are encouraged to adopt older children. One of the reasons that adoption from abroad has become so fashionable is because of the lack of babies over here, but even that's becoming harder.'

'You think people would be prepared to break the law?'

'If what you read in the papers is true, there are people out there who are prepared to do anything to have a baby. And they may not even realise that they're doing anything illegal. Zjalic is a smart and resourceful man. He'd make it sound legit. And it would be lucrative. What could you charge for a baby? Twenty thousand, fifty thousand? This could be far more profitable than prostitution.'

Knox was beginning to come round to Mariner's theory. 'Christ, no wonder these two girls weren't encouraged to have terminations.'

'No, instead they were sold some line about their babies being sent home to their families or to an orphanage, when in reality they are sold on to couples who are desperate for a child. The girls wouldn't be any the wiser. Realistically they wouldn't stand a hope in hell of tracing their child even if they ever succeeded in getting away from Zjalic in the first place.'

'But Nadia's baby wasn't sold. We know what happened to him.'

'But what's the other thing we know about him? He had a cleft palate.'

'He was damaged goods,' said Knox. 'So he couldn't be sold.'

'Perhaps Nadia realised that, feared for his future and refused to give him up, or perhaps the child died first and Nadia found out. We'll never know.'

'But where the hell does Christie come into all this? What was her stuff doing in Zjalic's house?'

'The last time Christie had those things with her was the night she was killed, so we have to conclude that someone who has access to Wilmott Road was involved with her murder, which in turn implicates Zjalic. She said she had something to tell you, and perhaps this was it. Christie had somehow found out about what Zjalic was doing. It would make sense of why she'd been on the internet looking at overseas adoption. She might have been checking out if what Zjalic was doing was legal.'

This was a step too far for Tony Knox. 'But how would she have found out about it in the first place? As far as we're aware she didn't even know Goran Zjalic.' He'd identified the missing link.

'It's something to do with Foundry Road, I'm sure that's the connection,' said Mariner. 'I wouldn't mind betting that the staff at Jack and the Beanstalk sometimes have to cover at Little Beans, so Christie must have worked there from time to time.'

'That still doesn't mean she knew anything about Zjalic. If she saw him in the street she wouldn't know who he was or what he did.'

'Unless Zjalic approached her.'

'But for what?'

'Christie worked in a nursery, looking after children. Perhaps Zjalic needed someone to help him out while he was holding the babies at Wilmott Road. Nadia and Sonja's babies are the ones we know about, but there may have been others. Christie was a bright girl. When she saw the setup she sussed what was going on and established through her internet research that the operation was illegal. She might even have tried to blackmail Zjalic.'

'She was playing with fire, if she did,' said Knox.

'It gives us a compelling motive for murder. When Zjalic wouldn't co-operate, Christie decided to report him to you. You said she had a conscience. Then when you didn't show up on Saturday night it occurred to her that she could make money from the intelligence in a different way and phoned Jez Barclay. Maybe she was going to anyway. She'd already told her nan that she would have enough money to buy a flat and she'd either get it through blackmail or the TV company, or both.'

But Knox still wasn't convinced. 'If Zjalic is as powerful as we think he is, I still don't think he'd be the kind of character to just walk up to a kid like Christie in the street and let her in on something as big as that. It's far too risky.'

'I don't think he had to. She could easily have worked it out for herself.' But they were grabbing at speculative straws and they both knew it.

'And at the other end of it, how does Zjalic make contact with couples who want to buy a baby?' Knox asked.

It was the bit that Mariner hadn't thought through, but suddenly it came to him. He scrabbled around on the desk until he came up with the orange flyer. Reading it again it made perfect sense. 'Take another look at this,' he said handing it to Knox. 'We made the assumption that it offers further fertility treatment, but the wording says nothing about "treatment." All it says is: *new hope for infertile couples.* What greater hope could there be than the offer of a baby?'

'Go on,' Knox was still dubious.

'This is the other end of the operation. Couples get these flyers, ring the number and Zjalic offers them a baby. Christie, it seems, wanted a baby, so the flyer's how Christie got involved. She found it or was given it, called the number and was offered a baby. The first step of that is some kind of bogus "clinic" appointment, which would explain the entry on her calendar. Until she kept the appointment she wouldn't have known what this offer was. She might even have got as far as meeting with Zjalic, then perhaps she recognised him from Foundry Road and realised what he was up to.'

'But where would Christie have got hold of the flyer?' said Knox. 'She hadn't been to the fertility clinic and we haven't seen them around anywhere, so where did it come from?'

It was the question Mariner couldn't yet answer. 'But all of this gives us two main priorities. Contact the immigration centre and find out if there are any other girls who have had babies in this country during the last twelve months, and had them sent home to their families or to an orphanage. And I want to find Goran Zjalic.'

* * *

Surveillance was an expensive option, but once Mariner had laid out his case, DCI Sharp could see its value. 'Whatever may be going on here, I think Goran Zjalic will be an interesting man to meet.'

Knox quickly came through with a result from the immigration centre. 'A couple of girls have come forward who were taken to other stations in the city and one from Stafford,' their agent told Mariner. 'One of them had her baby eight weeks ago. She had a picture that they've faxed through to us.'

'Do you think we could run it by the neighbours in Wilmott Street, see if they recognise it?' To him a baby was a baby, but maybe it was different for other people.

'We don't have to, boss,' Knox handed Mariner the copied sheet.

Mariner stared in disbelief. Even he didn't need any clues. There was no mistaking those big dark eyes. 'It's baby Ellie,' he said.

'Zjalic didn't need Christie to help look after the babies,' said Knox. 'He put them into the nursery while they were waiting to be adopted,' said Knox.

'It's like a holding station,' said Mariner.

'When I brought Christie up here to your office for the e-fit, she thought she recognised that picture.' Knox gestured towards the mock-up of Madeleine, still stuck to the wall. 'She thought she'd been into the nursery. At the time it seemed too far-fetched so I didn't push it, but maybe she was right.'

Mariner was thoughtful. 'We need to find out if Trudy Barratt recognises Zjalic.'

'He wouldn't do the business himself though, would he? The girl who was supposedly Ellie's nanny came to collect her,' Knox reminded him. 'Boss?'

But Mariner didn't respond straight away, because the understanding of what was really going on had ploughed into him like a ten-ton truck.

'Boss?' Knox tried again.

'Mrs Barratt knows Goran Zjalic, all right,' said Mariner, eventually. 'The nursery is all part of the scam.'

Chapter Sixteen

'I don't get it,' said Knox.

'Think back to the day of Jessica Klinnemann's abduction,' Mariner said. 'We ruled out the possibility that she had been taken in error, on the grounds that every mother knows her baby. But what if the mother who came to the nursery that afternoon *didn't* know her baby, because she'd never met her before. What if Goran Zjalic offers these babies for adoption and the nursery is a front for the handover?'

'So on the day Jessica went missing, the baby up for adoption was baby Ellie.' Knox was catching up and Mariner was encouraged.

'Ellie would have been brought into the nursery, like Jessica, early in the morning and handed over to Trudy Barratt. Without Trudy, the staff would have no way of knowing who the mother of the child is. The plan then is that sometime during the day the adoptive mother comes to the nursery and Trudy Barratt hands "back" the baby she has come to collect and is presumably handsomely rewarded for her trouble. The adoptive mother goes away with her new baby, and no one else is any the wiser.'

'But on the day Jessica disappeared Trudy Barratt wasn't there.'

'Exactly. We assumed that the woman's enquiry to Christie was to ensure that the manager was out of the way, but in fact it was the opposite; the woman needed Trudy Barratt to be there, to take her and introduce her to her new baby. When Christie told her that Mrs Barratt was out of the building and offered to take her to the crèche, the woman was left with no choice but to bluff her way through and take a baby. When she approached Jessica, Kam helpfully gave her the baby's name. And the lack of reaction from the staff when she approached Jessica may have led her to think that she had, by chance, even chosen the right baby. After all, she had a one-in-three chance of getting it right. Either way she had to brazen it out and walk out of the nursery with a baby.'

'But she took the wrong one.'

'Yes, she should have taken Ellie, which is why Ellie was left behind in the nursery long after the other children had gone, and was eventually collected by the girl Trudy Barratt said was the au pair.' Mariner recollected the so-called au pair who'd come to collect Ellie in the beaten up car, and how he'd compared her with Katarina. The similarity was closer than he'd realised. 'I'd lay bets that the phone call Mrs Barratt made when she got back to the nursery was telling Zjalic that there had been a cock-up, and urging him to arrange for Ellie to be collected. Otherwise she was going to have to account to us for a spare baby, which would have been pretty embarrassing.'

'It explains how naturally it came to the abductor to talk about "her" baby, too,' added Knox. 'She said it because in her mind she *was* collecting her baby, bought and paid for.'

'But if that's what happened, why didn't the woman who took Jessica come forward straight away when she realised what had happened? She must have seen or heard something. It was all over the news.'

'—because the mistake would have had to be explained. Potentially she would have uncovered the whole scam and jeopardised her chances of having a baby.'

'She'd go that far?'

'There are few more single-minded people than women who want a child but are unable to have one. I think these women are carefully chosen.'

'But how, and who chooses them?'

'It all comes back to the flyer. I think the reason we haven't come across any of these flyers is because couples are very carefully targeted. They'll be couples who are desperate for a child and who won't ask too many questions. They'll have gone through a lot to get this far and they're not going to give it up easily. Instead this woman waited and worked out a way of getting Jessica safely and anonymously back to us. Jessica had to be returned. With all the publicity, she could never have been absorbed into a family without arousing suspicion. Zjalic was probably behind that too. My guess would be that this woman, and probably her husband or partner holed up in a place somewhere until the fuss died down.'

'Betty Wrigley,' said Knox.

'Is that meant to mean something?'

Knox described his encounter with the holiday cottage owner. 'I dismissed her as a busybody, but if your theory's right then she could have been onto something.'

Mariner was inclined to agree. 'Renting a holiday cottage would be an ideal way of spending a few days with a new baby and getting to know it before introducing it to the family. The couple may have even had a cover story — that they were adopting from abroad. We should have a forensic team sent up to the cottage and go over it with a fine-tooth comb. And let's talk to Betty Wrigley again.'

'She'll be over the moon,' said Knox.

* * *

Mrs Wrigley's stone cottage lay in an isolated spot at the end of a rough track. Being supremely house-proud, she had made sure to give the place a thorough clean. 'At the moment,' Mariner told the forensic team, 'we're looking for any evidence that Jessica Klinnemann may have been here, or anything to link with the abduction.'

Meanwhile Mariner and Tony Knox went to talk to Betty Wrigley.

'Could you talk us through the transaction again?' Mariner asked.

Betty Wrigley visibly puffed up. 'I advertise in a number of magazines and on the internet. As generally happens, Mr Jones phoned at first to ask if the cottage was free for that week. He'd seen it online. It was available so I made a provisional reservation, and a few days later he sent me a letter confirming the booking and enclosing the cash deposit.'

'Did you keep any of the paperwork?'

'Of course. I file everything.'

But Mr Jones's letter brought no new information, there was no return postal address and nothing to identify the sender except for a Manchester postmark. With Mrs Wrigley's permission Mariner kept it for forensic testing, but he wasn't optimistic.

'Mr and Mrs Jones must have driven here,' Mariner said. 'Do you know what make their car was?'

'Yes, it was a nice black one. A hatchback,' said Joan Wrigley, certain that she was playing a vital role.

Knox and Mariner exchanged a look. 'Well, thanks anyway,' Mariner said, praying that the forensics team would turn up something. They were walking out of the door when Wrigley said: 'I wrote down the registration number. Would that help?'

A short enquiry to the DVLA identified both the car — a black Renault Megane — and its owner: a David Scanlon of 24 Goldfinch Drive, Salford, Manchester. A second vehicle was registered to his spouse, Paula.

'Talks like Deidre off *Coronation Street*,' said Mariner, quoting what Christie had told them. She'd had an ear for accents too.

* * *

Mariner and Knox drove across to Greater Manchester right away, arriving in the late afternoon. They notified the local force that they were on their patch but initially it was simply a question of watching and waiting. Goldfinch Drive was a cul-de-sac of pebble-dashed bungalows, the lawns neatly tended. There were no cars on the drive of number twenty-four, but dusk turned to darkness and eventually a small hatchback appeared at the end of the road and swung into the drive, continuing down alongside the house, past the front door to a side door. A woman got out, opened the boot and unloaded a number of carrier bags in through the side door. Emerging again, she went round to the passenger side of the car and took out an infant's car seat. Locking the car, she went in the house again, closing the door behind her.

'How do we play this?' Knox asked, as they got out of the car.

'Carefully,' said Mariner. 'Aside from taking Jessica by mistake, they may not even know that they've done anything wrong. The adoption might have been presented to them as entirely above board. Now that Jessica has been returned they probably think they're in the clear. Let's go.'

Paula Scanlon came to the front door almost immediately the bell was rung. Mariner held out his warrant card. 'Mrs Scanlon? Might we have a word?'

Her eyes were instantly wary. 'It's not really convenient. I was just putting the baby to bed. Could you come back another time?'

'Not really, this is important,' Mariner persisted. 'Can we come in?'

With clear reluctance, Paula Scanlon let them into the bungalow, along a narrow hallway past what Mariner assumed must be bedrooms and into a lounge/diner at the back of the house. A door opened onto the kitchen and Mariner could see the side door by which she'd entered the house. In a corner of the lounge was the baby in her car seat. No doubt about it, this was baby Ellie who, like Katarina, seemed to have grown since the last time they had met.

'And this is—?' Mariner asked pleasantly, smiling at the baby who gurgled in response.

'Lauren,' Paula Scanlon snapped irritably, but the irritation masked a deeper, darker fear. It was in her eyes. She was twisting her wedding ring round and round on her finger, leaving a white indentation.

'And when was Lauren born?'

'August 28. She's adopted, as I'm sure you already know.'

'Yes,' said Mariner. 'We'd like to talk to you about that. All right if we sit down for a minute?'

'If you must. I'd like my husband here. Can we wait until he gets home? He shouldn't be long.'

'That's fine,' said Mariner pleasantly.

'While we're waiting, can I get you a cup of tea?' The offer was grudgingly made.

'Thanks,' said Mariner cheerfully. 'That would be good.'

On her way out of the room she switched on the TV, for their entertainment presumably, though Mariner would have been content to enjoy the quiet. Paula Scanlon was gone for some time, during which they could hear taps going on and off and the clatter of mugs on a tray. Baby Ellie dropped the orange plastic teether she'd been holding and it fell to the floor. Mariner, who was nearer, picked it up and handed it back to her. 'Hello,' he smiled as he did so. Perhaps she recognised him because, at that precise moment, her little face crumpled and Ellie started to wail.

'What did I do?' said Mariner uncomprehending.

'It's what you said,' remarked Knox.

In any event the noise prompted Paula Scanlon's return. She practically threw the tray of mugs onto the table, urging them to help themselves, before hurrying over to baby Ellie, removing her from her car seat and holding her close. 'It's all right, darling,' she soothed. 'Mummy's here.' At the same time the lounge door opened and David Scanlon appeared, clearly startled to see such a gathering in his living room. Blond and bespectacled he looked shattered, his suit crumpled.

'These are the police,' his wife told him.

Even in this situation good manners prevailed and Scanlon, a tall man with unruly blond hair, shook hands with them before asking 'What's going on?'

'They want to talk to us about Lauren.' As Paula Scanlon spoke Ellie's crying rose to a new crescendo, competing with the TV. 'She needs to be fed and put down,' she said, making it clear that Mariner and Knox were causing a nuisance.

'Why don't you attend to that, darling,' said David Scanlon. 'I'll talk to the officers and you can join us when Lauren's asleep.' He leaned over and kissed the baby girl on her downy head.

'Go ahead, Mrs Scanlon,' Mariner said, if only for a bit of peace.

'Can you bring in her bottle when it's ready?' she asked her husband.

'I'll be through in a minute.' As he spoke, Scanlon sat down in the armchair opposite the two policemen.

Mariner thought about asking for the TV to be turned off, but knew that some people liked the background babble, and now that Ellie was out of the equation they were perfectly able to converse. 'Mr Scanlon, we need to know exactly how you came to adopt Lauren, and we'll need to see all the paperwork you have for her.' Mariner began. They'd come onto baby Jessica later. 'How did Lauren come to be with you?'

Unlike his wife, Scanlon seemed sanguine about it. 'We went through a private adoption agency. Horizons,' he told them, calmly.

'How did you find out about Horizons?'

Something bleeped in the kitchen. 'That's Lauren's bottle warmer. Do you mind?'

'No, carry on.'

'She's well-cared-for,' remarked Knox, when Scanlon was out of the room.

Mariner couldn't disagree. 'The irony is that, long-term, she may stand a better chance with them. But nonetheless, if we're right, she has a mother desperate to be reunited with her, and what they've done is illegal. Not to mention the small matter of abduction.'

Moments later Scanlon was back again to pick up the story. 'We were having treatment at the Queen Elizabeth Hospital,' he told them. 'It's a long way to travel but the unit does some pioneering work and our GP had referred us. We had undergone a total of four cycles of IVF and the consultant was worried that this was taking its toll both physically and mentally on Paula. He suggested that we talk to a counsellor, so we did.'

Another piece of the puzzle slotted into place. 'Sheila Fry,' said Mariner.

'Sheila, yes, that's right. Anyway, she recognised that we'd come to the end of the line where IVF was concerned, and suggested we come home and think about whether we really wanted to put ourselves through that again. She asked if we had considered adoption, which we had of course, but had been told that we were too old. Then a couple of weeks later, out of the blue, we received a flyer through the post.'

'Do you still have it?'

'I might. I'm not sure.'

'Is it like this one?' Mariner produced the orange flyer he'd been carrying round with him for the past week.

'Yes. That looks very like it. Anyway I rang the number and was told I was through to the Horizons adoption agency, who could offer us the opportunity to adopt a baby from an Eastern European country, in return for a payment for administrative costs. The woman at the other end sounded highly professional and explained that while this kind of adoption arrangement was not illegal, neither was it encouraged in this country, so discretion was important, but that she could offer us a quick and simple adoption process.'

'So you took it up.'

'I researched it a little on the internet and found that this has happened before, and I couldn't see why there would be a problem with it.'

'Didn't the level of secrecy bother you?' asked Mariner.

'We were told that the service wasn't publicised because if it was, the agency would be unable to meet the huge demand that would ensue,' Scanlon told him. 'We were told that we had been referred due to our particular circumstances.'

'But you'd also been "referred" without your knowledge. Didn't that strike you as odd?'

'Mr Mariner, Paula's whole aim in life has been to have a baby of her own. For the last ten years, ever since we got married, our lives have been completely dominated by that desire. I can't begin to describe what it's like. Since we were told that she was unlikely to conceive we've been through hell. Four rounds of IVF that have left us financially and emotionally broke. It hit Paula very hard. On one occasion she even tried to end it all. When you're that desperate it's easy to overlook the details. I'd have done anything for Paula at that stage and Horizons promised that within just a few weeks we would have our own baby. How could we resist an offer like that? And aside from the secrecy, which seemed perfectly explicable at the time, it all seemed kosher. We already knew a little about how the adoption process works and Horizons seemed to follow all the right procedures. A woman came and visited us to do a home assessment—'

'Do you remember her name?'

'I'm sure we have it written down somewhere.'

'Could you describe her for me?'

'Well, she was very smart and professional, blondish hair, about fifty.' Trudy Barratt. 'Then there were endless forms to complete. We were given a passport and birth certificate for Lauren.'

'Have you got those?'

Frank Scanlon went to a drawer and took out an envelope containing the documents. On first examination they looked like the real thing, but Mariner didn't doubt that their experts would find the flaws.

'They're forged, Mr Scanlon,' he said, with confidence. 'They're very good forgeries, admittedly, but sooner or later they'd be found out. Did these people tell you where your baby was coming from?'

'They said they worked closely with various orphanages in Eastern Europe, including one in Tirana, Albania. We were shown photographs of the place. We were told that over there many mothers abandon their babies because they can't afford to look after them. Lauren was one of those babies. We thought we were giving a loving home to an otherwise unwanted child.'

Mariner couldn't help but feel sorry for the man. In many ways the only thing he was guilty of was astonishing naiveté. It was the predators who had ruthlessly taken advantage of the couple's highly vulnerable state. Mariner wanted now to move on to the day of Jessica's kidnap. 'We really need to talk to your wife now, about the day Jessica Klinnemann went missing,' he said. 'Do you think the baby will be asleep?'

'I'll go and check.'

Scanlon seemed to be gone rather a long time and Mariner was just beginning to get itchy when he appeared again, alone. His face was ashen. 'She's gone,' he said. 'She must have slipped out of the front door while we were talking. She's taken my car.'

And they'd heard nothing, because the TV was on. Shit!

Chapter Seventeen

'Where will your wife go?' Mariner demanded.

'I've no idea.'

'Is she likely to do anything to harm the baby?'

'In truth? I don't know. Since all this started Paula's had some problems—'

But Mariner was already on his mobile, contacting the local police to put out an alert for the black Megane. He couldn't believe that they were going through all this again.

'Phone round anyone you can think she may go to,' Mariner said to Scanlon. Apart from that, all they could do was wait. Forty minutes later they got a call from local CID to say that Paula had been located at a nearby beauty spot, Heywood Bridge.

When they got there the Megane was parked up, surrounded now by police vehicles and with a team of divers standing by. A police helicopter hovered.

'Over there, she's all yours.' The lead officer at the scene raised his arm, and in the middle of the suspension bridge in the darkness, Mariner could see the lone figure of Paula Scanlon, hugging baby Ellie to her. A cold wind whipped around them and it was spotting with rain. They needed to get this over with. 'Mrs Scanlon,' Mariner called, edging slowly to the end of the bridge.

'Go away!' she shouted. 'You can't have her. She's my baby and I love her.'

Mariner walked forward a step.

'Don't come near me!' she shouted. 'If I can't have her then nobody will! I'm her mother. She needs me.' As Mariner looked on in horror, Paula Scanlon climbed unsteadily onto the parapet of the bridge, the icy waters rushing by under their feet, the dark current bubbling and swelling dangerously under the floodlights.

Mariner stopped walking. 'I only want to talk to you, Paula,' he said, trying to keep his voice soothing as he yelled above the noise of the angry waters below. 'Paula, I'm sure we can resolve this.'

'Will you let me keep my baby?'

Mariner couldn't answer her.

'Then I don't want to talk to you. If I can't have her then no one else will.' And with that she tipped slowly off the bridge, plummeting into the icy waters below.

Chaos ensued as the team of divers plunged after her into the water, with those on the banks shining floodlights and yelling directions. Amazingly, within minutes they had recovered Paula Scanlon, bringing her safely back to dry land and even more amazingly she still clung to baby Ellie, but when eventually she could be persuaded to relinquish her, the child was found to be barely alive.

She and Paula Scanlon were rushed to hospital for Paula to be checked over, after which she would be driven with police escort to Birmingham to be questioned. Leaving the Scanlons under the protection of the local police, Knox and Mariner went on ahead. They were silent in the car. 'Wasn't your fault, boss,' said Knox eventually. 'She'd have gone in anyway. She had nowhere else to go.'

'But what will it do to her head? We'll have to rely on the Scanlons to testify. We can appeal for other couples to come forward but if they do they might lose their children, so who's going to do that?'

'David Scanlon will be a good witness,' Knox said. 'We've got enough.'

Mariner hoped he was right.

Both Trudy Barratt and Sheila Fry had been brought in for questioning to Granville Lane but it was too late to start on that tonight, and Goran Zjalic had still not appeared. The following morning, armed with a search warrant, a team was sent to Jack and the Beanstalk nursery to search Trudy Barratt's office.

They came across a whole file pertaining to Horizons private adoption agency, including social services forms, paperwork and the names and details of a number of other 'adoptive parents.' The area office of social services confirmed that many of the documents were forgeries. Her computer files were encrypted and the hard drive was sent to the lab to be decoded.

'We also found this,' said PC Mann. He handed Mariner a copy of a letter sent to Emma O'Brien, a cheque enclosed, a pay-off from the nursery, 'in the hope that we can move on and put this terrible episode behind us.'

'I guess that's when Emma O'Brien changed her mind about the documentary,' said Mariner. Unsurprisingly, Trudy Barratt remained calm under questioning, if not protesting her innocence then feigning ignorance of what she might have done. Despite the hours in a cell her hair and makeup were as immaculate as ever.

'Tell us about the Horizons adoption agency,' said Mariner. 'How did it start?'

'Like lots of things, by pure chance,' Trudy Barratt said. 'I knew what went on at number thirty-three, you only had to watch the numbers of men knocking on the door at all hours. It would have taken an idiot not to work it out. But to be honest it didn't matter to me. No one there ever caused any trouble and they kept a low profile. I don't think any of our parents were aware, nor many of the staff for that matter. Then one morning I came down to the nursery for a routine visit and there was a girl outside sobbing her heart out. She didn't speak much English, but she managed to convey to me that she was pregnant, which, I imagine, didn't go down very well in her "workplace." She said that she would be turned out onto the streets and left to fend for herself and she wanted me to give her a job. She had no money and no legal papers. I couldn't employ her, but neither could I just ignore her so I took her into the nursery to calm her down and was going to call social services.'

'Weren't you the good Samaritan?'

'She was very distressed. I'm sure you would have done the same. Anyway, while she was in my office I remembered that some days previously I had been talking to one of our parents, Sheila Fry. She works at the fertility unit up at the hospital and had been telling me a dreadful story about a couple in their forties who had just had their fourth unsuccessful attempt at IVF and how desperate they were to have a child. The woman's health was suffering and they couldn't risk another cycle of fertility treatment, but they had left it too late for adoption.

'I saw a business opportunity, as simple as that. The young girl I had here in my office was going to have an unwanted child, and I knew of a couple who were desperate, but unable, to have a baby. It just seemed logical and to everyone's advantage that I bring the two together.'

'This has happened more than once though,' Mariner produced the details of the other couples.

'When I thought about it I realised that there may be other young women in the same situation. I persuaded the girl to introduce me to her Mr Zjalic.'

'I told him of my proposal. He was very taken with the idea. I thought it would be a one-off, but Mr Zjalic felt that there may be other opportunities in this direction. He was involved in businesses both in this country and in Eastern Europe where this was not an uncommon occurrence, though I understand that often the girls are persuaded to end the pregnancies. At the same time there was Sheila, who regularly met couples who were in a similar situation, so we decided to set up an agency that could help to solve two problems at once.' She spoke as if she was performing a public service.

'So how did it work?' asked Mariner.

'Goran would identify a girl who was due to give birth and arrange for her to come to the house on Wilmott Road to deliver her baby. Sheila would send out a flyer to any couples we thought might be eligible. If they got in touch, which all of them did, Sheila or myself would go out and interview them and do a background check to ensure that they would be suitable parents.'

'What in the world qualifies you to do that?'

'I used to work for social services, and I know what makes good parents.' She was so very sure of herself. 'When all the vetting and paperwork was completed, we set up the handover. Goran or one of the girls would bring the baby to the nursery first thing in the morning, and I would supervise the new parents to come and collect their child during the afternoon.'

'If this was all so above board, why not just hand the baby over?'

'It seemed a convenient way to do it.'

'And more acceptable for the staff.'

'Couples were advised not to engage with the staff.'

'I'll bet they were. So what went wrong on the day when Jessica went missing?'

'Usually I'm at the nursery to supervise the handover. But on that particular day, I was called to the other nursery on an emergency. I tried phoning and texting the mother to stall her until I could get back, but she had her phone switched off, so when she arrived, I wasn't there. Remembering what I had told her earlier, she took the child in the green babygro.'

'But the babies had been changed.'

'So without knowing it, she took the wrong baby. She and her husband did what they had planned and retreated with their baby to a holiday cottage. I didn't manage to get hold of them until three days later, when we could arrange to swap the babies.'

'How much have the Scanlons paid for Ellie?'

'You make it sound so vulgar. The parents make a donation to cover our expenses. It's entirely voluntary.'

'How much?' Mariner asked.

'I really don't remember. I'd have to check my records.'

'Don't worry, we're already doing that for you,' said Mariner. 'And I'm sure the Inland Revenue will be interested in them too. And that's quite apart from your involvement in the illegal sale of a child.'

'We didn't consider it—'

'You consider it what you like,' said Mariner. 'I call it selling babies, and you're in deep shit. Though it could be worse. Baby Ellie almost died.'

For the first time that day Trudy Barratt looked shaken. 'What do you mean?'

'Paula Scanlon tried to kill herself and the baby. Fortunately for you, they both survived and baby Ellie will be reunited with her birth mother, so that's one less tragedy on your conscience.'

'I don't understand.'

'Tell us about this girl, Nadia,' Mariner said, placing the photograph down on the table.

'I've never seen her before. Really.'

Mariner felt sure she was telling the truth. 'And where is Mr Zjalic now?'

'I really have no idea.'

* * *

'Know what the really fucking annoying thing is?' said Mariner afterwards. 'She'll come over all philanthropic, helping all these poor childless couples and girls who can't afford to keep their babies and probably get a suspended sentence.'

It was two days before they had further good news and Mariner came into Granville Lane to find a message waiting: Goran Zjalic had been picked up at Harwich, trying to board a ferry. He was being returned to them pronto.

Chapter Eighteen

When Zjalic arrived at Granville Lane the first thing Mariner arranged was for Valenka to come in and make a positive identification. DCI Sharp caught Mariner in the corridor. 'What's going on?' she asked.

'Valenka is coming in to do an identity parade.'

'Good. I've got that nasty little man Cahill coming in. I'll be able to tell him that we're making progress.'

Afterwards Mariner couldn't say what made him do it. It was just a hunch, pure and simple. He went down to reception to meet Valenka and Katarina, who had come in to translate for her friend. While he was down there he had a word with Delrose on reception. 'Could you let me know when Mr Cahill arrives?'

The identity parade went smoothly and Valenka didn't hesitate in her identification. Mariner was gathering further background from her, in one of the rape suites upstairs when he was paged. 'Let's take a break,' he said. 'Get some fresh air.'

The timing was perfect. As they got to the top of the stairs Mariner could see the carefully combed-over pate approaching from the floor below and was careful to position himself between the girls and the councillor.

Within a few feet of him, Valenka gave a little involuntary cry of fear and, forgetting herself, clutched at Mariner's arm. She retched. The exchanged glance lasted only seconds, but in that time Mariner could see the spark of mutual recognition, before Cahill hurried up the stairs to Sharp's office. When they got back to the interview room Mariner asked Katarina: 'Do you know that man?'

Valenka was silent, her eyes afraid.

'It's all right,' Mariner soothed. 'He's not a policeman. He's er, an official, someone who gives us a lot of trouble.'

'He was one of her clients,' Katarina said at last, and it was the first thing in days to make Mariner smile.

He lightly touched Valenka's arm. 'He makes me sick, too,' he murmured under his breath.

* * *

It was only as he was writing up statement notes later that Mariner noticed the date. It seemed significant for some reason but he couldn't think why. Then he realised it was the day that Anna was moving out. Rounding her street corner he saw with some relief that the removal van was still there. He parked up and went into the house. 'Anna!'

He was greeted by a total stranger. 'Hello, can I help you?'

'I was looking for Anna Barham, she's moving out today.'

'She's gone. We're moving in.'

The man was happy to let Mariner look around, but none of his stuff was there. Mariner went back to his home on the canal and could hardly get in the door. Everything from Anna's house had been dumped in the hall.

Katarina was in the kitchen, stirring some kind of beef stew. 'A woman brought it,' she said. 'She was upset, angry I think. She asks me to tell you: "I hope you will be happy." But she's not smiling when she said it.'

'No. I don't suppose she was.'

'It's your woman?'

'Not any more. It's finished.'

'Oh.' She smiled. 'I made stew. You want to have some?'

'Why not?'

Mariner was introducing Katarina to *Casablanca* when there was a rap on the door. He opened it to find Anna standing on the doorstep. 'I let the van go down without me. I couldn't just go, not without saying goodbye.' She looked beyond him into the lounge where Katarina sat.

'This isn't what you think,' Mariner said hastily. 'I'm only putting her up until—'

She managed a smile. 'I know. I talked to Tony a couple of days ago. It doesn't make any difference though, does it?'

'I suppose not. I hope you find what you want, Anna.'

'You too.' And with a soft kiss on his cheek she turned and walked back up the path.

THE END

Thank you for reading this book. If you enjoyed it please leave feedback on Amazon, and if there is anything we missed or you have a question about then please get in touch. The author and publishing team appreciate your feedback and time reading this book.

Our email is office@joffebooks.com

www.joffebooks.com

DI TOM MARINER SERIES

DEADLY LIES

DEADLY INNOCENT

KILLER LIES

BABY LIES

More coming soon!

75155747R00172

Made in the USA
Middletown, DE
03 June 2018